THE
HAUNTED
ZONE

THE HAUNTED ZONE

A HORROR ANTHOLOGY BY WOMEN MILITARY VETERANS

Edited by Sirrah Medeiros

TUNDRA SWAN
PRESS

THE HAUNTED ZONE

Collection Copyright ©2024 by Tundra Swan Press. All rights reserved. All stories and poems copyright © by their respective authors. All rights reserved.

This is a work of fiction. Names, characters, places, and incidents are products of the authors' imaginations or are used fictitiously and are not to be construed as real. Any resemblance to actual events, locales, organizations, or persons, living or dead, are entirely coincidental.

Printed in the United States of America. No part of this book may be used or reproduced in any manner whatsoever, stored in a retrieval system, or transmitted in any form or by any means, without written permission by the publisher except in the case of brief quotations embodied in critical articles and reviews. No part of this publication may be otherwise circulated in any form of binding or cover than that in which it is published and without a similar condition, including this condition being imposed on the subsequent purchaser.

Editor: Sirrah Medeiros
Cover Design: Kristina Osborn, Truborn Design
Interior Illustrations: Elize McKelvey, InkStickArt
Interior Design Layout: Sirrah Medeiros, Tundra Swan Press

Hardcover ISBN: 979-8-9852025-9-5
Paperback ISBN: 979-8-9852025-8-8
eBook ISBN: 979-8-9852025-7-1

Library of Congress Control Number: 2024900858

Published by Tundra Swan Press
TundraSwanPress.com

For our sisters in military service,
Past, present, and future,
We see you.

Brenda Huettner
Ella B. Rite
Janine K. Spendlove
Lee Franklin
Donna Zephrine

Proceeds of this book will be donated to the
National Veterans Foundation
a 501(c)(3) charitable organization.
For more information, visit
www.nvf.org

CONTENTS

INTRODUCTION

SIRRAH MEDEIROS

"Women, whether subtly or vociferously,
have always been a tremendous power in the
destiny of the world."

— Eleanor Roosevelt, *It's Up to the Women*

Several people threw a question at me early in the development process of this book: "Why *this* anthology?" I understood the question because I had asked myself the same thing repeatedly over a three-month period.

A question posed in the Horror Writers Association, Veterans in Horror Spotlight in November 2022 got under my skin, and I couldn't shake it no matter how much I tried. That question was, "Who are some military veteran horror authors you recommend our audience check out?" I rattled off a list of men with little thought, but not a single woman I absolutely knew for certain was a veteran came to mind. So, believe me when I tell you, I looked at every aspect before committing myself to the book and reaching out to others to join me. The answer wouldn't leave me alone—

and that answer was resoundingly that we should and must recognize women veterans for their contributions in the genre.

We don't traditionally think of women veterans as combatants, yet we live in an age where women fight alongside men on the battlefield every day. They also wage war in daily conflicts associated with being a woman in the military, often while not receiving the same respect from their peers, superiors, or society at large.

Add to the mix fighting off sexual advances or blatant assaults while working harder to garner the same recognition as their male counterparts on the job. These strong women then come home to nurture and raise children, support and defend their families, and they do it with a heavier commitment to military life than ever before. With the duty, sacrifice, and drive to protect and defend, the horror genre is the ideal arena for women warriors to express themselves. It is a must that we see them, not only to highlight who they are and their service, but for what they share with the community because of their talents and unique life experiences.

These women bring you classic horror as well as deeply haunting issues like domestic violence, suicide, traumas of war, loss, revenge, and the emotions entwined in these topics. They weave tales that bring us together in our humanity. Women warriors who express what we fear talking about with others, carrying the pack of societal burdens, at home and on the battlefield of life.

After giving the how and why much consideration, I couldn't fathom not doing this project. Gathering remarkable women together, full of talent, ambition, and heart in one never-before collection became the priority. It was a mission I had to complete.

At first, the thought of putting together an anthology was overwhelming. Not because of the tasks involved, I'd run the production of countless publications in the past, albeit within a different setting and target audience. But the hesitation was two-fold—a considerable time commitment was required of me and, as a returning horror writer after a decade-long break, I didn't know many people to reach out to for help or guidance. Thankfully, neither issue stopped me.

In preparation, I researched for days hunting for publications that highlighted women veteran horror writers. I found several submission calls from years past, yet no publications resulting down the line. The research took me back well over five years with disheartening results. This fueled the fire rather than squelched it. For all the earlier attempts that led to failure for unknown reasons, it became clear this project had to succeed.

According to the Department of Labor statistics, for every sixty-nine women you meet, you'll run across one woman military veteran. To find a woman military veteran horror writer, the odds are more remarkable. I don't have the figures, but I can tell you we are a tiny part of the horror writing community, perhaps the smallest. Yet, the life experiences and contributions to the genre by women veterans are astounding.

I am beyond blessed and honored to have served as editor on this amazing collection and have the immense opportunity to collaborate with each writer and artist. Every facet of this production—from the stories and poems to the covers and interior artwork—women veterans crafted every aspect of the book.

In addition, to honor and support other women veterans, we're giving back. We partnered with the well-renowned non-profit, the National Veterans Foundation, founded by Shad Meshad, who also graciously provided the afterword. Proceeds from anthology sales go to the NVF's Women Veterans Resources and Support Programs. Their programs assist women veterans and provide help in areas such as employment, family resources, counseling, suicide prevention, and homelessness.

I am delighted to share this amazing project with you and so enormously proud of the women warriors who joined me on this adventure. I'll stop prattling on now and let you get to their stories. It's an incredible lineup that is sure to please with award-winning authors and talented new voices in horror. So go on, turn the page.

Thank you for joining us on this daring journey through *The Haunted Zone*.

Love and blessings,

Sirrah Medeiros

WITCH OF DUNLORA

QUERUS ABUTTU

Bobby Ware's troop set up camp in the woods near an abandoned mansion. The building loomed like a hungry predator—its peeling white paint revealing a wood skeleton, warped and twisted. The windows were darker than the dense shadows in the forest. There was something off about the place that sent shivers down his spine.

Trees around camp leaned in around them. Strange animal cries echoed in the air, sounding like hungry beasts ready to pounce and make a meal out of them at any moment.

Yes, Bobby was scared of camping in this spot. Scared of camping here on Halloween. Scared of camping near the strange house with no lights on. But he couldn't shake the fear that gripped him. Still, he was twelve—practically a man. His pops said so. He wasn't supposed to be scared.

Scouting was supposed to help him transition to adulthood. Real men weren't supposed to be afraid of the dark, eerie noises or strange surroundings. Not afraid of nothing.

Bobby remembered his pops telling him of Uncle Roger. He had gone to war after being transferred to the Air Service. The Army even gave him a medal, a Distinguished Service Cross, when he came back. Bobby reckoned that meant that his uncle was brave. His mamma said so, and his mamma never lied.

As Bobby sat on a log facing the other boys in a circle, he was grateful for the small campfire in the center. Still, he couldn't help the wave of nausea that rose in the pit of his stomach when he glanced toward the mansion again. Its ominous presence overpowered his senses, and the fire's light failed to shake the feeling of dread away from him.

Bobby's Scoutmaster, Mr. Keppel, was always neatly dressed, like a military man in dress uniform. With a tight haircut and cleanly shaved face, the man looked like a soldier instead of a Scout leader. He strode over, placed a tin cup of hot chocolate into Bobby's hands, and sat on a log beside him.

"You are quiet tonight. Are you alright?"

Unable to think of what to say, Bobby only nodded.

When he looked at Mr. Keppel, he couldn't help but notice that the man's ears were huge. The tops of them stuck out from his head, and his nose was long and pointy.

Like Ichabod Crane, Bobby thought.

Bobby's sister would be the kind to tease the man about his ears behind his back, but Bobby reckoned the Scoutmaster was a good man. Big ears weren't no reason to tease a man.

He thought about his sister, Janny. She was at an All Hallows party tonight, ducking for apples. Supposedly, if she could catch an apple in her teeth three times in five minutes, she'd dream of her future husband.

It seemed like a silly thing to do, and Grams didn't like it, but Janny was headstrong. Somehow, she always got her way, so she got to go to the party.

No, it was better that he was out camping. Practicing archery, learning to hunt, and knowing how to skin and cook animals helped Pops when winter food stores were low. Pops said it was a better use of time, being with the Scouts. He said it was better than going to some old Halloween party. Bobby reckoned Pops was right.

"I hear birthday congratulations are in order," said Mr. Keppel. "Thirteen, right?"

Bobby was shaken out of his thoughts. He opened his mouth. A squeaky "Yes" escaped his lips.

"Well then," Mr. Keppel slapped his thighs, "we shall have a birthday breakfast for you that can't be beat! Nothing is as good as a camp morning breakfast." He yelled with vigor, "Right boys?"— gathering the attention of the circle of Scouts sitting on other logs, sipping their cocoa.

The boys turned their eyes on him.

Bobby felt like they were studying him, weighing him on uneven scales. It made him feel very self-conscious. Especially under the discomforting stare from the oldest among them. Carter Fields.

Of all the other boys, Carter was the strangest. Sure, he helped the Scout leader. But it was clear that the other boys tried hard never to be alone with him.

When Carter asked a fellow Scout to help him pitch a tent or gather firewood, that boy would always ask another boy to go with him.

"Many hands make light work," they'd reply.

Words Bobby often heard his mother say.

An owl hooted right over their heads, startling everyone.

Mr. Keppel chuckled and stood. He strode to the center of the group, taking a stance by the fire.

"While everyone's finishing up their cocoa, I'll tell a story. What shall I tell?" He looked around. "Hunting story?"

The boys' faces were solemn.

It seemed to Bobby the boys weren't in the mood for a hunting tale. Probably many of them were thinking about their families and the trick-or-treating and Halloween parties going on tonight.

Sure, it was Monday, and many kids had to be in school tomorrow morning, but that didn't stop the festivities. And each Scout had permission from their parents and teachers to be out of school the next day. They simply had to make up their schoolwork before Friday.

Mr. Keppel grinned. "Hmm. Not a hunting story. Love story then?"

Sour faces bloomed around the circle. Some of the younger Scouts stuck out their tongues in distaste. The fire crackled and the moon, just shy of dark, barely lit the tops of their heads.

"No love story, eh?" The Scoutmaster paused. He stroked his chin. "Well, it *is* All Hallows. A *scary* story, maybe?"

Bobby watched several heads slowly bob. His own head nodded almost against his will. But yes, a scary story. It was Halloween, after all.

Mr. Keppel rubbed his hands together.

"Well, let me think." He walked a complete circle around the fire, looking in the direction of the house in the meadow.

"Once upon a time," he began, "there was an old house that sat right by a haunted forest. A mansion."

Everyone's eyes flicked to the large, darkened home across the way. Their gaze returned when the Scoutmaster spoke once more.

"It's said that an evil woman by the name of Ida Dunlora lived in that house. Some folks say she was born on All Hallows—at midnight—in the middle of a graveyard. The year was 1720. Her mother was very wealthy, and rumor was her mother was a *witch!*"

Mr. Keppel raised his hands shoulder-high. He wiggled his fingers, bending them in the shape of claws.

There were nervous chuckles all around. He smiled knowingly and went on. "You see, her mother had fled her German homeland to come to America. Times were hard then, even for people with money, and the witch mother—so it's said—would bleed the farm animals and feed their blood to her newly birthed daughter, Ida, to keep the babe healthy and strong."

Here, the Scoutmaster paused, and Bobby quickly glanced around to see all the other Scouts rapt with their attention upon the man.

Mr. Keppel continued. "Some say her mother would even place spells on men passing by. She'd capture them and bleed them so her baby could suckle on their warm, sweet blood. Then, she would cook and eat their flesh. Other folks say she would make a meal of anyone who dared to trick-or-treat at her home, mesmerizing unsuspecting children and their parents."

One of the younger Scouts, Little Bill, piped up with a question. "But who was the baby's father? Couldn't he stop her?"

A glint from the fire made it seem as if Mr. Keppel's eyes sparkled with mischief. "No one knows. But it is said that the baby was the child of Lucifer himself. Satan's own brood."

Silence fell upon the group, and the tension among the boys was tighter than a violin string.

"Now," Mr. Keppel went on, "The baby grew into Ida Dunlora, and when she turned fifteen, she was famed to be the loveliest girl in town. By the time she was nineteen, word of her beauty spread throughout the lands of Virginia. She had many courters call on her, but word was if they stepped upon the lands of Dunlora, those men were never seen or heard from again."

There were sharp gasps from many of the boys.

"That's road apples," Carter sneered. "Everyone knows there's no truth to that bull pie."

Mr. Keppel placed a finger to his lips in a silent, *Hush, be quiet.*

Carter crossed his arms and leaned back, a contemptuous half smile on his face.

"In fact, Ida Dunlora's mother disappeared when Ida turned eighteen. It was never known what happened to her—but some folks speculate Ida had turned against her own mother on All Hallows night and ate her right up!"

The trees surrounding the group rustled as a sudden wind blew through the branches, and several golden leaves floated to the ground like a fireworks finale.

"Ida never took a husband and remained reclusive. No one in town ever saw her go shopping for food or wares. She was never seen after her 20th birthday, and anyone who's ever gone to the mansion to inquire about the woman never returns. Even a small cavalry of Union soldiers was reputed to have stopped there to pillage the place for silver and food. No one ever saw the Union men again."

Mr. Keppel pointed toward the mansion. "And that house right there, boys. That very one is where the Dunlora Witch is said to live, even to this day. Whether she lives there or haunts it, do not go near it!" His voice was a dark, hissing whisper now. "Don't even *think* of climbing those steps or contemplate looking inside the windows." He finished with a weird rhyme that sounded like something made of old legend. "No midnight excursions to find out if it's true, or the Witch of Dunlora will make a meal out of you!" He clapped his hands together loudly at the very end.

All the boys jumped, and Mr. Keppel let out a belly laugh, and each of them, except Carter, allowed a sheepish smile to cross their faces.

"Well, you boys wanted a scary story," he said. "I think that will do for the night. Let's clean up and hit the hay. We've got an early morning birthday breakfast to make for Bobby. We'll check our snares to see if we've got a rabbit to add to the meal, and whether yes or no, I've packed a few things that will fill our bellies."

"I can wash the cups, Mr. Keppel," Bobby volunteered.

Mr. Keppel nodded and gave him a salute, then disappeared into the dark.

The boys rose from their logs, leaving Bobby alone. He collected the tin cups to wash them out—thirteen in all.

"Let me help you with that." He hadn't heard Carter come up behind him. He mentally kicked himself for letting the other Scouts go without asking someone else to help.

"That'd be fine, Carter. Thanks," Bobby said.

They used a bit of water in a pan they'd carted from a stream to rinse out the cups and turned them upside down to drain on a cloth.

Carter surprised Bobby with a chuckle when they were done.

"You buy any of that stupid story?" His eyebrows hitched up a bit with the question. It would have been impossible to see him, except each boy had a kerosene lamp they carried at night.

Bobby looked up into the night sky. It was dark now since the fire had died down to glowing embers.

"Hey," Bobby felt a hand shake his shoulder. Carter raised his voice. "You hear me? You buy any of that story?" Bobby's lamp barely lit Carter's face, but the tone in Carter's voice held something that Bobby didn't like. He decided it was best to say nothing.

A voice in his head said, *Get to your tent, Bobby. Get to bed.*

"Well, now. Ain't that interesting?" Carter grabbed his shoulder again and spun him around. "See that?"

Bobby did see it. And he didn't want to. There was a light on at the Dunlora house. If, indeed, that *was* the Dunlora house.

Carter chuckled. "Bet that's really Mr. Keppel. Trying to give us one last scare." He made fun of Mr. Keppel's final warning with a mocking tone. "No midnight excursions to find out if it's true, or the Witch of Dunlora will make a meal out of you!"

It *was* curious. Bobby didn't argue that, but he held with Mr. Keppel's warning. Best get to bed and leave well enough alone. He turned toward his tent.

"Hey!" It was clear Carter wasn't going to leave this alone. "Don't you want to know? If it's Mr. Keppel, or maybe if it really *is* the ghost witch? She can't be alive—long as it's been."

"Nope," Bobby said in a voice that he thought would sound firm, but when it hit the air, it sounded more like a feather floating on a breeze.

"You *scared*, that it?" Carter's voice dripped with venom now. "What if he is?"

Bobby looked over to see the kid everyone called Mouse. He earned the name on account he rarely said anything. It was surprising the kid was taking this moment to speak up. "Wha-what if he is?" Mouse questioned again. "Ain't no crime in being scared. Scared keeps you alive 'cause you don't wait around to see what happens next."

"That right, pip-squeak? Mouse, right? What does a mouse know? Nuthin'." He grabbed Bobby's shirt. "Well, we're going. Check it out, that's all. Back in three shakes of a stray dog's tail."

By now, quite a few boys had crawled out of their tents. The commotion outside had drawn their curiosity.

"What's going on?" It was Watts. A nickname he'd earned on account of his last name was Watson, and he was always investigating something, just like the Dr. Watson in the Sherlock

Holmes stories. He had huge glasses that seemed to cover his entire face.

Mouse spoke up before either Bobby or Carter could get a word in. He pointed to the old mansion with the light on upstairs. "Carter says that's Mr. Keppel up there."

A few more lit kerosene lamps flared and surrounded Bobby and Carter.

Watts pursed his lips. "Well, I'll see if Mr. Keppel is in his tent. That'll solve one thing."

Whispers of "Don't" and "Come back" came from the lips of several of the boys, but the words hit empty air as Watts disappeared into the night. He was back in less than two minutes.

"I checked everywhere," the boy said. "Mr. Keppel is gone."

Silence fell upon the group of boys, and they stared at the old building with the light shining on the third floor. The only discernable noises were the wind and the creaking of trees as they bent their trunks over, sounding much like an old woman's knees might after too many years gone by.

"Well, let's go see," Carter taunted. "It's just a silly old house. Stupid story. If that's Mr. Keppel up there, he's probably just wanting us to go over and get scared. Like a second part of the story where they always tell you—stay tuned 'til next week."

Carter grabbed Bobby's shirt and dragged him along. The other boys looked around at each other, and there were calls of, "Wait up!" "We're coming too!"

It both warmed and chilled Bobby's heart. They were protecting him in a way. The only way they knew how.

The snarl on Carter's face told him he wasn't pleased to have the other boys come along. Then he grinned, and Bobby got the feeling Carter had just come up with a horrible idea. An idea that would launch all the kids into a terrifying night.

"I'm not waiting," he said. "You want to come along; you follow soon as you can, and if you get lost, it's on you."

The boys all peered over at the light inside the Dunlora house, and each one knew that if that light stayed on, no one would get lost. Carter continued to drag Bobby with him into the dark. The field grasses were long, and the air gripped him with that autumn chill and the scent of all things dying after a frost. All living things in nature struggle against death before the coming of the first snow.

Carter continued to prattle as they went along.

"You're a fraidy cat, Bobbers. You wait and see. If there *is* a Dunlora witch, I'm gonna feed you to 'er. If it's Mr. Keppel, you are gonna, well," Carter sneered, "owe me ten dollars."

Bobby's brain whirred. "But I…"

"You WHAT?" Carter pulled him so close that Bobby nearly gagged. Carter's breath smelled like a rotting dead deer in the thick of summer.

"I didn't make a bet," Bobby whispered, choking back tears. Part of him knew full well that it didn't matter if he'd bet or not. Carter would hold him to an imaginary bet in the worst way.

A sudden tug on Bobby's shirt propelled him in front of Carter, and then Carter pushed between his shoulder blades, catapulting Bobby across the field grasses and onto the ground. His lamp hit the ground, flickered, and the light went out. Carter hadn't brought a lamp.

"YES, you did. And by the time I'm done, everyone will have heard you make that bet. Count on it." Carter stalked by him, jerked him up by the arm, and pulled forward on his shirt again. Bobby wondered how in the world Carter could see—the night was so dark. That one lighted window at the Dunlora place was bright as a moon, but it didn't help him see where to step. At least the sky was clear, and there were stars overhead.

The march toward the house seemed like forever. As they approached, Bobby noted two old oaks on either side of the front of the house.

Guardian Trees, he thought.

Carter pushed him forward. "Go up the steps and into the house. If I don't see you stick your head out of that lighted window and wave in five minutes, I'm gonna slice off one of your fingers with this. He pulled a knife from his pocket and flipped it open, continuing to press his threat. The knife had an ebony handle. Bobby had seen it before. The blade was long; he knew that much.

"C'mon, Carter," Bobby pleaded. "I can't see in there. It's dark. There's no light." And then his heart sank further than it already had. A group of lights bobbed toward him. As they got closer, he saw it was Watts, Mouse, Donny Whittle, Rudie Green, and another boy, Stephen.

"What's going on?" Watts said. Bobby could tell Watts wanted to sound strong. The light from his kerosene lamp flickered against his glasses.

Carter turned, not acting surprised that some of the boys had followed him.

"Our Bobbers here was just getting ready to go inside and find Mr. Keppel. You guys want to join him?"

The lights didn't move forward, then one did. It was Watts.

"I will," he said. "There's no way to see in there without a light. Not till you get upstairs, anyway."

Come in---

The hairs stood up on Bobby's neck. He spoke in a hushed voice. "Did anyone else hear that?"

"Hear what?" Carter was almost laughing, but Watts nodded. So did Mouse, Donny, Rudie, and Stephen.

"Yes," said Watts. "It said *come in.*"

"You guys are not pulling one over on me. Get in there, Bobbers. Find Mr. Keppel. And then you owe me ten dollars."

The other boys sucked in their breath.

"Yep, you guys heard him, right? Our bet? Ten bucks, it's Mr. Keppel. Not some old ghost witch."

Bobby looked at them. Each of the boys' faces was blank, but they spied the glint of Carter's knife. They all nodded slowly.

Watts stepped up beside Bobby so they were both on the first step.

"Let's go," said Watts. "Nothing to be afraid of. If anything, it could be a transient. Maybe from the rail yard?"

Bobby breathed in deeply and whooshed out the air. At least he wasn't going to be alone. And at least they had light now. The wind picked up, blowing their hair askew. Another owl screeched eerily in the trees above. Or was it the same one?

When Bobby pressed the metal thumb-plate on the door lever, the front door swung wide open.

Not locked.

And it wasn't too surprising. Especially if the house was supposed to be empty all this time. Watts swung the lamp forward. Dust and cobwebs met their eyes. Broken pieces of wood furniture were strewn across the floor. The main staircase greeted Bobby's eyes, shadows flickering along the bottom steps which rose higher into the darkness.

"We're coming too!" It was Rudie's voice. Looking over his shoulder, Bobby saw Rudie, Mouse, Donny, and Stephen stepping forward.

Bobby relaxed a bit. There were five lamps total—and light had a way of chasing evil out of the shadows, didn't it? If anything, it helped chase away fear—fear of whatever the dark held within it.

But if evil were chased out of the shadows, that didn't mean it went away. It only meant it was easier to see.

He swallowed, his throat feeling ever so dry.

"Let's go," Watts urged. "Get this over with. If it's Mr. Keppel, then har-har, he had a good laugh drawing us all into the house after his story and all. And if it's not…"

Bobby nodded and finished his sentence, "… then we'll deal with whatever it is when we get there."

Bobby's foot hit the very first step, and it creaked loudly. He cringed. There'd likely be no element of surprise as they ascended.

He turned to look back and saw the rest of the boys. All except Carter had completely entered the house. A gust of wind, this time from inside the house, blew hard against their faces and slammed the door shut. Their lamps rattled.

Carter's laughter outside carried a malicious tone. "Go on, fraidy cats!" they heard him yell. "I want to see your face pop out of that window, Bobbers. No one's going home 'til I see your peepers! Got that?"

The staircase seemed to go on forever, and on the landing, it split—half the stairs going to the left and half to the right. They all stayed together, climbing the left staircase. The walls were covered with peeling wallpaper. Some kind of red and gold print, curling in some places and torn in others.

As they reached the second floor, a large wooden desk blocked their way. Bobby glanced over at Watts, but couldn't see his face well in the dim light. He decided to scramble over it and Watts followed him. The others did likewise, except for Mouse, who wriggled under the piece of furniture and met everyone on the other side.

The stairs rounded again to form a central stairway to the third floor, and the shuffling of their feet echoed off the bare walls. A piece of plaster fell from the ceiling, startling everyone, and Rudie called out in surprise.

Donny covered Rudie's mouth. "Shhhh…" he whispered.

Bobby didn't think the noise would make any difference by now. After the door slamming so loud, if there was anyone up on the third floor, they knew someone was here already.

Please let it be Mr. Keppel. Please…

Again, the stairway split at the central landing, and Bobby went to the right this time. The lighted window, he remembered, would be on the far left, facing the house. If he took the right staircase, he'd be on the far right of the hallway and have more time to see if anyone, or *anything*, was waiting for them.

It was then that he heard a low, muffled moaning and the sickly sound of something wet smacking against—what? He couldn't tell.

As they arrived at the top, Watts held his lamp high so they could look to their left down the hallway. Nothing. The sound was definitely coming from the opposite side—the side where a light shone through a doorway at the very end of the corridor.

Bobby took a deep breath, noting his hands were trembling. Most of his troop was with him, but he was still afraid. Again, he heard his father's voice, "… not afraid of nothing!"

You'd be disappointed, Pop. I'm afraid, alright.

"Might as well get this over with," whispered Watts. "The sooner we check this out, the sooner we can get back. Let Mr. Keppel have his laugh."

The rest of the boys chuckled nervously behind him. Bobby nodded and stepped forward, his knees shaking, Watts at his side. They reached the doorway. He turned to look at the others, and Donny jutted his chin.

"G-go on," whispered Mouse.

Bobby took a deep breath and craned his neck around the door entrance.

And there was Mr. Keppel! He almost laughed out loud. They'd been right! He was sitting on the floor below a kerosene lamp on a table. Mr. Keppel had played—

Then, Bobby stared at the floor, and sudden terror gripped him. In front of Mr. Keppel lay a heap of something, but it was shiny. Wet. Red. And there was something round next to it.

Stephen shuffled forward, "What…?"

The rest of the boys gathered in the doorway, each of them staring at Mr. Keppel, whose eyes were closed. He was sitting, almost crumpled, in a crossed-legged position on the floor. His usual meticulous clothing was rumpled. Untucked shirt, sleeve torn and smeared with—

"What is that?" Stephen said out loud, and then he yelled. "Mr. Keppel?"

Bobby heard the boys calling out around him, but his stare was fixed on the ball next to the slick and shiny mess in front of Mr. Keppel. Then, he realized the awful truth. He was staring at a head. And not just any head. He was staring into Carter's lifeless eyes. Something was stuffed in his mouth—a sock.

But Carter is downstairs…

Mouse pushed by him. "Mr. Keppel!" He ran over and shook the man. Mr. Keppel's eyes suddenly snapped open, and his hands jutted forward. Mouse screamed, and Bobby couldn't tell what—

Mouse crumpled to the floor, and Mr. Keppel slowly stood. And there was something in his hand. Was that—?

No. Carter's knife! He'd stabbed Mouse with the knife!

Bobby knew it was Carter's. The six-inch blade. Same ebony handle with brass bolsters and pins.

But Carter was on the floor, mutilated. Strips of skin and muscle peeled off the bones—peeled with his pocketknife.

Someone behind him retched. Bobby heard footsteps—someone running away.

Mr. Keppel was looking at the bloody knife in his hand, screaming, "No, no, nooo!" He backed against the wall, cowering in the corner, muttering to himself. All his clothes were covered with blood. Carter's blood. And now Mouse's.

Boards creaked from behind the door, and Bobby—frozen in position—could only stare as another Carter moved in front of him. He stared as it faced him.

"You didn't look out the window." The voice was malicious, thick, and sinister.

But this can't be Carter. Carter is—

"Outside?" Laughter poured from the vision in front of him.

Watts—yelling in his ear— "RUN!"

Bobby drew back, still transfixed—staring into the eyes of the thing that played at being Carter. Eyes flickered red. Or was that a trick of the light? The thing that looked like Carter lunged for him.

Watts yanked him away—pulling him, dragging him toward the steps. "RUN! We gotta get out of here, Bobby!"

And finally, Bobby broke away from the horror, the terror that was not Carter—and Bobby ran.

On the stairs, he and Watts nearly tripped over something they could barely see. Stephen and Rudie lay on the steps, both necks twisted at impossible angles, their lanterns broken. Fire from their spilled kerosene had released flames that spread across the wood floors, then up the dry wallpaper. At the very bottom of the stairs, before they could reach the door, they found Donny.

In their shock, Bobby and Watts paused for a second, taking in the scene. It looked like someone, or something, had stuck a large kitchen knife through Donny's right eye. Their eyes riveted toward each other and in horrified agreement they dashed for the way out.

They tried to open the front door. It wouldn't budge, no matter how hard they pulled. Only then did Bobby realize he and Watts were both screaming.

Watts grabbed a broken chair leg. "The window! Break the window!"

Bobby snatched another piece of wood—something that maybe once belonged to a table.

They beat their makeshift clubs against the large window, breaking the glass all around.

Bobby backed up, not even thinking about how far the fall would be. His only thought was, *I have to get out. Get out!*

With all the fear he had in him, he launched himself through the open space, scratching his arm on a jagged piece of glass, landing hard on the overgrowth in front of the house.

There was a crash. It was so dark, Bobby couldn't tell what had happened at first. Flames leapt up in the window. Then Bobby stared in horror at Watts. His body was hanging half in, half out of the window—a large wedge of glass piercing through the center of his body.

A howl of laughter rose from the lighted window upstairs as flames started licking the sky.

Bobby wasted no time turning and running as fast as he could away from the Dunlora house in the direction of the camp.

The Children's Preventorium in Charlottesville admitted Bobby Ware three days after Halloween. He'd been found wandering in the forest two days after the parents of the boys in the Boy Scout troop reported the Scoutmaster and children missing.

The missing Scouts were found dead in their tents, mutilated. A bloody, black-handled knife was found in the Scoutmaster's tent.

The Scoutmaster, Mr. Kevin Keppel, was found wandering alongside the road leading out of the Dunlora forest days after the tragic incident. He was said to be muttering incomprehensible words and had to be heavily sedated. When he was committed and admitted to Central Lunatic Asylum, the physicians recalled he repeatedly ranted, "No midnight excursions to find out if it's true, or the Witch of Dunlora will make a meal out of you!"

Bobby was rendered mute, completely unable to speak. Doctors debated if Bobby Ware should be considered a child or not since he was thirteen years old. In the end they decided it would be best if he remained on the children's ward to prevent him from catching tuberculosis.

He remained there for the rest of his youth until he started a fire that consumed an entire wing of the asylum—a fire where he died screaming while surrounded by the flames—screaming his first words since he was found wandering in the forest, "The Witch of Dunlora is alive!"

The Dunlora Mansion bore no trace of fire that anyone could tell from a distance, despite the tirades of Mr. Keppel who sometimes screamed about the flames, but investigators never went inside the place. And anyone who ever heard of the macabre mansion history dared not set foot near the windows or doors.

Passersby are still reported missing from time to time; however, the local law enforcement refuse to cross onto the Dunlora land. The house, partially claimed by the forest now, is said to have a light upstairs that still shines from the third-floor window every Halloween night.

Dunlora remains under the sole possession of a landowner who desires to maintain her anonymity.

33

ARACHNE'S SHADOW

RACHEL A. BRUNE

*H*e's going to kill you.

Three days after the fight, Octavia returned home from her part-time library job to find the back door unlocked.

"Hey, Tavy." Evan had not only cleaned the few dishes she'd left in the sink from her last few microwaved-leftover meals, but he'd put a pot of water on to boil and chopped vegetables.

The back door opened into the kitchen, with a pony wall separating the eating area from the cooking area. Octavia paused, still in the threshold, aware of the knife in his hand, glinting in the kitchen light like the dull stinger of a wasp. One foot in the bright light of the dining room. One foot back in the dark, keys clutched, purse clenched across her body.

"Evan." She smiled at him, shaking off the voice in her head. "You cooking?"

He grinned sheepishly, his smile as crooked and beautiful as ever. "Yeah. I've got one recipe, but it's a good one." He dropped the grin, turning down his face, mouth, eyes in practiced contrition. "I'm so sorry, babe. Top told me I'd be the world's biggest idiot to mess this up again."

Octavia nodded. He'd spent three days at the barracks. Not the longest time he'd ever stayed away. The keys in her hand dug into the soft skin of her palm.

Inside, at the kitchen table, sitting on the tablecloth she'd thrown over the scars the knife left—a large package wrapped in her favorite color, bright yellow, with metallic gold ribbon tied in a bow.

She took a final step into the room, closing the door behind her, and ventured closer to the table. "This for me?" A slightly smaller package sat next to it—a large, reusable tote from her favorite craft store, tissue paper sporting rainbow-colored owls poking out the top.

"I found it at the thrift store on post." His voice had a curious buzzing whine. "Go ahead, open it!"

From the kitchen Evan watched her un-tape the corners, unfold the paper back, revealing the item that took half the table.

"So?" he prompted her. "Do you like it?"

"I love it!" She did not ask, "Where did you find the money for this?" She also did not ask, "Which bill won't I be able to pay this month?" She refrained from pointing out, "I don't have the money to buy the things I need to use this."

Instead, she opened the craft store tote, pushing aside the rainbow owls to find what else he had chosen to bestow.

"I figure, once you learn how to use it, you can make things to sell with it, maybe get a table at the farmers' market down at the museum on Saturdays." Evan grinned and returned to chopping vegetables, the knife making soft *sshhh*ch *sshhh*ch sounds. "Maybe make a baby blanket or two."

Octavia nodded, taking in the gift, the unspoken messages behind it. For the slightest pause, long enough, but not too long,

Evan held the knife above the board, making eye contact, his wide grin projecting affability and charm.

"I love it, Evan," Octavia said. "Thank you."

She smelled a strange, sharp soap—not his usual scent. And then, he shooed her away, to spend time with the gift, appreciating it fully. Appreciating him.

Rigid Heddle Weaving.

The thin book didn't contain a great deal of detail, but Octavia thought she could use it to start. Evan was in bed; she'd delayed joining him, claiming since he'd cooked, it was her turn to clean the kitchen. And then, after, she couldn't wait to start using the gift he'd gotten her.

In the darkened house, the sole light above the kitchen burned as brightly as she needed. The rest of the house was dark. As midnight ticked on, she read the book from cover to cover, taking in the instructions and the pictures. Finally, as the digital clock on the microwave clicked into the next day, she put the book down and began assembling the loom.

"Evan?" Octavia half-whispered. She froze, listening.

The sound came again, the flutter-movement from the shadows. Had he gotten out of bed and come to check on her?

The dark stretched around her in the old house, the shadows resting against the fifty-year-old linoleum and ratty carpet the landlord hadn't gotten around to replacing. The dim light hid the pet stains next to the couch from the previous tenant's dogs and the lone cockroach that tapped its tentative way across the kitchen floor.

Whoorwhooor...

Something beat against the back door, and Octavia jumped. Her hand shaking, she got up to open the door.

Outside, the night was breezy, but not too hot for late summer in North Carolina. The slight wind rustled through the trees bordering the property, bringing with it the hint of autumn to come. On the side of the porch, a golden orb-weaver spider sat merrily spinning its way through an intricate web.

Octavia nodded to her fellow crafter. "Evening." Laughing to herself at her fright, she went to close the door.

The rush of wings came again, this time so close she ducked and squeaked, expecting feathers, curved beak, talons reaching and tangling. She closed her eyes, frantic, waving her arms above her head.

"What the hell are you doing?" Evan stood in the kitchen, staring.

Silence. Octavia gingerly straightened and lowered her hands. Next to her, the orb-weaver continued knitting its gossamer lace.

"Sorry, I…"

"Get in here and lock the door." He shook his head. "Can't believe this, opening the door in the middle of the night."

Disgusted, he cast an eye over the half-assembled loom, then back to her, waiting.

Octavia stepped inside, letting the door close behind her. In the moment before she turned the bolt, she once again heard the rush of wings and the soft hooting breaking the night's silence.

"He bought you a loom? Like, a weaving loom?" Penelope snorted, her derision ringing clear through the library's landline. Technically, Octavia wasn't supposed to use it for personal chats with her sister, but Evan checked her phone regularly and had played back snippets of conversations. Penny wasn't shy about sharing her opinion of Evan, and Octavia was tired of bearing the brunt of her sister's bleak honesty.

"Yes, a weaving loom." Octavia pulled the last book out of the return bin and stretched her back. "And a bag full of all different colored yarn."

"Like, in pioneer days?" Penelope's voice crackled a little. "So what, he wants you to stay home and weave a blanket or something? Make a hope chest for your future eight kids?"

"He thinks maybe I could make something to sell at the farmers' market." Octavia scanned in the returns, not taking the bait, wishing she'd never said anything to her sister about Evan and his big family plans. *Beep, beep, beep.*

"So, he gets to say 'I'm sorry' with a gift that means you can quit your job."

"It's not like that," Octavia said, knowing Penelope was completely correct. She paused. The next book in the pile was a children's nonfiction book about spiders, the front graphic a giant, golden orb-weaving spider perched in the middle of its intricate web. Evan had torn down the one on the front porch on his way to morning formation, complaining he hated spiders, as he flailed against the sticky strings reaching for him.

"It's exactly like that," Penny said, breaking the silence that stretched over the line.

"No, I mean, it's not a big pioneer days loom," Octavia said, scanning in the book and continuing through the rest of the short pile. "It's a tabletop rigid heddle loom, and a pretty nice one. Thirty-two inches wide. I can make some nice things with it." She thought back to the night before, reading through the book. "And people do love homemade towels and placemats. I'm looking forward to trying it out, anyway." It was time to change the subject. "How are mom and dad?"

Now the silence came from Penny's side. Across the library, the head librarian gave Octavia a meaningful look.

"Sorry, Penny," she said. "I have to go."

"They miss you."

But Octavia was already hanging up the phone, and she might have heard her sister say something else.

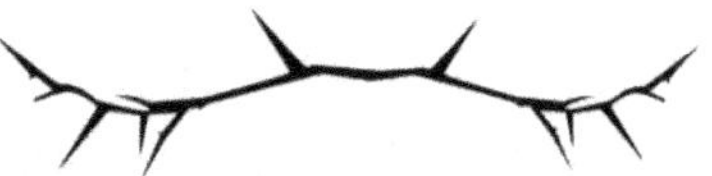

The house was empty again. This time, Evan had a field exercise that would take him away for two weeks. The loom still sat on the table. Eventually, he would grow sick of it and complain she spent all her time with it and not him. But for now, he was on a bus on his way to Louisiana with the rest of the men and women in his unit of combat engineers.

The wooden frame of the loom stretched across the table, the heddle that would lift half the warp threads at a time suspended on its block between the warp and cloth beams to the front and rear. Octavia neatly arrayed the tools around the loom—the dowel rods and C-clamp and the little hooked needle the book said would be used for pulling the warp yarn through the small holes in the heddle.

Peering closely at the book, she used her finger to trace the instructional graphic that showed the path of the warp yarn, the back-and-forth strings that served as the foundation for the weave. She'd do alternating stripes of red and white, the regimental colors of Evan's combat engineers. Maybe it could be a shawl she could wear over her dress to the next military ball, picking up and complementing the deep red accents on his dress uniform.

The mercerized cotton yarn snagged under the rough pads of her hands as she unwound it, pulling out long lengths to place on the table alongside the loom. As she worked, the shadows grew longer, and the sunlight grew richer and then dimmed as the night fell. Octavia ignored the murkiness that crept in, hovering just over her shoulder, as if to sit back and observe her careful work.

She'd never attempted weaving before. Crochet, yes. She'd learned that skill from her grandmother, making quick work with her hooked needles, knotting and looping intricate webs of doilies and cupholders and scarves for the charity tree at the church. Knitting, too, she'd cast her hand at, learning mostly from instructional videos on the internet and the occasional trip to her local yarn store.

Octavia had stopped crafting. Even if the church supplied the materials, Evan complained about the time she spent, the money they could save, the unfashionable old-lady-ness of making things for your home.

Why, then, this gift in particular?

She picked up the first set of warp strings, tying a string on both sides of the "X" cross, holding it firm between her fingers as she slipped the first string out.

Barely ten strings into the warp, her back and neck began to complain. Her eyes, too, teared as she squinted against the gloom. How had people ever stood to go through this process on the huge looms she'd seen in pictures? If a spider's weaving process started as onerously, it would be a surprise if they hadn't all starved to death.

Ah, sister.

Startled, Octavia almost dropped the strands she held. At the last moment, she tightened her hand convulsively, then forced herself to relax. If she tangled the yarn, she'd be there all night.

"Penelope?"

It wouldn't be above her sister to show up uninvited. She'd done it before, but then again, not for a long time.

A soft laughter, barely more than the gentle shuffle of wings, fluttered outside her line of sight. Octavia squinted into the gloom of the rest of the house.

"Evan?"

In response, the darkness grew silent, drawing in on itself as if in disgust. For the first time, Octavia found herself uneasy in her solitude. A chill seized her shoulders and upper back, and she shivered, jerking the warp strings. The loom shifted on the table, and Octavia forced herself to relax, swallowing against her dry throat and tongue.

No.

A low *hoot* accompanied the unspoken word.

What? Octavia's mouth formed the word, though she didn't say anything aloud. If there were an owl in the house, she would know. She would see it. The kitchen area opened to a small living room, and then the hall led to the bedrooms. There was a small laundry room off the dining area with a back door to the driveway and the unattached garage. No place for a giant bird to hide.

Also, she was only a quarter of the way through the loom and too afraid to put the strings down mid-warp, for fear they would tangle and ruin her work. When no further sound came, she bent back to her work. Reverie set in, a peculiar liminal state of half-conscious creation Octavia had experienced before.

Her sister's distaste at her use of the gift was unsurprising. Octavia's parents had reached out less and less after the wedding.

Her parents never felt comfortable around either Evan or confrontation. They chose, instead, to slip away from contact with their oldest daughter rather than voice concern or confront his snide put-downs and the deprecating humor he turned on her in social situations.

Penny, though, had no problem making her thoughts known regarding Evan's jokes and their focus on his wife for their punchline.

Octavia reached for the next thread and came up empty-handed. Somewhere in her reverie, she'd finished stringing the last of the warp thread. Her eyes had gone dry, with little crusties forming at the corners as she rubbed them with the palms of her hands. She yawned, cracking her jaw and her spine against the muscles that had tightened from standing hunched over the table as she worked.

What time was it, anyway?

"Holy shit, it's two a.m." Octavia groaned. She'd be at the library all day tomorrow, and her work alarm was going to come in a few hours. Sighing, she left the loom where it lay, promising herself she would finish the warping tomorrow. Again, she wondered, *How did women do this over and over and over again?*

A sad rustle washed around her, even as she turned the lights off, checked the door lock, and headed through the dark house to bed.

Behind her, the rustle gained form, stature. A light not visible on any spectrum grew around the table, calling its sisters to it, surrounding the cotton and wood and metal. With many arms and deft fingers, they quietly reached for the strings.

"Hey, babe, hope I didn't wake you." Evan's voice came through glitchy with digital artifacts. "We're not supposed to have our phones, so I didn't want to call until everyone was asleep."

"I'm awake," Octavia said, trying to force the cobwebs out of her brain. "How's the exercise going?"

"It's fine," Evan said. "It'd be better if Sergeant Haskell would get the fuck off our case."

"What happened?" Octavia asked. It was all the prompt Evan needed.

"Jesus Christ, well, get this…" Evan kept talking, telling her all about his squad and their mission and how his squad leader was an idiot and his team leader was cool but wouldn't stand up to him, and how their platoon sergeant had it out for him, and his platoon leader was a bitch who did everything higher leadership told her to instead of what was best for the platoon but of course, she was looking out for her career and how he was going to keep his head down and try to make it back without getting another negative counseling about his attitude and work ethic.

Octavia listened and muttered supportive noises occasionally. She hadn't met any of the people Evan was talking about—he wanted to keep work and life separate. But he needed someone to vent to, and she was there to listen. She was zoned out, halfway back to sleep, when she realized he wasn't talking about work.

"…and I really think we're in the right place, you know, babe?"

"Sorry, Evan, the phone cut out right then. What were you saying?"

"Kids, Tavy." The slightest edge undercut Evan's words. "You said you wanted them, and I'm about to go to the board when we get back. Once I get my P status, you can quit your job, and then you know, maybe do the farmers' market on weekends instead."

"No, Evan, I—"

"You what?" The edge in his voice sharpened to a blade. "Don't want kids because why? What do you do all day?"

Octavia stayed silent. The dark room took on a brooding aspect. She shivered. She was alone—why did it feel like someone was watching her? Judging her?

"I—maybe we can talk about this when you get back." She kept her voice soft, still, neutral. With any luck, he would forget he even brought it up.

From the other, distant side of the conversation, Evan swore sharply. The phone cut off. Had he ended the call? Signal dropped?

Evan had a temper, although he managed to control it most of the time. He hadn't raised his voice or given her the silent treatment since they'd made up with the gift of the loom.

Is that what it is? A gift?

It wasn't her voice in the back of her mind. It was the voice that had grown increasingly insistent that she recognize its existence. She had ignored it all day and gone to bed, hoping it would go away.

The same subtle laughter drifted through the bedroom. Octavia gave up and threw off the covers, dragging herself out of bed. It was too late to go back to sleep, too early to get moving on the day's errands.

Instead, she shuffled out of the room, down the hall, and off to the kitchen to make a pot of coffee, throwing the light on to warn off any of the giant North Carolina cockroaches wandering around in the darkness. She'd stepped on one, once, and didn't care to repeat the experience. If she *were* an expert weaver, she'd weave a giant web around the house and kill every single disgusting one.

Carefully, Octavia measured and poured water and grounds, hitting the BOLD setting button on the machine and waiting until it started dripping through.

Was it a gift? Or an apology?

Both, she supposed.

Does he use them to make you feel better? Or him?

Also both, she guessed.

And is he both generous and sorry?

"You're as bad as my sister, Penelope," Octavia finally said aloud. "At least I can hang up when she gets too annoying."

Again, the scattered laughter, sounding almost like nightbirds calling. But the voice stayed silent for a little while.

"What the hell?" Octavia, fully awake now that caffeine had hit her bloodstream, and the sun had lifted over the horizon and was pouring in the kitchen windows. "Who…did *you* do this?"

She still wasn't sure who she was talking to. The voice (voices?) could be anything—hallucination, ghost, dream, sudden psychotic break with reality. But it spoke to her. And now it answered.

We replace what is taken.

"What does that mean?" Octavia drew her fingers along the warp strings. Someone or something had picked up where she left off, tying off the warp, weaving two long, thin pieces of polished wood through the bottom of the warp to arrange the strings evenly. They had even prepared a shuttle and woven the first two lines of weft yarn. Octavia wasn't an expert, but it looked as if she was all set to go; she only had to sit down and begin.

Weaving is not a solitary pursuit.

"I disagree." Octavia wasn't planning on spending her day at the table, but now she was sitting, coffee placed carefully to the side, left hand reaching for the heddle to lift it up. "You ever see a pack of spiders working together?"

Peals of laughter greeted her, making her think she had missed the punchline of a joke she didn't realize she was making.

"Fine, laugh it up," she muttered. Awkwardly, she shoved the shuttle through the open shed. It snagged on a warp string halfway through. Muttering under her breath, she pulled it back a little, unsnagged it, and finished slipping it through the strings.

The wooden shuttle only made it halfway through the pass. There wasn't enough slack string to allow it all the way through. At first, Octavia tried to unwind the string with the shuttle still mid-weave; that resulted in strings tightening and frustration until she pulled the shuttle all the back out of the weave and threw it on the table.

"This is stupid." She frowned. The shuttle was back in her hand. "I didn't even want this stupid gift."

The softest touch on her hand, as if she had reached for something in the dark and disturbed a spider's web. Far from disturbing her, the gentle stroke calmed her and then came to rest, an invisible helpmeet to guide her.

Octavia unwound the string and passed the shuttle through the open shed again. This time, the added slack allowed easy passage. Still under the guidance of the invisible, soft hands, she lowered the heddle, opening the next shed. She picked another polished piece of wood and inserted it into the strings, pulling it down against the previously woven strip. Firmly, the wood shoved the strings into place, and she prepared to pass the shuttle through again.

She repeated her previous actions once. Then twice. Then again, settling into a comfortable rhythm. The gentle touch lifted as she grew more at ease. Now and then, she felt it at her lower back, urging her to sit up straight, to raise her bowed neck, lest she cramp and tighten at the loom.

The day brightened outside, and yet she continued at her work. What would she do with the final product? Would she sell it at a market? Would she put it aside as a blanket for a future child? Would she gift it to her sister, Penelope? Or would she finish it at all?

Is this gift truly so cursed? This time, the voice came layered with so many sounds, as if an entire chorus waited behind her to ask her that question.

"What do you want from me?" Octavia asked aloud, even as she opened the shed, beat the weft, passed the shuttle, opened the shed. "What more do you want from me?"

What do you want? A single whisper, a hair's-breadth from her ear.

At last, the crux of the matter. She'd buried the question so deep for so long, she grew upset just thinking of it.

No. She wasn't upset—she was tired. Tired of her sister, tired of sympathetic glances and condescending offers of salvation. Tired of knowing they were right, but too tired to do anything about it.

Octavia had read a story once, about a frog slowly boiled alive in a massive cooking pot. The frog stayed, not knowing—or not believing—what was happening until it was too late, until the skin sloughed off it into the heat of the bubbles and the brine.

She didn't believe that story.

When she was younger, she had gone, once, to the beach with her mother and father to visit her grandparents. They'd gone crabbing off the edge of their long dock, casting their traps out in the bay, and caught a mess of unusually huge blue crabs that year.

They barely fit in the pot.

But fit they did in a huge, cast-aluminum Dutch pot with a heavy lid. Her grandmother had put the water in and started it on the stove. Even though it boiled slowly, ever slowly, the crab had begun to shake—to panic—to claw inside the darkness of the pot, stepping on each other, panicked, trying to find the light, the cool water in which they had once found refuge.

Octavia didn't believe in the slow boil anymore. There were so many times she could've looked back. She could have unpicked her weft, rolled her ball of twine and gone home. But now, as the daylight darkened into twilight, she stayed and would stay, not moving from her table and her work as she put the shuttle through, lifted the heddle to open the shed, beat the weft, passed the shuttle, lifted the heddle, beat the weft and on far into the dark and the night. And always, beside her on the narrow bench, the echoes of women who kept the watch at her side.

"Tavy—*Tavy?*"

Evan's voice ripped through her reverie, slicing her awareness with the serrated edge of his anger.

"I…didn't hear you come in." Octavia blinked against the sudden glare, refocusing, aware of the dishes piled in the sink and on the counters, the coffee cups standing like sentries along the table, the cockroach ambling along the top of the pony wall. The smell of her own body.

Dimly, she remembered the voices and the invisible hands guiding her to the refrigerator, to the microwave, the coffeemaker and then back to the bench—always back to her seat behind the loom, as she wove throughout the day and night.

"What the hell is wrong with you?" Evan dumped his rucksack on the floor. He'd carried it in his arms, wearing his big duffel bag on his back. "You didn't answer—dammit, I had to ask Sergeant Haskell for a ride when we got back."

Octavia blinked at him, then back down at the table. Needle in hand, she made a final loop and pulled it through the end of the fabric stretched across the table and over the loom. She remembered finishing the weave, then removing it from the loom, deciding on the hem stitch to avoid the ends unraveling. She'd found the instructions in the book; the hands that had guided her had gone strangely silent.

"I didn't hear the phone," she said.

"Goddammit." Evan threw his duffel to the ground, then kicked it. "What the hell were you doing? Were you playing around with that?" He stomped to the kitchen, pausing at the pony wall to slam his hand down on the roach. "Look at this dump. Is this how you live when I'm not home?" He flicked it to the floor, and Octavia cringed. "Disgusting."

Evan took in the kitchen, the dirty dishes, the un-swept floor. His face flushed. The silence in the house took on a life of its own, drawing around them. Octavia had to swallow, but she couldn't.

With a *crash*, Evan swept a stack of dishes to the floor.

"How about that?" he shouted into the aftermath of the splintering porcelain.

Another violent gesture, and the coffeepot landed on the floor, the glass breaking into a million shards, flinging dark brown drops against the cabinet.

"Can I live like a pig, too?"

Octavia froze as Evan threw another dish, and then another. He grabbed a cast-iron frying pan off the stove, egg remnants still clinging to it, and bashed and bashed until the kitchen counter cracked and began to sag.

"Is this enough of a pigsty for you, you goddamn dirty, filthy fucking pig?" he screamed.

A white haze formed in front of Octavia's gaze, a haze that dampened the noise and drew her attention back to the work laid out in front of her.

She had begun the project with a simple intention—a plain weave, in red and white. But what stood before her now was not plain, nor was there a single color anywhere.

Instead, a band of woven white cloth began under her fingers, a cloth with a brocaded pattern, almost unnoticed until the light caught it. Had she picked up the strings, lifted each one in the precise sequence necessary to create this pattern?

Here, under her fingers, a band of geometric diamonds and squares. Next, above that, a set of ancient armor against which a circular shield rested. On the shield, a nest of snakes, their heads poised to strike, their nest the head of a woman who stared off to the side where Evan raged.

Who had moved her fingers through this work, guided her as she wove ribbons of water and wheat, fields of battle, a forest at midnight where an owl, wings open in flight, waited to pounce?

Octavia passed the fabric through her hands, noting the imperfections along the right edge, how it rippled in and out where the tension was not quite even.

It is our gift. It is your choice. The voices spoke in unison, drowning out another scream from her husband, the heavy tread of his footsteps, for the first time, the blow of his hands landing on her— ungentle, grasping, choking.

Will you accept it?

The voice grew and thickened, split and shattered. The shards of sounds skittered across the room on multi-jointed legs, taking form, weaving their shadows until the strings of their essence revealed them—tall, electric.

Evan whimpered and tried to draw back. Octavia didn't notice.

Here stood three women holding a single string, their ages evident in the wrinkles of the crone's hand, in the fresh skin of the child, the eternal worry and love of the mother.

Across the room, five women clad in garments of leather armor, sharp swords safely hidden in scabbards at their sides, manipulating the intestines and viscera of a battlefield's worth of men as they wove their dark tale of cold winter slaughter.

Again, from another corner of the room, a fierce, gold light shone down on a chorus of women who bent to their work, plying a fine, linen sheath many ells long, as sacred cats twined around the weights of their looms.

Beside them an old woman clad in wool and fur sat behind an inkle loom made of boards and thick round pegs. A young girl watched, eyes glistening as if in reflected flames, intent on the warp strings that danced as her grandmother twisted cards, opened the shed, passed the shuttle, twisted the cards, and beat the previous shed, weaving a narrow band, giving life to dragons and flames and flowers blooming from the wool.

Beside Octavia, sitting on the narrow bench, a young girl dressed in a fine robe, holding the other edge of the fabric. She was the one who posed the question, and its ripples spread through her dark, shining eyes.

"Yes."

In unison, the women smiled and came to the table. Clasping the newly woven fabric, they lifted it high above their heads. Wordlessly, they released the long, white piece. It hovered, lingering in the air for a moment.

Evan shouted and tried to step back, escape, find a way out of the impossible situation that couldn't be happening in the destroyed kitchen.

The edge of the weaving reached him, the intricately embedded design stretching and elongating into lace, resembling the strands of a spider's web, reaching and entangling him as he tried to run.

"Tavy?" Evan whispered and reached for her.

She stepped away.

He held her gaze for one long, terrible moment, and then the shroud took him in a blizzard of frenetic activity, winding its way around him, the white passing before Octavia's eyes. Evan's eyes, hair, skin, limbs and hands disappeared under the layers, his screams choked as the wadding pushed into his mouth and down his throat. He struggled against the cloth binding him, suffocating him, soft little sounds escaping even after he ceased moving.

After what seemed hours, Evan thrashed once more and lay still.

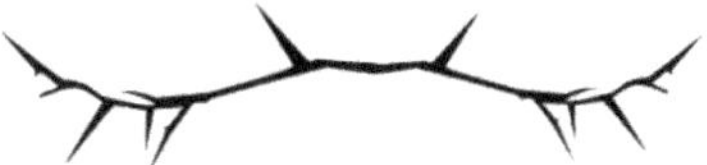

Night fell again. The kitchen was silent, empty, except for the corpse that lay, moldering, within the woolen folds of its shroud.

At the table, alone once again, Octavia ignored the mess rotting in the kitchen, the roaches skittering in the shadows. Her phone had stopped ringing—having lost charge weeks ago.

Under her fingers, the gossamer threads stretched and danced, catching and refracting what bits of light made it through the window into the dining area. Dust sat thickly on the surfaces in the rest of the house.

The soft hoot of an owl broke the silence, but not her concentration. The figure gently brushed her lower back, remind her to sit up straight, relieve the tension and ache. Octavia shifted on the bench, but did not pause, her long, black limbs dancing across the loom, weaving her web, another silent, white shroud in the company of her sisters.

RAYON

K. P. KULSKI

Big girls don't get scared. They don't cry when they get a scrape, or when they watch the strange sunrise on Highway 5 over a cracked windshield and mom's vacant unblinking eyes. They don't scream, they don't anything, even when dad cried and cried and cried.

Kitty hugged her doll, Buddy, to her chest, making his plastic face glow with a sickly green light that reflected against the dark picture window. Outside, the maple tree clung desperately to the soil through driving rain. Click-clack-scratch against the house. Thunder rolled like galloping horses over the pitch-blackness of the sky and in response, lightning brought the world to daylight for the space of a breath.

"Let's play hide-and-go-seek," she said, tugging on Daddy's sleeve, forcing him to put down the beer he'd been nursing. Light from the television flickered over his gaunt face—blue, then red, and against the *tal*-Korean shaman masks that Mommy hung when they first moved in—to scare away the bad spirits.

He let out a long sigh and slumped his shoulders. "Sure, Kitty."

Kitty sensed his resistance, his exhaustion, and glanced at the screen. Sears dress sale. Women flicked their hair and walked confidently, half smiling through the screen. Women that never looked like Mom. Kitty didn't think she'd grow to look like those women. Would that be okay?

"You don't haff to though—"

"You hide, I'll count. Ready?" Daddy said.

"Really?" Kitty's heart soared. He lifted his eyes, watery blue and haunted. Dad had barely spoken for days except through the telephone as he ordered pizza. Solidifying grease and cheese in lukewarm dough, the thought made her stomach turn. She missed *japchae* and *kimbap*. But that didn't matter right now. Daddy was gonna play hide-and-seek with her, just like he used to. Just like before—

Another peal of thunder rocked the house. The lights sputtered.

"Yeah. Go hide."

Big girls don't get scared.

Kitty ran, a bubble of laughter rising in her. With the sound of counting behind her, she cataloged potential hiding spots before ducking into the nearby cupboard. Pushing aside a jar of spaghetti sauce, she shut the little door behind her, grinning into the dark. Daddy would never find her here.

His rough voice faded away to soft creaks across the floor. She'd have to remind him later that he should say, "Ready or not," after counting. Her foot pushed over a tin of Spam with a clatter and Kitty froze, holding her breath so her giddiness didn't emerge as a stream of giggles. She imagined Daddy throwing open the cabinet with a gush of happy surprise and he'd say, "there you are! I found you!" Then he'd pick her up, tickles and laughter would break the silence. Kitty hugged Buddy close, waiting for it all to happen.

But nothing did. Only the sound of thunder and the smell of the wood cabinets and some long forgotten and dead spice, imparting its last scent forever into the tight space.

Buddy leaned against her in worry.

"It's okay," Kitty whispered.

Kitty cracked open the cabinet and peered out from her hiding place. She'd hidden here before, a long-ago time, when Mom had hauled buckets of clams and mussels newly gathered from a trip to the shore. Each bucket a self-contained ocean, the contents waiting to be cleaned and dropped into a pot of boiling water.

Stepping out of her hiding place, the house felt impossibly still. The darkness wrapped around her, folding her into its secrets, trying to swallow the memory of her very existence. She tiptoed and stole back into the living room. Absent of the television's light, everything had transformed into silhouettes and blackness. The window an oculus to the strengthening storm. A siren sounded somewhere close by, whirling a tired warning. No Daddy here. Maybe he hid too, waiting to pop out and scare her. It would be okay because he made her laugh whenever he did stuff like that.

"Taking a long drive," Mommy had said on the day of the accident, piling thick mink blankets in the backseat like a bed.

A trip. Trips were fun and Kitty had been so bored. Nothing much fun had happened since her dad deployed. Just school and playing alone in her bedroom. The military made Dad go away a lot. Kitty was used to it. When he left, the house would turn garlicky. English would give way to only Korean words from Mom and her friends, who exclusively watched Korean news and shows.

The commercials had women selling dresses, too. These women looked like Mommy, all dark hair and eyes. Kitty didn't think she'd look like them either when she grew up and she hoped that would be okay too.

Sometimes Dad called. Last time, Mom's voice sounded harsh and afraid, pushing fire through the phone receiver. Daddy's voice garbled back in loud stabbing tones. Their voices rose like a chorus of rage, firing back at each other, heavy with disappointment and frustration. The phone clicked and Kitty cried. "I want to talk to Daddy."

Mommy wept. "We have to go on a trip, Kit-kat."

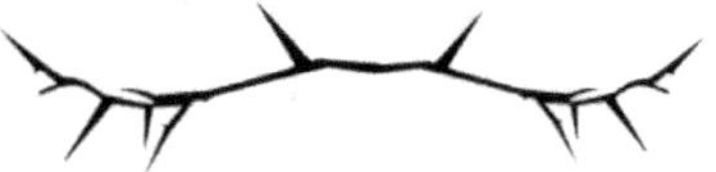

A figure emerged too close to the window, solidifying in the moment between a flash and blackness.

It looked in.

White T-shirt, clean-shaven, hair high-and-tight, his fevered gaze burrowing into Kitty's center, the soft place inside where she still remembered mom's protective arms encircling her.

"Daddy?" Kitty whispered, hugging Buddy so hard that his face lit up with his faint green light.

The figure shook, rain parting like a curtain around him. The maple threw its branches wildly at the house, knocking frantically as if it could suddenly uproot and run. Daddy looked up at the sky and yelled, a raw, unintelligible noise that pierced the thunder.

Kitty was a big girl. Big girls don't scream.

Buddy's glow went out.

A lamp flared to life behind her. Daddy on the couch, a pool of red on the rug. He turned to look at her, half his face a mangle of blood and meat. One eye burned bright as he rolled the lamp switch between his fingers. The light flashed on and off.

Click, click, click-click-click.

"Time to hide, Kitty." The remaining half of his lips said. His words hung heavy and stifling, like a rain-soaked blanket forgotten on a laundry line. "Hide real well now. 1…2…3…"

Shapes of swaying trees shadowed along the floor of the tiny glen. "Look, Kit-kat. See how the *kosari* curls? This is when it is good to eat." Mom gently pushed forward the tip of a fern. Kitty leaned in dutifully. The *kosari* pulled in at itself, desperate to keep its tender leaves from the chill of the world, tucking until it swirled into a spiral. It wouldn't do it any good. That made Kitty a little sad, but Mommy had already snipped the spiral and added it to her basket.

The damp scent of dirt and green leaves blew through, rattling and humming, almost masking the sound of cars from a nearby highway. Mommy moved on, checking for more *kosari*, moving like royalty, at least it seemed to Kitty. Mommy's midnight hair tied back with a handkerchief, dressed in jeans and T-shirt. A queen in hiding. Kitty didn't understand why some people talked to the queen with loud voices and sneers, as if her mom didn't understand. Kitty wanted to shout at them. Make them listen to her mother's soft words and hard meanings.

It didn't matter now.

Mom had died. But queens aren't supposed to die.

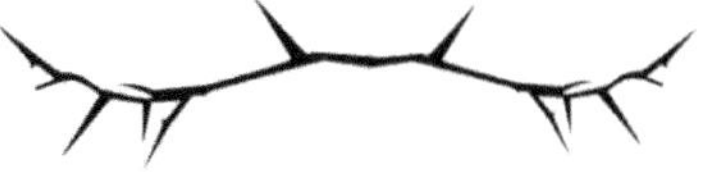

Kitty sprang and threw herself into the hall, pumping her legs hard, one hand out, the other wrapped around Buddy. Thunder rolled again, gaining speed, and finished into a crack that sucked the air from her ears.

She made for her bedroom, for the safety of lavender walls and frilly bedspreads. The lightning saturated the hall as she reached the doorway, clipping from white to darkness, creating still frames of her bedroom door slamming shut. The other doors followed suit, throwing themselves toward and away from their frames in wild crashes.

Kitty's heart jolted, panic threw shocks of cold into her limbs. Buddy reignited, squealing out Mary Had a Little Lamb in alarm. She dared to turn. The doors stilled, each sealed like walls, except for her parents' bedroom. The outline of the open closet door within seemed to elongate in the dark. She ran for it instinctively.

Hide real well now.

She tumbled into the closet, pulling the door shut behind her, and sprang a hand toward the light switch, fumbling along the wall blindly. The cool, smooth drywall went on for miles. Finally, she passed over the bump and flicked it on with one neat motion.

Nothing.

Big girls aren't afraid of the dark.

She flicked it again and again with shaking hands.

Big girls aren't afraid.

"Mommy," she whispered into the darkness.

A peal of thunder shook the house. Footsteps stalked outside the closet. Kitty held her breath, keeping each muscle still. She no longer wanted Daddy to find her and tickle her. Now she prayed he wouldn't do any of those things at all.

The pacing gave way to agitated shuffles. Then nothing.

Kitty's shaking legs forced her to sit, the old carpet itching bare skin. Buddy lit up again, illuminating the forest of Mom's dresses. The blue one with white tiny flowers and green vines snaking along the hem, Kitty used to dress up in that one to play pretend. The scent of the ocean rose up strong, and cloth rustled gently as if trying to shake out the wrinkles of disuse.

"Come'ere Kit-kat, come'ere Kit-kat, kat, kat."

Click-clack-scratch, the maple tree knocked into the house wall again. This time slower, less frantic.

A face peered out between the hanging clothes. A chill fell from Kitty's stomach to her toes with prickly pins-and-needles. She opened her mouth, but only a puff of air came out, giving only a faint rattle against her vocal cords.

Cast in Buddy's green light, the face bore the unmistakable expression of concern, the kind full lips, the dark eyebrows that wrinkled when she said Kitty's name.

Mommy.

"Kitty." The soft, pale oval glowed translucent, as if barely able to exist at all.

Buddy released a few chimes of concern.

"Come'ere, Kit-kat," the face said.

Kitty put Buddy under her arm and took a step forward. The green light extinguished on the second step, and on the third something soft pulled her into the rayon and cotton darkness.

Fabrics tickled her face, unseen hands compelled her to walk far into the rows of old dresses. Department store faux satin slipped past her ears with whispers of reassurance. She let it all push in around her, pressing cool against her brow, a living sea of things that once made-up the essence of her mother. Hands urged her forward, silk palms pushed down until she lay prone, cheek to cheek with the carpet, face to face with Buddy, whose light came alive in her hands.

"Hide," she whispered to him, and his light went out.

Click-click-click-bang.

Kitty waited for a long time. Soon the sound of the wind grew gentle, the thunder receding. Through the night she dosed, dresses stroking her cheek, settling protectively over her like the wings of some great brocaded bird.

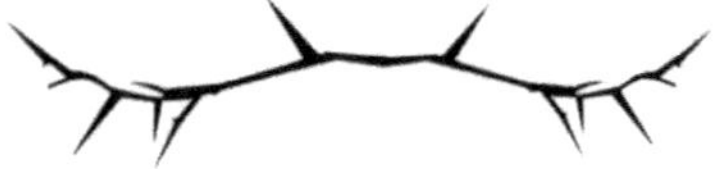

Kitty jumped at the sound of an unlatching door and sunlight filtered in around the shape of unfamiliar shoes. Mom's dresses had fallen still and lifeless.

A buzz of static and a fuzzy voice, "Confirming report, ten-five-six."

"Standby," the shoes said.

Then those shoes turned into knees and the knees turned into a face. A man crouching down to peer at Kitty. "Come out, sweetheart." His black uniform all shadows against the badge on his chest, glinting in the morning light. He put out a hand. "Come'ere."

Kit-kat, kat, kat.

"It's okay," the officer said.

Kitty took his hand. A dress slid past her face, pushing back her hair with a sigh.

"The kid's here," the officer yelled to the movement in her parents' bedroom.

"Daddy," she started.

The officer shushed her gently. His eyes went soft and sad. "We'll talk more about that soon. Let's get you out of here, okay?"

She nodded.

More voices in the hallway.

The officer gathered her to his chest. "I want you to bury your head here, okay? Don't look until I tell you to."

She didn't respond, turning her head to fit into his arms and stared blankly at the dresses in the closet. They swayed goodbye.

"Sweetheart, do you hear me? Don't look until I tell you, okay?"

"Okay," Kitty said. Grown-ups always wanted to hear okay to questions like that.

She squeezed Buddy. He played a little for her, his green light faint in the morning sun. The officer smelled unfamiliar, like metal and starch, but maybe, the way he acted, he smelled just right to some little kid back home.

She peered over his shoulder as they moved into the hallway, just like he said he didn't want her to do.

Kitty was a big girl. Big girls did what they wanted.

The coverlet looked as if a can of scarlet paint had spilled. Her daddy lay slumped over the bed, as if he had crumpled from exhaustion. Flecks of fleshy matter decorated his white T-shirt, a revolver still gripped in his motionless hand.

Kitty took one good picture with her mind and then closed her eyes. Big girls don't get scared. The officer's shoes hit the sidewalk with a soft pat-pat-scuff.

"What's your name, sweetheart?" The man's voice came out strained.

"Kitty." Kit-kat-kit-kat.

He nodded, motioning to another officer. The woman's mouth set in a straight line, her eyes watery, as if she tried to layer serious over sadness to make it go away.

"Hi Kitty, I'm Officer Choi." The woman stuck out a hand. She looked like Mommy, but not really at the same time. She looked like Mommy the same ways Mommy's friends looked like her.

Kitty's insides tumbled and lurched. She concentrated on holding her eyes wide so she could act the way grown-ups wanted her to act. "Hi," she said, taking the hand.

"Kitty," Officer Choi said. "Do you know where your mom is? Was she in the house?"

Kitty scrunched up her nose in confusion. The memory of the pale oval of her mother's face still glowed in her mind.

"Your mom called dispatch for help."

Kitty blinked, silence spread out between her and the officers, hanging in the air before she could answer. "My mom died— twelve sleeps ago." The words moved over her lips like a garden slug.

The officers glanced at each other.

Kit-kat-kat…kat…kat.

"How long have you been in the house… alone?"

Kitty didn't know. "I was hiding."

Officer Choi nodded. The other officer shifted his weight.

She hugged Buddy so tight that the first chime caught in a tinny loop.

Officer Choi sat gently on the curb and put an arm around Kitty. "You know, it's okay to cry."

Tears slicked Kitty's insides, turning her stomach sour. "But I'm a big girl."

"I know. I can tell. But even big girls need to cry sometimes."

"Do you?" Kitty said, staring at Buddy.

The officer gave her a squeeze. "More times than I can count."

The maple tree swayed.

Tears pushed out of the hollow inside Kitty, a sea of boiling water emptying in hot, frantic gulps. Her self-contained ocean.

Kitty was a big girl. Big girls are afraid, they cry—and they remember the whisper of rayon and the horrible silence that follows a gunshot.

SAPPHO AT SEA

SAM CASEY

The sheath is mightier than the sword,
As the warship slices through the unruffled sea
Land-loving inhabitants suffering short sleep
As moonlight coats the liminal horizon.
What goddess of oceans deep accepted
This Trojan gift that invades the sacred plane,
Slicing stillness and leaving gashed wake?
Oh, serene siren, reflecting the void of skies above,
Soundlessly promising eternal silence,
Forgive me, for I have sinned,
And in sinning sought refuge in thee.
The solace you provide is slick with guilt,
Your Silence deafening besieged ears,
Coaxing the sword from restless sleep.
Blissful slumber starts with just one step.
Darkness providing warmth at last,
Wedding bells chiming all the way down.
If freedom remains free with sword unsheathed,
Then freely do I commit my remains to thee.

NEVER THE PRINCESS

ELLA B. RITE

Charity clenched the hood of the cloak tight against her head. Blonde tendrils of hair escaped and tangled with her thick eyelashes. An icy gust of wind whipped around the dense, twisted trees and slapped her pale cheeks, leaving them red and sore. She cursed and glanced at her older sister. Grace's long red hair danced on the breeze. Each auburn strand highlighted by the orange rays of the waning sun. Grace strolled along the leaf-covered path like a queen enjoying the royal garden.

"Please move faster," Charity begged as she stamped her satin-covered feet on the frozen ground. "We should have left Fairyton weeks ago. I hate the cold."

Grace smiled and opened the cloak with a flourish. The emerald-green ball gown matched the color of her eyes—the bodice cut far lower than expected on a proper lady. A layer of steam clung to her body like an aura.

"Is it cold? I hardly noticed. Besides," she plucked a yellowed leaf from a tree limb. "You can't visit this town without a stroll through the enchanted forest."

"You wanted to visit the fortune teller," snarled the younger sister.

"Of course, I did. She could tell us the location of your next murder victim, umm," Grace gave a little cough into her hand, "I mean, husband. Isn't that the whole purpose of this Sisters Trip?"

Charity whirled to face her sister. "I will find another husband. One who will accept me for my strengths and who appreciates my independence," she hissed.

"Didn't your last two husbands share those traits? I mean, before their untimely deaths."

"They wanted me to submit, like a trained puppy." Charity's fists shot to her waist. "Michael dared to strike me across the face and Donald expected me to clean his cottage, launder his clothes and cook him dinner while he spent time at the brothel. I will never tolerate abuse. Mother taught us better."

"She did indeed," admitted Grace. "So here we are, strolling through the enchanted forest to find you a husband. One who you won't need to annihilate." She shrugged a shoulder. "And folks call me a hothead."

"Michael left a bruise," replied Charity. "He deserved it."

"Of course," said Grace. "Let's return to town. Maybe drink a cup or two of ale and leave this place."

An old man stepped from behind a gnarled maple tree and blocked the girls' path. He raised a bony finger to his thin, cracked lips. A long ax dangled from the other hand. The silver blade caught the light of the setting sun. A wolf bayed in the distance and the man sneered, showing small yellow teeth. Crisp leaves danced in the wind around the girls' heavy cloaks.

"You are in danger," said the man in a deep voice. He leered at their low-cut bodices. "This forest is filled with creatures that would tear your limbs from your body. Your pretty little screams would never be heard."

Grace stared at the man, blinked, and raised her velvet-covered hands with the palms up. "That's it? You pop out of the trees, looking creepy, wielding an ax, and that's your line?" She placed her hands on her hips and turned her wide green eyes toward her sister. "I'm offended."

Charity stomped her satin-covered feet against the cold dirt. She pulled the hood at the neck as tendrils of blonde hair danced on the icy breeze. The wind smacked her face long enough to redden her cheeks and water her blue eyes. "Can we be offended and warm?" Vapor escaped her mouth with every exhalation. She should have changed her outfit after the Yule Ball at the palace, but Grace didn't think it necessary.

A long howl carried on the wind. The man turned in a slow circle, his long grey hair tangled in the wind. An owl hooted in the distance.

"The wolf is free. You are in danger." Fall leaves crunched beneath the man's boots and he turned to scan beyond the trees. The shadows of the tree lengthen as the sun fell. The skies purpled.

"That what's she said," said Grace, pointing a thumb over her shoulder. A cloth-covered caravan stood in the clearing. Folding her arms, she cocked her head to the side and sighed. "So, what's your scam? You and the fortune teller," Grace performed air quotes with her fingers, "set up shop in the middle of the forest. Then spread word that the old biddy is some oracle who can see the future. When folks dare to visit, the witch declares imminent death and danger? Once the victims flee the van, you appear with your little ax. Then the victims flee and tell the tale of the haunted witch in the woods. That's one weak con and I'm disappointed," she pouted. "Charity, handle this."

Charity groaned and rolled her eyes. "Dammit, Gee."

"Fair is fair," said Grace, tucking her auburn hair behind her ears. "I did the witch, and that heifer put up a fight."

The old man blinked. "What did you do to the sorceress?"

The women ignored the man and continued their tiff.

"She threw a crystal ball at you," complained Charity, "and missed."

"I won. That's all that matters," Grace grinned and pointed to the woodsman. "Now you get to handle the help."

"Fine, at least warm my hands." Charity removed her gloves and held her hands in front of Grace's face.

"What a baby," said Grace, but she leaned forward and exhaled a thick plume of steam on her sister's fingers. "How's that?"

Charity bent her fingers and beamed. "Perfect."

The man stepped one pace toward the girls and demanded, "What happened to Margette?"

The wind died and silenced the sounds of the forest. Something howled. The old man raised his ax to a two-handed grip—one hand at the base and the other hand gripped below the blade. He bent his knees and narrowed his eyes.

"What are you?" he rasped.

Grace shrugged a shoulder. "Just a couple of fair maidens navigating a cruel world."

Before the man could respond, Charity retrieved a dagger from the folds of her cloak. The blade glinted as she tossed it in the air, grabbed the blade between her thumb and index finger, and cocked her arm. The knife momentarily froze behind her right ear before she snapped her hand forward and released the blade.

The man's head whiplashed back as the knife lodged in his left eye. He stood a few seconds (enough to make the girls nervous) before falling to his knees. He dropped the ax and removed the dagger. Blood mixed with creamy eye fluids poured along his ruddy cheek and thin lips. He pointed the knife at the sisters as his good eye evaluated them.

"Wha, woo, wha, woo," he said before falling dead into the crunchy leaves.

"I think he was calling you a witch." Grace sauntered forward. She stooped, removed the dagger from the man's fingers, and wiped it clean on his sleeve. "I think I'm offended again."

Charity replaced the knife within the folds of her cloak. "You prepare the bodies. I'll get the horses and supplies."

"Fair enough," said Grace. She removed the ax from beneath the dead man and passed it to her sister. "Two hours tops." She grabbed the man's leg and dragged him toward the caravan.

Hours later, Charity strolled to the campsite. She had changed into leather pants and a heavy shirt. Her hair pulled into a pony tail. She nodded at the scene.

The bodies of the old man and the fortune teller hung, naked and upside down, from a tree branch. Their bodies fileted open from pelvis to collarbone. Grace had three different fire spits, each at a separate temperature based on the meat: low for liver and heart, medium for spleen and kidneys, high heat for lungs.

"Looks good. How much longer?" Charity tossed a bundle of clothes at her sister's feet. "The caravan is packed and ready."

Grace removed her dress and began donning the heavy pants and shirt. "How's the inventory? Please tell me she had herbs."

Charity strolled to the body of the old woman. "We're good." She ran her fingers through the coarse, grey hair. "Herbs, spices, salt. The old bat even had a fishing pole." She turned to her sister. "What she didn't have was a cauldron."

"What a bitch." Grace sat on a log to lace her boots. "Food will be done in a few minutes. We should be on the road within the next half hour."

Charity removed a parchment from her satchel and strolled to one of the spits to use the light of the fire. The juices of the spleen dripped into the fire and sizzled. The aroma watered her mouth.

"So Fairyton is a bust," she twisted her mouth and glanced at Grace, "just like Neverland."

"Fine," said Grace, folding her arms. "You were right, and I was wrong."

"Twice," said Charity. "Now we go where I want. Camelot, here we come."

"I don't like knights," Grace pouted. "Who wants a tin-can man? Especially during the cold season."

"Fair is fair," said Charity, rolling the parchment.

"I guess," said Grace, rolling her eyes. "It'll take a fortnight and 4 portals to get there."

"Good thing we got so much food," said Charity, smiling brightly.

The sisters broke into a fit of giggles.

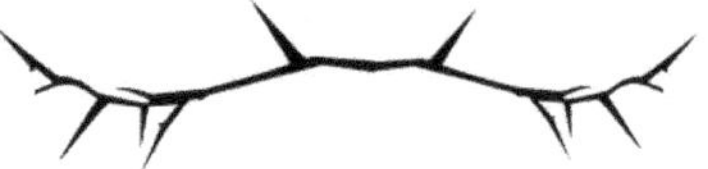

The wolf hid behind a twisted hedge and watched his prey. They had killed 'The Witch' and 'The Hunter,' which freed him from the moon curse. He could change into his man form and return to his homeland.

The icy breeze combed through his fur. The scent of blood and lavender reached his nostrils–his nose flared. He opened his mouth as the flavors danced across his tongue as he panted. He made his choice.

The wolf stalked forward: his knees bent, belly close to the ground. Women have been the bane of his existence. First the witch who cursed him and now the women who taunt him with their delectable smells.

Kill the fire girl first. One bite to the neck should do it. He may dance with the knife thrower for a time before dispatching her to the gods.

The forest is a dangerous place for girls.

THE PHONE IN THE WOODS

SARA CROCOLL SMITH

For Maximus, a most loyal companion

Deep within the woods, you will be measured, you will be weighed. Will you be found wanting?

Christie stepped out of her car, shading the screen of her phone from the glaring sunlight. She flinched at the ping of another work email. When squinting didn't help her read it, she found herself halfway back into the car to look before shaking her head, slamming the door, and marching toward the entrance to the hiking trail.

She shoved her cell in the back pocket of her shorts and slowed by the trail sign. There were tattered postings for lost dogs tacked several layers deep, like the fraying skin of an old onion. What was once something she'd never paid attention to had, over the past couple of days, become forever burned into her memory. Her fingers traced the newest member of the collection. Christie frowned to see the fresh rains had also eaten at the edges of the poster she'd poured her heart into.

"Domino." The picture wasn't great. She'd been surprised to realize she didn't have as many good ones of him as she thought. Grainy, her fawn-colored whippet, stared out from the poster, his amber eyes bright and cheerful. Christie frowned, popped an antacid from her small fanny pack, and rubbed at the ache in her chest.

Footsteps approached from the right. "Still no luck?"

An older woman, perhaps in her sixties, with a glamorously gray-silver bob, breezed out of the trail toward Christie, a sympathetic look on her face. Embarrassed, she couldn't remember the woman's name. Christie sighed. "No. He's got to be out here somewhere. He's not the type to run away."

The woman nodded and briefly squeezed Christie's shoulder. She gestured skyward. "Lucky the rains have come through. Give him something to drink. You'll find him today. I have a feeling—"

Christie's phone buzzed behind her, its obnoxious default melody piercing a thrum of anxiety through her entire body. Her face reddened as she withdrew it from her pocket. "Sorry."

The older woman moved on, but Christie hardly noticed. She gazed down at the screen, her boss's name flashing alongside the button, dancing and demanding to be answered. Her chest constricted. The world turned dull and gray around her as the screen pulsed wildly neon, and Christie sank against the trail sign to the ground. Frozen. She couldn't answer, she couldn't *not* answer. Echoes of the call bled strangely into the sounds of the forest. Electric birds morphed into nonhuman voices, until finally melding into a chittering whine, like the one she'd ignored on the day Domino went missing. A day, like any of a hundred others, she'd taken the call from her boss during her walk, in between repeatedly attending to emails and hardly looking up.

A sharp bark snapped everything back into an effervescent green. Christie sprang up and scoured the underbrush for any sign of Domino.

Nothing.

The phone bleated again. She let out an exasperated cry, stomped to her car, and threw her cell into the front seat. "Can't I get a few hours of my Sunday to search for my damn lost dog?"

Pivoting on her hiking boots, she made a beeline down the trail. Her spine tingled with frustration and fear. Her boss wasn't known for patience or mercy when he wanted something, regardless of the actual urgency of the task. Christie slapped a mosquito from her arm and came away with a dab of her own blood. She grumbled and stalked further into the woods.

As she searched the usual trails, she couldn't help but replay all the instances in the past couple of years she'd meant to spend more time with Domino, yet didn't. Something was always more pressing. More work to be done. Housework. Creative side hustles. Family. Friends. After all of that busyness during the day, Christie couldn't be bothered at night when she was exhausted. The walks on the trail were about the only thing she did with Domino. Christie bit her lip, irritated at herself.

She slowed where a lightly worn path branched off the well-trod ground, near where Domino had disappeared. She'd never been down it, nor really ever noticed it before, but that didn't mean he didn't find something good to sniff that way. Besides, she'd covered the rest of the area already.

Christie hadn't seen any other hikers lately. She glanced both ways down the main trail, then dipped through the brush onto the path. The trees huddled close, branches clasped together and vines knitted tight. Dodging gnarled roots, she advanced farther. The sun penetrated the dense forest and trickles of light that should've seemed like rays from heaven instead mocked her for having any hope at all. Did she really think she'd find her dog out here? A dog that never once had to find food or water on its own. A dog that didn't have a remotely feral bone in its body. Exactly the things she loved about him were what most assuredly doomed him on his own.

Ahead, the path came to a bend. She'd gone much farther than she'd planned and without knowing how far this trail went or where it led, Christie would have to decide to go back soon. The waning day had taken on an agonizing late summer heat, crushing with humidity that called mosquitoes to her skin like a siren. She cursed herself for not putting on a stronger bug repellant as the urge to scratch prickled in select spots on her arms and legs.

Just a quick inspection around the curve and then time to turn back. Christie stared down a short corridor that opened on one side to a spectacular view of a lively river that was a good thirty-foot steep drop. She adjusted her sunglasses and shielded her eyes with her forearm as the sun hit the water at a blinding angle. Once she took in the sight, she noticed that on the other, shrouded side of the trail, an old rotary phone was mounted to a simple wooden pole.

Curiosity piqued, a jarring discovery in the otherwise untouched forest. She moved closer to inspect it. The black telephone hung there expectantly. A sign nailed beneath it read:

> *This phone is for you. Speak to the one whom you never got to say goodbye.*

Tears gathered at the corners of her eyes as the intention sank in, the leaves blurring in a green haze in the periphery. Hands trembling, feeling slightly silly, she lifted the handset off the hook and put it to her ear. For a minute, maybe two, no words came.

"I miss you," she whispered. Christie closed her eyes. "I'm so sorry, Domino. I thought I was doing my best to juggle everything. And I missed you. I took our time together for granted, thinking you'd always be there. But no one is always there, are they? I'm just so freaking *sorry*."

Her words trailed off in soft sobs. She wiped at her wet cheeks and runny nose. As she removed the receiver from her ear, the chittering returned–like the tip of a branch, skipping across a rough surface, it seeped through the earpiece.

Christie stiffened and pressed the phone against her ear. The soft sound appeared to creep closer to her as it grew in intensity, forcing her to take an irrational glance behind her. Fear, like ice, spread to her fingers and toes. Then, a low keening replaced the terrifying chittering. She'd know that whining anywhere.

"Domino!" She grasped the handset, desperate for any other signs or clues. But the whining no longer came through the phone.

It came from farther down the trail.

Dropping the phone to hang itself by its springy cord, she sprinted as fast as her legs would take her. "Domino! Come here, boy! Where are you?"

The whining veered off to her right, off trail. She bounded in the direction, stumbling over branches and decaying tree trunks. The sound kept moving and she couldn't imagine her dog going that fast, but she wouldn't forgive herself if she didn't keep up, not when he was this close.

A fawn-colored tail whipped around a craggy oak. "Domino!" she screamed. When she came around the tree, Christie skidded to a stop, teetering on the edge of a deep, muddy pit. A bouquet of putrid, bile-summoning aromas wafting from below hit her like a truck. Her stomach churned. She covered her nose and scoured the bottom for Domino, afraid to jump down as there were no points of egress she could see.

Leaves rustled behind her. A branch snapped. Giddy, she was ready to pivot and draw Domino into her arms and give him the biggest squeeze of his life. But as she turned, the chittering returned. Her pulse sped up. The sound morphed into a strange clacking, hollow in a way that set her teeth on edge.

It was *close*.

Christie rolled her shoulders back and faced toward the unsettling sound. It could be anything. Probably just another hiker. "Hello?"

In the space between heartbeats, she realized she held her breath and her lungs burned. Sweat trickled down her back. A mosquito landed on her leg, and she resisted the urge to smack it, afraid to move a muscle.

From between two trees, something moved. Not tall enough to be a human, but much too large to be a dog, it ambled forward, a pronounced hunch arched with odd protrusions at regular intervals. It used a long, bleached staff to aid its ungainly gait. What she'd assumed were leaves rustling were actually the noise it made when it moved and as it approached, she saw the bulk of its body was composed of moldy, rotten leaves compressed together like sinew. The thing's head was covered with a hood of dark green moss, and Christie would've done anything to avoid seeing the face of the horrifying being before her.

She inched backward as it came closer. The dank musk of the creature battled with the odor of the pit behind her. Christie put her hands up to slow it. "Whoa! I'm just looking for my dog…"

The moment she spoke, the creature halted, returning to a stillness that rivaled the surrounding trees. It blended into the forest with such adeptness that Christie, rooted to the spot, questioned every hike she'd ever been on, the sensation of its empty gaze bleeding into her past like judge, jury, and executioner.

When several minutes passed in this manner, she could endure it no longer. "I mean no harm—"

The decomposing atrocity raised its staff a foot from the ground and slammed it down. From around its back, four mangy dogs burst forth, snarling and viciously growling at Christie. They were almost on top of her. She toppled backward and fell into the pit, landing with a force hard enough to knock the wind from her body.

Christie wheezed, gripping her midsection, as the wild dogs barked ferociously down at her, yet remained safely at the pit's edge. She heard another thump of the staff and the dogs retreated. Rolling onto her side, she coughed and hyperventilated until her vision faltered and darkness crept in.

When she came to, by the angle of the sun, she couldn't have been passed out for long. The rotten essence curled up her nose, causing her to dry heave. She had to get out of this pit and return to the trail. Put as much distance between her and these woods as possible. Nothing hurt too much, aside from some aches and pains. Still, she ran her muck-covered hands along her arms, her stomach, and then her legs, to be sure she hadn't broken anything.

As she reached her legs, her right leg seemed unusually warm. Was she in shock? If she'd broken her leg, she would never get out of this pit. Her mind raced. She didn't have her cell. No one knew where she was, and no one would be looking for her. She could die. In fact, it was highly likely.

"Help!" Her scream was weak and raw. Christie bit her lip and pushed herself up to force herself to assess the damage. To her surprise, her leg was fine, at least as far as she could tell. Yet something nestled against her. Caked in mud, it was warm on her thigh. Unrecognizable, she scrutinized it, terrified of it being a creature like the one she'd just encountered.

Its surface rose and fell with a breath. *Alive!*

Christie jerked away. The creature hopped up and stared at her with bright amber eyes, tail wagging eagerly behind it.

She blinked several times. "Domino?"

Domino sniffed her hands and licked her cheeks. Christie laughed, relief flooding through her system. She hugged the whippet around the neck. "Oh, thank goodness," she breathed into his dirt-laden fur. She wrinkled her nose. "We're both going to need one heck of a bath, buddy."

Christie pulled back and scanned the rim of the pit. On all sides, they were surrounded by at least eight or nine feet of sharp incline. She struggled to stand in the slippery mud and looked down at the dog. "How are we gonna get out of here, boy?"

She searched the walls and found the least steep area. "Even if I get up, how will I get you out? And what about that… thing?" The urge to cry crushed against her sternum, stealing her breath. She slumped into the muck and threw up her hands. "What are we going to do?"

Domino whimpered and shoved her in the shoulder with his snout. She brushed him off, trying to think of a solution. He jostled her again.

"What?" she asked, exasperated. Then her eye caught on something about the mud. It was irregular in places, angular, bumpy. She'd taken it for rocks or the like. But now, she wasn't so sure.

Crawling closer to a clump, she dug her fingers into the sludge and wrapped them around a smooth, hard object that was long with a bulbous end. She lifted it out of the mud and quickly wiped off the excess. Her eyes widened and a frightened scream erupted from her lips as she threw it as far from her body as possible.

It was a human bone.

Gleaming ivory on the parts unmarred by soil, it sat there, mundane, surreal. Domino poked his nose at it.

"No. Leave it alone," she commanded.

Domino ignored her, instead opening his jaw wide and scooping the large bone in his mouth. He trotted over eagerly and dropped it at her feet.

Christie looked from the dog to the bone and back again. Then she cocked her head in consideration. "Do you think the ground is firm enough, though?" she asked him.

The dog answered with a short, encouraging bark. Christie picked up the bone and walked to the edge. She arched back, aiming the end perpendicular to the pit's bottom, about waist height, then slammed it into the ground. Locating another bone, she used it as a hammer to secure it into place. After she was reasonably sure it would hold, she repeated the step with other bones, refusing to tally what the amount of bones in the pit truly meant.

Christie admired her handiwork. Three carefully positioned bones should allow her the leverage to escape. She patted Domino on the head. "Well, boy, I think it's do or die time." The attempt at levity rang hollow, despite her best effort. She lifted Domino onto her shoulder and climbed. No problem on the first one, only a slight struggle to maneuver them up to the second. Her muscles ached to lift them both. Christie reached for the third and her hand slipped. She shoved Domino the final few feet before she fell back into the muck with a sickening thunk.

She wrestled to regain her footing and squealed in pain, unable to put much weight on her ankle without coaxing forth agony.

Pressing both hands against her prison, she peered up at the edge. Domino was nowhere to be seen. "Domino?"

Christie strained to hear her dog. Nothing.

Then it started again. Quiet, slow, before the malicious metronome of its clacking increased, fast, loud. Close.

Domino whined.

"Domino!" Adrenaline bathed her muscles with renewed fire. Christie climbed with fear and fury, her ankle screaming in protest. At last, she clawed herself over the edge of the pit, then froze at the sight before her.

The creature stood not three feet away, with its four faithful dogs in a semicircle behind it. Each dog stood like a statue, their eyes watching her. The creature was equally still. Christie's mouth hung open at the realization that the protrusions on its back were jagged, exposed spine bones cascading down into a long, grotesque tail. Human hand bones connected by grime and filament gripped the staff—no, not a staff—a femur. Whether it was human or animal, she couldn't tell. With the other hand, the creature lifted its moss hood, revealing its ghastly visage.

The hair on the back of her neck stood at attention. The air grew hot and cloying with the scent of carrion. A tidal wave of dread washed over her.

This thing was not human.

The elongated skull of a dog stared at her with empty eyes. Lifting its snout to the sky, it rattled its teeth together as chittering rang out. Then it turned toward her.

It gestured to her and to Domino, who cowered in front of it. Christie's eyes widened and her muscles tensed as the creature raised the bone staff to strike Domino. This thing wanted to take her dog from her.

No.

Christie gritted her teeth, then snarled in a way that quickly became a roar. She rushed in between the creature's blow and Domino. The bone staff struck her in the shoulder, and she collapsed at its feet. With defiance and great effort, she pushed herself up enough to glare at it.

The four dogs at its back howled, but the creature put out a hand to stay them. It glowered at her for several moments before tipping the staff in the trail's direction and bowing its head briefly.

Not tearing her eyes from it, Christie scooped up Domino in her arms and hobbled as fast as she could to the path. She couldn't help but look back as she escaped. When she did, the creature pointed at Domino with one impossibly long skeletal finger. A warning.

Covered in dried mud and sweat and streaked with tears, Christie emerged from the trail and into the parking lot, with Domino safely in her arms. Only when she stepped onto the blacktop did Domino lift his head from her collarbone and give her several sloppy kisses. She laughed and hugged him tight.

Once Domino was settled in the back seat, Christie eased into the front. Her ankle throbbed dully and every bone in her body groaned for some serious rest. She sighed and pulled on her seatbelt. In the relieved quiet of her car, listening to her dog's relaxed panting, the ringing of her phone shattered the calm.

Frowning, Christie tapped the decline call button and gave Domino a pat on the head in victory. Yet, as she put the car in reverse, she unlocked her cell on instinct and pulled up her messages, scrolling through them. The car shifted back into park. She began typing out a reply to an urgent text.

It started.

Quiet, slow growling, before it increased—faster, louder.

Right behind her.

In the rearview mirror, Christie spied Domino, teeth bared, foaming at the mouth, ready to attack. Cemented to the spot with blood curdling terror, she locked and tossed the phone in the passenger seat.

Ever so slowly, she rotated to look at Domino. His cheerful eyes greeted hers with no trace of malice. He was her happy, tired dog, in need of nothing more than a good meal and bath.

Christie let out a big exhale. She bit her lip, patted his head again, and resumed pulling out of the spot and getting onto the main road.

When her phone rang again, she chucked it out the window and watched in the rearview mirror as it smashed to pieces, sparkling metallic like an eruption of stars on the asphalt behind her.

ON GUARD

BRENDA HUETTNER

I see Evans rounding the corner of the last storefront of the East wing, and I let out the breath I didn't realize I'd been holding. We meet, as planned, in the center of the mall, right by the two-story pile of concrete that used to be a gurgling fountain.

"So exactly how long does it take to get used to all this vacancy? I swear the shadows pulse like living things."

Evans snickers at my skittishness. "I'll let you know when I find out. I'm still startled whenever that blasted furnace thumps on, and I've been on this graveyard shift for over a month now. Sounds just like someone trying to break in."

"Has anyone tried to break in?"

"Not that I know of. We're in the middle of nowhere here. That's partly why so many of the stores have gone out of business. And the few that are left, well, there isn't much there worth stealing."

"But what if someone does try something? What do I do?"

"Just call me. I'll come help. Don't forget, there's no cell reception here, so use the two-way radio. I'm on channel two. But don't worry, Chris, nothing's going to happen."

And with that, we go our separate ways, with Evans taking the first floor this time around and me trudging up the motionless escalator to the second floor.

It takes an hour or so to walk the maze of hallways and weird little corner areas. I sweep my flashlight across the glass of the windows that aren't covered in plywood, just to make sure there's nothing going on that shouldn't be. I'm glad Evans mentioned that about the furnace—it thumps loudly both when it kicks in and when the fan shuts off. I just need to learn what the normal sounds are. In the restroom, I open the door to the first stall. The bang of the door hitting the wall behind it echoes across the broken tiles. When I catch a glimpse of movement to my right, I stop for a minute—only a minute as we're supposed to keep moving—to see myself in the mirror. The uniform makes me look older than I am, I think, and makes me feel kind of important. The weapon at my side looks ominous to me, despite my three days of armed security guard training.

The food court encircles me. The protective metal shades above each counter are like a dozen eyes watching everything I do. The whole place smells vaguely like french fries, even though a cleaning crew came through a while back. There's a hum from the TCBY—from their freezers, I guess. And there is a drip, drip, drip coming from the Orange Julius. Should I write that down? Probably not. It's a waste of water, but it isn't a security risk. In a way, I find these noises comforting, because I can identify the cause for each and not panic that it might be a thief or druggie or some kind of dangerous intruder I'm supposed to handle.

I'm really glad it's almost time to meet Evans back at the center of the mall. We only exchange a few words each time, but it gives me–gives us both, I guess–a touchpoint of human contact that helps mark the slow passage of the night.

"Boo!" Evans jumps out from behind the fountain and laughs when I jump. "Hahaha, I got you good there."

"Not funny, Evans. Not funny at all."

"Aw, lighten up man. I gotta entertain myself somehow!"

I walk another round. The hallways are short, feeding off each other in a weird set of branches that leads to the different anchor stores. Which means there are tons of corners that could hide I-don't-know-what. I picture my yoga teacher leading us in deep, calming breaths and I try to imitate her long, slow, inhale and exhale, but I'm happy to manage any kind of breath—just keep breathing! I pretend to emulate the old-time TV detectives I used to watch with my grandma: Rockford, Baretta, Kojak, Mannix. They wouldn't fear an empty building. As I approach the next corner, I press my back against the wall and raise my weapon in both hands, doing my very best Magnum impression. Another deep breath, and then I jump into the hallway, spinning 180 degrees and aiming directly at the heart of…well, nothing. There's nothing here but empty space and closed up shops. There *is* a weird shimmery blue light coming from the Spencer's Gifts, but that's normal enough for them.

I see the escalator as I approach the center of the mall, but no Evans yet.

Crap. There's a rustling, scraping sound coming from my right and slightly behind me. I spin around and my light smears across the plywood walls and disappears into a corner niche I hadn't noticed before. The shadows *wiggle* when they should be still. I raise my weapon and croak out a warning, scared almost speechless. But one shadow elongates out of the corner, creeping slowly toward me.

I try to remember the protocol, but come up blank. I freeze in place, yelling for the shadow to stop, and for Evans to hurry down from upstairs to back me up. But my voice comes out a shaky whisper. The blood is pounding in my ears, and I can't hear a thing except a sort of raspy murmuring coming from the shadows. I feel the hot sweat dampening the hair at the back of my neck—a slow dribble soaking my collar. My flashlight wavers as I fumble to draw my gun and aim into the darkness, but I am engulfed, and I can no longer see the shadow or whatever it was that made it. I remember I have a radio, and try to raise Evans while juggling the flashlight and the gun without taking my eyes or my aim off the impending shadow, but my hands are shaky and sweaty and the radio slips from my grip and tumbles down the escalator. I can hear a shuffle, and a click, and I think I hear someone or something laughing—a slow, deep, mean kind of laugh. I fire a warning shot. The sound bounces around the stillness and multiplies and repeats until I can't hear my own voice anymore. Everything…goes…black.

I don't know how long I was out. A few seconds? A few minutes? When I open my eyes, I see the ceiling much further above me than it should be. I'm flat on my back, down on the first floor. Did I fall down the escalator? Is that what knocked me out? I sit up slowly, checking for broken bones or bruises, but I don't feel any pain. My ears have stopped pounding and everything is quiet again.

I thought I was scared before, but now I'm sliding right into terrified. Did whoever or whatever it was get to Evans, maybe before coming for me? Did I shoot someone? Or maybe the bullet went horribly astray in the darkness? It's past our meeting time. Why hasn't Evans shown up yet? That shot was certainly loud enough.

I still have my gun and my flashlight, so I carefully, slowly, head back upstairs to look a bit closer at that dark corner. There's nothing there. No damage, no intruder, no boogie man. Maybe it was a bird or a rat or something and my imagination got away from me. Were the gunshots all in my mind?

I take a couple of deep breaths to calm down, but it doesn't help. I watch for any sign of movement, waiting for my sanity to return. I know I should tell someone what happened, but I don't want to leave my post until I am properly relieved. I figure if nothing else, Evans ought to show up soon. We can discuss what to do then.

Evans doesn't come. I decide to look for that fallen radio, backing away from shadows, feeling for the handrail of the escalator, doing a full 360 with the light, before taking each step. Nothing's going to sneak up on me now. Down on the first floor, I look back up and realize there's no way the radio would have survived a drop from such a height. I check under the stairs, look down into the cracks between the treads, scan the entire surface of the dried-up fountain, but oddly, there's nothing. Did it bounce? I widen my search, but no radio.

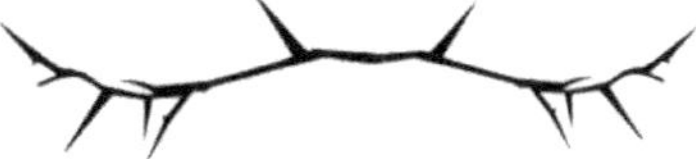

I've been alone for—I don't know how long now. I've lost track of the rounds I've done—one hour upstairs, one hour down, like I'm supposed to. Each pass blends into the next, so they all seem exactly the same. I sweep my flashlight across the glass of the windows that aren't covered in plywood. The furnace thumps loudly when it kicks in and when the fan shuts off. There's a hum from the TCBY freezers. And there is still a drip, drip, drip coming from the Orange Julius and the eerie blue glow from Spencer's Gifts. And every round, I wait a bit longer at the escalator, hoping to cross paths with Evans.

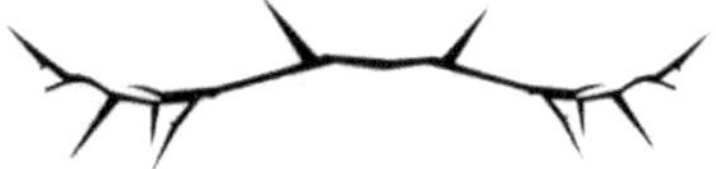

I'm looking for the dawn, for whoever is on the next shift to come and relieve me. Surely, it's time to make the donuts or something, and the place will start filling up with the early morning staff. Until then, I keep making my rounds among the hums, thumps, and drips.

Finally, I see a silhouette next to the fountain. I'm not scared anymore, only relieved I'm no longer alone. I call out, "Who's there?" but the shape doesn't move.

As I get nearer, I see that it is Evans, but without the smirk I'm used to seeing. And, oddly, out of uniform.

"Evans! Where have you been? Are you ok? Why don't you answer me?"

Evans takes a deep breath and, without looking at me, climbs the escalator steps. I follow, trying to explain what's been happening.

"Oh, come on, Evans. Don't be mad at me. I haven't been ignoring you. I lost my radio. Well, I dropped it first, so it's probably broken, but I don't know for sure because I couldn't find it. Can I get another? Like, is there an extra one somewhere, or a backup?"

Evans doesn't say a word, but heads straight for the corner where I had that little misfire a while back. I take a few steps closer. Evans looks terrible, thinner and more gray than I remember.

"Chris, can you hear me?"

"Well, of course I can hear you. I'm standing right here."

"Chris, if you can hear me, wherever you are, I came to say, I'm sorry." Evans turns slowly away from me and addresses a spot on the wall where the plywood looks newer than the surrounding boards. "I'm so, so sorry."

"What the heck are you talking about? You mean about missing the meetups all night? I admit, I was spooked, but you're here now. How about we do the next round or two together?"

Still talking to the wall, Evans keeps apologizing. "I shouldn't have tried to scare you. I thought it would be funny, honest. I knew you were jumpy. I just didn't know you'd react so badly.

"No biggie. I'm just glad—"

"Then, when your gun went off, I guess I panicked and acted out of instinct. Chris, you must know I didn't mean to hurt you."

Evans walks to the top of the escalator and looks down, this time talking to the floor below. "I've had a lot of time to think about it. You don't know it, but I ended up pleading guilty. They called it involuntary manslaughter, and I did my time, but I won't ever forgive myself."

"What are you saying? And why are you talking to that spot on the floor, not to me?"

"I'm really, really, sorry. I'd give anything to take back that shot. I didn't mean to kill you, I swear. I only hope that you're in a better place. Rest in peace, my friend."

BABY BOY

DONNA ZEPHRINE

My baby boy
Born premature.
My adorable
Precious baby.

What a delicate color he has.
His skin is flawless, lighter than mine,
His perfect smell—delicious.
Pleasant little nose
This poor tiny nose loaded with tubes
Tubes coming out of his nostrils and mouth.

The doctors are talking to me,
telling me if he survives,
he will have serious complications.
I can hear their words,
but I'm not processing what they're saying.
They must be wrong.

I have a fever.
Maybe I am imagining this.
They're still talking.
This is real.

They say words like infection and sepsis,
asking me questions,
the worst question I've ever heard.

Do I want to *pull the plug?*

No!
No, I don't want to *pull the plug!*
What kind of question is that?
Unthinkable, disturbing, horrifying.
Yet, I know, I see it in their eyes.

I start to make sense of their words.
All the doctors looking at me,
looking at my baby.

Bright lights,
beeping sounds—awful sounds.
All of this makes it hard to think.
I don't know how much time passes.
I know I have to make the most inconceivable decision.
I must remove life support.
It is the only way to give my son peace.

I hold my son for his final moments.
The greatest gift I give my son.
He is at peace with God forever—
A perfect little angel.

THE BEAST

T. R. WHITNEY

The night was pitch black. The moon hid as the shadows loomed from random starlight penetrating through the dense forest. Ernie Jackson walked hesitantly, looking around, though he couldn't see beyond the length of his arm. The trees whistled in the quiet wind. Their spindly branches reached up and out like clawed arms. An owl hooted as it lifted into the sky with its wings clapping in the air. The grass rustled as the night animals scurried away from the threat.

He just wanted to get out of there. Why did his car have to break down on this lonely stretch of highway? Maybe he should have waited in his car. But no, he decided to walk, hoping to find a store or a house along the way to call for help. It was a cliché of every horror movie he had ever seen. Kids in the woods on a dark night being chased by a maniac with a chainsaw or knife—or ghostly beings that materialize out of the misty haze. The sweat dripped down his temples at the thought. Unnerved by his imagination, he moved to the center of the roadway.

Stop it, you idiot. There's nothing to fear.

He jumped as something large came crashing through the trees behind him. Poised to run if needed, his eyes swiveled from side to side. Shaking his head in relief, he relaxed as a deer ran past.

Ernie turned back, only to find a colossal shadow in front of him. It was a mean-looking inhuman beast, unlike anything he had ever seen. A deformed horrifying monstrous being seven feet tall with glowing red eyes. An ugly white puckered scar running across a hairy cheek and bulbous nose marred the grotesque face. A stream of moonlight peaked out from behind the clouds, gleaming off the fang-like teeth. A low growl rumbled from its chest.

Ernie's mouth opened to scream, but nothing came out. His eyes widened as he looked into the menacing crimson orbs of a sinister savage. Battling the most abject fear he'd ever experienced, nausea burned in his throat and tightened his lungs. He couldn't speak, couldn't move. He could only watch in horror as the beast moved toward him. The rumbling from the monster's chest intensified. His body quaked with fear as his clothes became drenched with sweat.

Oh God! This is it. I'm gonna die right here.

This was not a character from his niece's favorite movie *Beauty and the Beast*. He passed out as the monster reached for him.

When Ernie awoke, he was in a damp, musty cave. It was too dark to see more than shadows. So, he lay as still as possible, listening. He reached around looking for an escape, only to realize he was in a cage. He crawled along the edges to find a way out. His hands shook as he fumbled, searching. Something stopped him from going any farther. As he groped the obstacle, realization dawned on him—it was a skeleton.

Oh shit!

The quaking started in his chest, working its way throughout until even his teeth chattered in rhythm. He clamped his jaw tight to temper the hard shaking of his body. His mind whirled with questions. He scrambled backward until he came up against the wall of the cage.

I gotta get out of here!

Ernie heard a guttural grunt but couldn't place its proximity. He waited as the next couple of minutes passed in silence. Standing, he moved around the edge to the other side, searching for the door. His hands slipped on the wooden poles. It did no good to wipe them on his clothes. It would only make them sweatier. Finally, his hands grasped what felt like a door.

Now, how do I get out without this grotesque creature catching me?

Even though the cave was dark, Ernie noticed a tiny sliver of light filtering in from the cave opening. Once his eyes adjusted to the dimness, he focused on the construction of the cage. What he thought was a door turned out to be a hatch like those in the cages where he kept his rabbits. An odor of filth and decay permeated the area. Now he knew what his rabbits experienced.

The hatch was secured with a rope tied in a weird knot. Needing something sharp, he scanned the floor of the cage but found nothing useful. He glanced over at the skeleton. His heart dropped as he made out the human form. The bones were scattered with the skull tossed on top.

His body went cold.

Oh God! Oh God! Oh God!

The stench of raw, bloody meat assaulted his senses. Straining to locate his captor, he spotted it sitting off to the far side of the cave. A flame suddenly flared, and Ernie could see it holding something over the fire. It was the leg bone of an animal, though he couldn't be sure. The object was as long as his lower leg from knee to ankle.

Obviously, the leviathan was physically powerful. Strong enough to tear apart its prey. He watched in horror as it gnawed on the bone with a mouth full of long, vampire-like teeth. The fire snapped and danced as pieces fell from its gaping mouth into the flame. Ernie looked back at the skeleton in the cage.

The fire cast enough illumination for Ernie to see the bones more clearly. He studied them and then wished he hadn't. The pinkish-hued bones had bits of tendon remaining, and it was missing a lower leg bone. Hearing movement, he quickly skirted to the far recesses of the cage. Pulling up into the fetal position, he prayed as he watched the shadow of his horrifying captor move toward the cage.

God! This is a nightmare! Please let me wake up and it be morning! I can't take this! I don't want to die! Please, please make this nightmare end!

His heart did its best to squeeze out of his chest in terror. As the feral being worked to open the knot, Ernie knew this would be his only chance to escape. He'd rather die fighting than wait to be chopped up for this creature's supper. Taking a deep breath to calm his nerves, he formed a plan.

The beast opened the top hatch. Dropping the lower section, it reached in to grab its prey. Ernie stayed low to avoid the outstretched claws as he inched closer to the opening. Grabbing two fistfuls of dirt, he tossed them at the glowing red eyes. It emitted a guttural scream that chilled Ernie to the bone. Kicking at the savage behemoth, Ernie landed a foot or knee wherever he could to get past the massive hulk blocking the opening. Blocking his freedom. He drew in a deep breath and lashed out with a foot that caught the horrible beast in its leg joint. With a thundering roar that tore the air, it slumped to the side. Wasting no time, Ernie sprang for the cage opening.

As he scurried by, the gigantic monster blindly slung out his arm. Its claws connected with Ernie's shoulder. A deep, searing pain raced across his body, but Ernie kept moving. Reaching the cave entrance, he glanced over his shoulder to see the creature searching, throwing the cage and debris around its home. Turning away, Ernie squinted against the brightness of the day. As his eyes focused, he raced out of the cave and scampered up the side of the cliff. His terror mounted with every step. He knew he wouldn't be able to outrun the colossal hellhound. Ernie prayed its climbing abilities were limited.

Ducking behind a boulder, he waited for the merciless predator to emerge. Pumped full of adrenaline, Ernie's stomach lurched and spasmed before it clenched, and he thought he would throw up. As soon as it came into view, Ernie picked up a rock and threw it as far as he could into the trees. Hearing the clunk when the rock landed, it turned and headed in the direction of the noise.

Ernie waited until it disappeared before coming out from behind the rock. Dread gnawed at his insides as he determined the safest direction to go. It felt as if the world was spinning out of control. Everything in him screamed to move faster and as far away as possible. Suddenly the beast returned—its nose sniffing the air like a bloodhound.

Ernie dropped back down. He didn't dare move. His heart leaped into his throat when he heard rocks falling to the ground. Ernie peeked over the boulder. The color drained from his face, leaving it as ashen as the boulders surrounding him. The savage creature was trying to climb up the side of the mountain.

Ernie's mind ran rampant with options. He didn't have much time to decide. All he could think about was the need to escape. Seeing a rock the size of his hand, he reached for it. He wasn't much of a pitcher in high school, but here he had a bigger strike zone. Rising, he took aim and hurled the rock down onto his objective. As the beast slipped to the ground, Ernie climbed higher, zig-zagging his way across the face of the cliff.

The monster growled and shook his arms. Ernie threw another rock and clipped it in the head. Every few feet as he tried to get away, Ernie tossed another rock, keeping the creature distracted from his direction. Finally reaching the top, he crashed through the trees to find himself at the edge of a paved road.

What now? Which way? Come on, come on, think!

He had to move. It wouldn't take long for the monstrous savage to catch up with him. Mentally paralyzed, a sense of helplessness pervaded his thoughts. He took off running downhill opposite the threat, with no idea how far it was to safety or even in which direction would lead him to help. Ernie only knew to run away. His chest heaved with effort as he sprinted as fast as he could and prayed as he ran.

Please, God! Please help me!

Breaking into the open, he heard a ferocious growl, but Ernie didn't bother to look back.

Please, please somebody help me!

He was running out of time. His lungs burned from the thinning oxygen as he struggled to breathe. Ernie sensed the hideous beast coming closer as his pace slowed. With legs feeling like jelly, he scanned the area for a place to hide. Every shadow, every swaying branch was suspect. Movement out of the corner of his eye jerked his attention back to the road. A truck appeared on the opposite side. Ernie switched into the lane, waving his arms to get the driver to stop. Even if the truck didn't stop, he'd rather be roadkill than captured by that horrifying creature again.

Second by second, the two converged on each other. Ernie closed his eyes as the truck neared, expecting a collision. The squeal of tires on the pavement registered in his panicked mind. Realizing the truck had stopped a few feet away, Ernie rushed to the passenger door and jumped in.

"Go! Go! Go! It's after me!"

"What in the hell is wrong with you? Were you trying to get yourself killed?"

Ernie looked at the old man sitting in the driver's seat. "We'll both be dead if you don't get us out of here!" Ernie screamed.

The old man stared at Ernie as though he were crazy. "Have you lost your marbles—"

"Please just drive! I'll tell you once we get out of here. PLEASE!!"

The old man shifted gears and put the truck in motion, all the while mumbling about idiots and crazy people.

Ernie frantically searched out each window of the truck but couldn't find evidence of the beast. Adrenaline pounded his pulse in his ears. He prayed his attacker had skulked back into the forest. Earnie relaxed as the truck headed farther and farther down the road. Lowering his sweat-drenched head against the car window, Ernie let the coolness from the glass wash over him.

Late the next morning, Ernie awoke. It was unusual for him to oversleep even on his days off from work. However, last night's nightmare had him tossing and turning. Never had he had such a vivid nightmare. If he hadn't awakened in his own bed, Ernie would have believed the whole thing had been real.

Probably a result of bad takeout food last night.

The bedsheets twisted around his body, trapping him as though he were caged. The numbers on his clock shone brighter than normal, glowing red like the eyes of the beast in his dream. There was an odd smell in the room he couldn't place. *When was the last time I emptied the garbage bin?* Breathing a tremendous sigh of relief, he stared at the ceiling.

Thank God! It was only a dream.

He unwrapped the sheets from around his legs and rolled out of bed. His whole body hurt as though he'd run a marathon.

Must have been all the running I did in my nightmare.

He chuckled and gingerly shuffled to the bathroom. Leaning over the sink, he raised his head to stare at his weary face. Raising his arm to scratch his stubbled cheek, he winced in pain. Lowering it, Ernie twisted around to stare in horror at the mirror.

Across the back of his shoulder were three evenly spaced, bloody claw marks.

HAUNTED APP

PAMELA K. KINNEY

"Whoever first said it is right," said Jake as he peered over Neri's shoulder. "There's an app for everything, even a gaming app with ghosts to haunt the gamer."

Neri nodded. "Yeah, this game will be cool to play tonight, navigating various haunted spots. I have always wanted to go on a paranormal investigation. It's just staying up all night in some yucky, haunted, former insane asylum or a bug-infested cemetery in the summer was something I balked at before. But curled up in a cozy corner in my condo at night searching haunted places will be fun."

Jake hefted his book bag over a shoulder. "Cool. I gotta run, or I'll be late for World History class. I'll search for the app in the Google store this weekend and add it to my phone."

Neri shook her head. "Lily emailed me the website link last night, but I hadn't downloaded it yet. She's playing the game, too, and told me it's unavailable on Google or the Apple Store. I'll be glad to text you the link so you can join. Lily said to let all my friends know."

Jake grinned. "Sure. That's fine with me. Bye."

Neri tossed her trash in the trash can nearby. She slipped her phone into her crossbody purse and headed across campus to the hall for her English class.

Finally done with her homework, Neri stuck it into her book bag on the desk. As she began putting pen and paper away, her phone made a ding, indicating an update. Good, that meant *Haunted* finished downloading.

Neri got off her chair and crossed over to the bedstand beside her bed, snatching up her phone after unhooking the charging cable. As she returned to her chair, she let her fingers dance across the screen to bring up the app.

Haunted. She remembered the app's description: Do you dare to be haunted? Survive the ghosts in several haunted spots in the game, banishing the spooks before losing the game.

The app never cost her a dime—it was free. Free was always good on her college budget. Her G.I. Bill paid for college, but she still had to pinch pennies.

After setting her phone on the bed, Neri undressed and slipped into her pajamas before crawling into bed. Laying her head on the pillow, she picked up the phone and opened the app.

Spooky music played as she picked an avatar to use. There was a character that looked like her, but in a cartoonish way. Since the avatar looked like her, she made it exactly like her in real life, a college student. Reading the rules, she realized it was not a Triple A game. Anywhere she looked, she couldn't find the name of the gaming company. Well, nothing significant to worry about, because from what she witnessed and read, the game appeared top notch.

If the game proved crappy, she could just delete it. She had virus protection on the phone, so it was safe to play a game or two to test it out.

A shadow person image appeared, and a deep male voice broadcasted, "Okay, it's time to get haunted. Will you banish the entities or lose and end up added to the game forever? The game starts now."

Kinda creepy. How would she be added to the game forever? Neri snickered. *It meant my avatar, not me.*

Her avatar stood on the mat at the front door of the haunted house, the first leg of a haunted spot she had to win to go on to the next part of the game. Instead of WELCOME, the mat said UNWELCOME. Her avatar inserted a skeleton key into the lock, and the door slowly creaked open.

Neri snorted. How cheesy, using a creaky door like in a trillion haunted house movies. So far, the game is a typical scary game.

Her eyes blurred for a second, and when they refocused, she swore it was like she was the avatar, looking out of its eyes up at her. Puzzled, she blinked a couple of times, looked around, and saw not her bedroom but the inside of the haunted house.

What's going on?

What sounded like the male voice from the game whispered in her ear. "You wanted the game to be something you never encountered before."

She scrambled up and off her bed. "What the—"

"Bad choice, foolish mortal," said the voice. "The first ghost has tagged you."

Her hand hurt. As she was about to look at it, suddenly Neri found herself back in her bedroom. Her eyes widened as she stared down at her hand clasping the phone. She realized something had happened to the back of her hand. She'd been scratched. Looking at the sore closely, it appeared a sharp fingernail or a claw might be the cause.

Her heart fluttered like a bird in a cage, and she tapped herself out of the game. Fear drove her to shut her phone off and stick it in the desk drawer, slamming it shut with a bang. Shaken, she headed to the bathroom to put healing ointment on the cut and pressed a bandage over it.

Neri stepped out of the bathroom, puzzling about what happened. It's just a game. Typically, she would explain it all away, telling herself it's only her imagination. Ghosts didn't exist. But there's the nasty scratch on her hand. It hurt and had bled. Spirits were not real in the game and, honestly, since she didn't truly believe in them, not in the real world, either.

Most likely, she scratched herself, maybe by something sharp at her desk.

"Come, mortal; the specters are waiting for you."

She shrieked. Neri turned and saw the phone on top of the desk, its screen lit.

I had shut off the phone! I stuck it inside the drawer.

"Join the game—now!" demanded the voice from the phone.

"No, I won't!" she screamed back. "You're not real. Just a stupid app I am now deleting!"

Neri reached out to grab the phone. Dark shadows flew out of her phone and surrounded her, and she lifted into the air, screaming. Suddenly, she was no longer in her bedroom but on her feet in a dark forest. Things like this happen in horror films, even fiction novels, but never in real life.

She punched at a tree trunk with a clenched fist to prove the tree nearest to her was fake. That she imagined it all; instead, she hit tree bark, heard bones cracking, and felt terrible pain. The skin of her hand ripped, bleeding, and her fingers were throbbing, two looking like they might be broken, and since it had been the bandaged hand from earlier, the bandage was gone, and the scratch was bleeding worse than earlier.

She wished she had never gotten the app. Haunted? Forget haunted! Hell, the app proved to be a curse. And Lily wanted her to share the link with her friends? What kind of freakin' friend was Lily that she shared it with Neri? Had she known this would happen?

"The stupid mortal is in the notorious, haunted Dark Woods. If she thought the house was full of ghosts, wait until it's night. The forest contains more of the dead than the house—all angry for getting caught and dying here. The longer the time, the eviler the spirits became. And our brave fool only has an EMF meter we furnished her—not much protection to go on." Maniacal laughter filled the woods.

Neri realized she clutched the working meter in her other hand. It began flashing in a sequence, repeating over and over. No matter where she pointed it or, as she was moving on, or stopped, it kept blinking its colorful lights. She heard a growl behind her, and she turned, locking eyes with the mad red eyes of a tall shadow. It must be at least over six feet. Suddenly, more growls plus moans surrounded her. As she twirled around slowly, she saw a lot of shadows.

The shadows rushed her. She needed to do something, but what? All she had was the dumb meter. Only a little good it could do her. Or it could help.

What can a meter do against ghosts? EMF meters detect electromagnetic energy in the area, and electromagnetism occurs when electric current changes or moves.

That must mean through her phone. She smiled. If she got all these ghosts to attack, it might bring up the charge and possibly burn out her phone. Not that she wanted to ruin her phone or die in it, but it could get her out and back to her bedroom. She could always buy another phone.

She waved the meter in the air. "All right, stupid phantoms. Quit fooling around and let's see what you got. I'm betting on next to nothing." She flashed them the finger. "Forget next to nothing; I bet it is nothing, just like all you ectoplasmic thrift store bedsheets!"

Screams filled the air, slamming into her ears and even busting her eardrums. She felt moisture leaking from her ears. Not taking any time to check with a finger and see if the wetness was blood, Neri whipped about like a merry-go-round on steroids, dodged around trees, and ducked down to avoid the dark shadows and white, glowing orbs that materialized too. She punched at each one with the meter and hoped it racked up points for her every time the meter touched or went through a ghost. More entities appeared until they filled the woods, and she couldn't find anywhere to hide. They covered the trees and bushes and, yes, even Neri herself. She couldn't breathe. It looked like she might die when she heard crackling in the air. The crackling became a thunderclap that hit the air with a sonic boom, and when she woke up, she lay on the floor of her bedroom, the phone within reach of her fingertips. She sat up. Her body hurt everywhere. Neri picked up the phone. The screen had burned black; she saw several cracks in the phone's body.

"Dead," she said, "and all the apps, too, especially that one." She laughed. "But I'm alive!"

Tomorrow she would go to the phone store and get a new smartphone. She doubted they would use her insurance to get a new one; how could she explain what had happened to the old one? She could see herself telling them that an app she put on her phone inserted her into a game. They would think she was nuts or lying. If she had to pay for a new phone from money out of her savings account, it served her right for downloading that app.

Neri found a plastic store bag and slipped the phone inside. She placed it on her desk before heading off to shower and then bed.

The following day, after a stop at Starbucks for a latte and a breakfast sandwich, she drove to the phone store. She didn't see any customers inside, which shocked her as it was a Saturday. The phone store was always busy, especially on Saturday. Only a man dressed in a blue T-shirt and khaki pants stood behind a counter. She took the phone from the bag and placed it on the counter before him. Neri noticed the name tag on his shirt, and her eyes blurred when she peered at it to get his name. She rubbed at them. Funny, as her eyes seemed fine earlier.

"Hi," she said. "My phone got into an accident. Can I get a replacement? I bought this one through you."

The man picked it up and peered at it. "Looks like an electrical fire, or maybe the battery did this?"

Phew. The battery is a good out for me, instead of a haunted app being the cause. No way he would ever believe me.

Neri nodded. "Yeah, I think it might have been the battery. It seems like these battery problems have been in the news a lot lately, haven't they?"

He put it down and walked over to a phone on the wall that looked like her dead one. "I assume you want another like it. That's all your insurance will cover for you."

"That'll be fine. Will it cost me any money?"

His mouth quirked up at the corners into a grin. "Not at all. Let me go to our storeroom in the back and get another. The one on the wall is just for display."

He stepped through a doorway. Neri waited, checking out the other phones on the walls and the displayed tablets. It was toasty warm when she first walked inside, and now it felt cold. It became so cold it made her wish she'd worn a sweater. She shivered.

"Here it is."

Neri turned and saw the man behind the counter, holding what looked like a twin of her phone.

I didn't hear him come back.

He handed the phone to her. "There it is, and now you're ready to return to that game you played last night on your old phone."

Neri asked, "What did you say?"

"I said, you can get back to playing *Haunted*. I loaded the app on this phone for you."

She looked down at the lit screen of the phone, and her hair stood up at the back of her neck as she saw the app there—the only app.

The young woman dropped the phone on the counter. "Uh, no. First, I don't want that app on my phone, and two, how did you know I played that game or even had the app on my old phone?" She peered at his name tag again and her eyes blurred like before. "What is your name? I seem to have a problem reading your name tag."

Neri wiped at the tears and saw his grin. How white his teeth seemed.

He leaned over the counter and said, "I am the gamemaster. I collect souls for the Devil himself. He has found this to be an easier way to harvest souls for Hell. Mortals are really stupid. They never question a free game app offered to them that isn't sold at the

Google or Apple stores." His voice had grown more profound, like the male voice from the app last night.

An icy finger traced along her spine as her heart thudded, growing louder with each thud in her ears. The palms of her hands grew moist as her stomach clenched. "No, this can't be happening. I'm not playing that horrible game ever again because I beat the ghosts in the forest. I won."

"Oh, but you never escaped. You are still inside the game app. Except now, you are not a player. You are one of the haunts." His grin widened, and she noticed for the first time how sharp his teeth looked. "Never met a player yet that could beat the game. That'll teach you to download apps. Oh, wait! Too late, you're dead!"

Neri bolted from the store. As she stepped outside, she found herself not in the shopping center but inside the haunted house, floating up into the air. She passed another spirit and saw it was Lily.

The front door creaked open, and someone stepped through the doorway. It was her friend Jake. Neri guessed he'd gotten the app on his phone.

The gamemaster spoke in her head. *There are no friends once you are dead. You'll learn after a while—just players to haunt and scare them into losing. Now get haunting. We still need a thousand more souls for the app.*

THE DEAD'S GRIN

SIRRAH MEDEIROS

I sat in thought within the wood,
Whilst wind blew me oft left to right.
As darkness settled, as it should,
Then slumber softly does the light.

Whispers raced through the chilly air.
Gathered in wicked bursts—my ears.
Caught in flight by my hair.
Nerves, muscles—taut in fear.

The voices constant in the night
My body rigid as the wind held tight.
I could not flee without a fight,
Its embrace grew harsh with malicious smite.

Against my cheeks, it hissed and lashed.
Blood oozed with each fresh whip of late.
My eyes blurred and my body thrashed.
Heady figures revealed my fate.

Haunted by the dead's angry breath,
It shared with me its vile pitch.
Now I knew a tortuous death
Was close at hand—I must switch.

I sank limp with the stunning truth.
Thus, eased control did the horror's hold.
Rushed was I to survive a sleuth,
I wiggled and writhed—now a spirit bold.

Doom tattooed my soul forever.
The devil's foul ink twisted my fine skin.
No matter—I shall endeavor,
Marred evermore with the Dead's grin.

SHAFT ALLEY

SAM CASEY

I look down the ladder that goes deep into the ship's belly. The lights are out. I look around for a light switch until I figure out there isn't one. Someone must have tagged out the power source for maintenance and, considering no one was here doing maintenance, failed to restore the switch when they finished. *I expect nothing less from this damn shipyard availability.* I pull out my black, three-inch flashlight and check the bulb before making my descent.

The first few steps are easy, my arms yet to feel the strain of the intermittent weight of my body shifting from one side to the other as I immerse myself in blackness. The light from the passageway above gets smaller as I descend the narrow ladder. Each level opens to a magazine, an office, a space filled with useless stuff before closing in around me. My teeth clench around the flashlight providing a cone of vision that follows my head movement. The uncirculated air becomes staler, drying my nose and throat the deeper I go. My breathing gets heavier as the light above grows distant.

I stop five levels down and four levels up from the bottom. Stillness allows me to take stock and feel the dampness of the space below the waterline. To my left, one of the far carabiners is not fastened onto a safety net. Grumbling, I grip the ladder between my bicep and my forearm, freeing my other arm. I stretch out past the safety of the ladder, half my body dangling above the infinite darkness below. The flashlight illuminates my fingers, almost reaching the clip when my arm disappears.

Damn flashlight's going out.

Repositioning, I take the flashlight in one hand and shake, the rattle echoing off the walls like a child's laughter. The flashlight does not turn back on. I shake it again and the laughter continues to echo after the movement stops. I don't remember ever fearing the dark. Looking up, I see the twinkle of the passageway light. Looking down at my destination, the darkness obscures my judgment of distance. Logically, I know it is less than the distance above, but my eyes belie my mind. I squint at a fleeting reflection shimmering on the hull floor from pooling water before returning to the task at hand.

I shake my flashlight and the light returns, dim. *Hopefully, it lasts long enough to fix that damn safety net.* Armed with the light in my teeth, I stretch out again, fingering the clip so its clasp kisses the grommet. Applying all the feeble force I can with my lack of structural support, I almost fasten the clip when the flashlight fails again. I know it's fatal this time. *Fuck it.* I drop the carabiner and return to the ladder with both hands.

Unfamiliar wetness moistens my hands, thick with a faint metallic smell, but without being able to see, I assume it must be residual grease on the ladder. Reaching into my pocket, I grab my back up light, forgetting about the safety clip. It's smaller than the first and requires the silver button to be continually pushed to light up. *Good enough.* After testing it and placing it back in my pocket, I renew my descent slower now that I've lost my sight. The metal rings clink with each limb movement. The further I go, the darker it gets. Each level's opening gives me a temporary reprieve before the shaft rushes in around me, hugging the small space that separates my body from the metallic walls. The enclosed space is temporary, preventing me from getting accustomed to it. Instead, the descent is a constant closing and opening, my breath becoming ragged as I feel more constricted, more enclosed in a laddered tomb. The shaft breathes slower than I do, as each opening is faint, lacking circulation with the air feeling fresh for a moment before the stank of the constricted space dries in my throat. I move faster, hoping to reach the bottom, trying to suck in more and more stale air as I lose stamina and light. My boots hit each rung quickly as I beg for stable ground. When I finally reach the bottom, my panic overshadows my joy at the solidness of the metallic grate under my feet in the near total darkness. I fumble and remove my flashlight and light up the shaft alley.

I move and check the space. *CO2 extinguisher is out of periodicity and looks like it needs to be replaced.* I have no envy for the sad Sailor who has to carry a new one down and the old one up, although in reality it will probably be me. The small lock on the ship's man-sized shafts remains in place, preventing the propellers that drive the ship through the water from turning. The bilge has water from the moisture condensing and an oil sheen from equipment leaking. I notice new scaffolding in the corner. As I approach it, I hear the subtle drone of marine life just outside the ship's skin. Getting closer, I see the damaged lagging that they put the scaffolding up to replace, partially burnt and giving the air an acrid smell. Below the scaffolding, there is a dark pile. Sweeping my flashlight over it, I see writing on the wall, faint but discernible. Flowers, now wilted and dried, were placed in front of the writing by hands unknown. I walk toward it, my boots resounding and echoing across the small space. I run my hand over the painted, faded writing and can barely make it out. Scarcely above a whisper, I read it out loud. *Lost at sea: Foster.*

Roaring to life, the sound of metal trying to shear metal resounds through the shaft alley as the shaft struggles to rotate against the lock. Startled by the sound, I jump back, lose my footing and slam into the metal grate. The skin on my palms tears and I cover my ears to try to block out the noise. The grinding is so loud I can't think, can't breathe, as I press my bloody palms tightly to my ears. I press my finger firmly on the flashlight, as I cling to the single light I have this deep in the ship. In addition to the cacophonous metallic din, I hear laughter. The laughter grows louder, resounding joyously throughout the space. I back towards the exit as my heart beats at an erratic pace. The laughter turns to words as something calls out my name in a high sing-song voice.

"Johnson. Johnson. Johnson."

The threat of the shaft breaking free and whipping the hoses and equipment around the small alley is imminent. I need to get out of here! The equipment will destroy the alley if the shaft breaks free. I'm still holding my flashlight as I jump up and rush to the ladder. Dropping the flashlight into my pocket, I touch the first rung. The noise stops. While adjusting to the sudden darkness and silence, I calm my fast-beating heart at the base of the ladder with a deep breath of the bitter air.

The ambient drone of marine life is replaced by the stale stillness of silence. As I slow my breathing before beginning my ascent, I question my memory of what had just happened. *Is another Sailor playing a damn prank on me? Or did I imagine the voice? Now that the shaft is still, I can quickly finish my tour.* I remove the flashlight from my pocket and light up the space. I train the light across the empty space and notice everything is the same, except for one detail. The dark pile below the scaffolding is bigger. My flashlight shines on a figure huddled in the corner with hair covering her face. The air smells of iron, possibly from the scraps on my palm. Slowly, the figure's head turns toward me, showing her face mangled and bruised from a fall.

"Johnson. Stay with me. Please stay."

My body froze. I study her dirty Naval uniform, her unkempt hair, her bloody hands, her rotting flesh. Any empathy I have for this Sailor asking for companionship dries up with the fear stuck in my throat. The girl rises and I notice my light shines through her ethereal body. Coming closer, she reaches out a decomposing, shriveled arm to me. She is no farther than three strides away before whispering, "Help me." Her rotting flesh assaults my senses. I can't move and she gets closer still. She touches my cheek and I notice she was really quite beautiful, if not for the abuse of time and neglect. Her skin begins to heal before my eyes, her bruises fade and she almost looks healthy. While I am admiring her transformation, my breath gets shallower, my mouth begins to taste of ash and my eyesight blurs. She lets out a soft sigh and her icy touch warms as I struggle to breathe, my body convulsing as I fight to get air into my lungs. When I pitch forward, her contact is broken and a rush of sweet air enters my body. In an attempt to make space between us, I swing my arms out and it chills as it sweeps through her body. I drop my flashlight and turn to flee up the ladder. Once my eyes are no longer on her, the girl lets out a sobbing scream.

The sweat and blood from my hands slicken the rungs before my boots reach them as I hurriedly ascend. I continue to climb as fast as I safely can, face front, seeing more and more the closer I get to the soft patch of light at the top. I don't stop and look below until I am a safe distance above. Then, the constant clicks of boot and ladder stutter as I pause to catch my breath. *What was that thing? How long had it been there? And who else had seen it? Why had no one told me before I did my rounds? Do they even come down here?*

Cursing the other watchstanders for not warning me of the specter, I continue my ascent. I pass the safety net without pausing to attempt to attach the unclamped clip. I pass the halfway point. I missed things on my tour, but I won't go back. I look up again and pray for the end of my watch. Quicker than before, I continue until my foot slips, followed by the other, one hand giving way while the other clings. Dangling, I picture myself falling, breaking through the safety nets that haven't been inspected in God knows how long, and lying at the base, crippled but alive, waiting for help that would never come. Suddenly, a shrill screech breaks me from my thoughts before devolving into cackling laughter. I pull myself up and try to rush up the ladder, but the moldy darkness coats my skin, entering my nose, my mouth, my lungs, filling my chest until I can't bring air in or out. I desperately try to get air into my lungs, clinging to the ladder as the laughter continues. Like a child singing a lullaby, the specter taunts me.

"No one will help you, Johnson. No one cares, and no one will know you're even here!"

Shocked from my frozen state, I catch my breath and start again. Struggling, I heave myself up the ladder, finding more sure footing. The constant clicks return and drown out the girl's morbid laugh. The metal hull lets out an uncomfortable groan. One level away, the passageway light radiates above me. Feeling safer, I venture one last look. The darkness seems shorter now, like I could jump down and land at my destination unharmed. I see a reflection again, not as fleeting as it was before, two tiny eyes waiting for my next descent.

As I reach the top, my hands on the cusp of the watertight hatch held open by flimsy blue wire, I know I will never go down there again. In the light and on stable ground, I'm grateful I never again have to know the icy darkness of the shaft alley.

"One need not be a chamber to be haunted. One need not be a house. The brain has corridors surpassing material place."

— Emily Dickinson

GUILTY CONSCIENCE

TARA MOELLER

Amanda hated Saturday mornings. Her head usually hurt after a night of binge drinking and her hair and skin reeked of smoke from the bars visited the night before. Her stomach wasn't her best friend, either, threatening to retch if she stood up too quickly.

"God! Why don't I learn?" Amanda rolled over but didn't even attempt to sit up, leaving the twisted pink sheet draped over her naked body. She watched the slowly rotating fan centered over her bed and tried to remember what had happened last night. She could remember going into Stoney's tavern, but nothing after that. Only vague images of beer bottles, colorful frosted drinks, and toilets. She could smell a faint tinge of sweat beneath the smoke, as well as the sweet-sour stench of vomit.

Carefully, she moved onto her shoulders and looked for the TV remote. It was usually buried in the sheets and blankets of her bed, since she usually fell asleep listening to the drone of the late news every night except Friday. Finding the wayward device, Amanda turned on the local news channel and flopped back onto her pillows, groaning when the impact sent sharp shards of pain through her temples.

She was only half listening to the news when a description caught her attention. "… the car was described as a late model, black BMW, and the driver as a dark-haired female, wearing her hair up. She had been noticed weaving in her lane prior to the accident and drove away quickly after hitting the two pedestrians and brushing along a telephone pole. One victim was reported dead on the scene, while the other is in intensive care at Mary Compassion Hospital. Police are asking that anyone seeing a black BMW with damage to the right front fender and quarter panel to call Crime Stoppers immediately."

What did you do? The voice that sounded like her father's, hoarse and raspy from cigarettes and booze. It was a familiar voice; she'd grown up with it, the rasping cough that accompanied it a harbinger of what would follow.

Shaking away the memories, Amanda stared at the screen, not seeing the following story about the new bears at the city zoo, or the big tax cut the governor was promising if he was re-elected for the next term. She just kept hearing the description of the hit-and-run driver over and over again, then thinking of the brand-new black BMW that sat in her condo's private garage. She had gone out last night directly from work, leaving her long brown hair up in the professional-looking bun she wore at work.

Oh, God! Had she killed someone last night? She would know as soon as she went downstairs and looked at her car. The reporter had said the car also hit a pole and had damage to the right fender. She would just have to go check out her car. She would see that it wasn't damaged and would then know that the woman the police were looking for wasn't her.

You don't have the guts to go look.

Amanda stood up, dropping the sheet to the floor and grabbing clean underwear from the top drawer of her dresser. She rushed to throw on a bra and underwear, putting her panties on backward the first time, quickly turning them around so the thong part was to the back. Pulling a sundress from the closet, she tugged it over her head, for once not worrying about showing bra straps. She almost forgot to put shoes on, but she tripped over the heels she had kicked off the night before, so she tucked her feet into a pair of flip-flops before grabbing her keys and running out her door.

Her headache was gone now, replaced by a horrible, pressing dread that made her whole body heavy with ache, a pressure that stole the air from her lungs. The keys in her left hand seemed to weigh a ton, anchoring her to the spot rather than allowing her to go see the proof that she was innocent.

Amanda licked dry lips, standing in front of her garage door. It was a building separate from the condo itself, with a long row of garage doors and storage spaces for the inhabitants. At the end of the building was the tall privacy gate that led to the communal pool, sauna, and exercise room. Amanda could hear the laughter and splashing of neighbors enjoying the sunny day.

They'll know what you did.

Surreptitiously, Amanda looked around, trying to act nonchalant and disinterested. She gripped the key tightly in her left hand, the coded edge of the key biting into the skin.

She didn't want to open the door.

Open the door.

Looking skyward, Amanda berated herself in whispers. "You're being silly. That wasn't you last night. Just open the damn door and take a look."

Hand shaking, she placed the key in the lock, but had trouble turning it. The soft click told her it had unlocked, but still she hesitated. The truth was, she couldn't remember what had happened last night, and she was afraid of what she might find in her garage. What would she do if she found a damaged right fender on the front of her car? Would she call the police? Would she turn herself in?

Amanda pushed the door. It was already nearing noon and hot air rushed at her from inside. She never woke early on Saturdays. Today, she wished she was still asleep and unaware in her third-floor bedroom.

Flipping on the light switch, Amanda edged herself around the right side of the car, her skirt snagging on something sharp in the wall, tearing the fabric, drawing blood.

She barely noticed.

The car was parked crooked, the rear end closer to the wall than the front, so she had lots of room after she had tugged her skirt free. Halfway to the front, Amanda paused, her stomach cramping into tight knots. There was a telltale crumple and streaks of silver metal showing from beneath the shiny black of the new paint.

Oh, God! Her front right fender and quarter panel were damaged. Shuffling closer, she peered around the front edge. A perfect half circle was imprinted in the right part of her fender, just as if she had run into a pole.

Bad child; evil child.

Amanda crumpled to the floor, her legs giving way beneath the concrete weight on her shoulders. She had killed someone last night, and possibly severely injured another. She had done that, hit a pole, then drove away, as if nothing had happened. How could she have behaved in such a reckless manner? How had she let her life get to this?

"I'll fix it." She whispered, staring at the huge dent in the front of her car. "I'll fix my life. I'll never drink again. I won't ever let myself get to that point again." Amanda stood up, wiping her sweaty palms down her thighs. The key was on the floor. Amanda stooped to pick it up, wiping the dust on her skirt of her dress, the smear resembling dried blood.

There was only laughter from the voice.

Taking deep breaths, Amanda backed away from the car, locking the garage behind her. She would take the bus to work on Monday and never drive the vehicle again. If it didn't ever come out, it would never be seen, and no one would ever know that she had been that hit-and-run driver. None of her friends or co-workers knew she had bought a new car.

No one would ever have to know what she had done.

Amanda closed her eyes briefly, pressing the key to the garage to her lips, then nodded before turning to re-enter the condo building.

"'Morning, Amanda. You're up early for a Saturday."

Amanda shrieked in surprise, dropping the key so it clanged on the hot black asphalt. She hadn't heard the resident handyman, Earl Smith, walk up behind her. Shaking, she smiled and bent down to retrieve the key. "Yeah, I woke up this morning and realized I had left something in my car last night. I really needed it this morning, so I came right down to get it."

Calm down, Amanda, he'll suspect something. You don't want him to know how bad you are. He can't know what you've done.

"Have a good time last night?"

Amanda jumped a little at the question, staring into the unshaven face in front of her. It was no secret she went out on Friday evenings and didn't return until the wee hours of Saturday morning.

"Yeah, about the usual." Amanda started to slide past him, gripping the key to her chest. "I really have to get in now. I…I think I'm going to lie down for a while, now that I have what I needed from the car."

Amanda was nearly at a run when she reached the side door to her building. Glancing over her shoulder, she saw Earl Smith staring after her, his dark bushy eyebrows bent in a deep frown. Casting a quick wave in his direction, Amanda ducked into the shade of the inside hall. Gasping a little to calm her breaths, Amanda pressed back into the wall.

He knows. He knows what you've done. He knows the evil that lurks in your veins.

Amanda spent the weekend waiting. She jumped every time the phone rang or someone knocked on the door. Mrs. Pinterly, who lived across the way, was worried because she hadn't seen Amanda out and around and decided to check on her. Amanda had almost thrown up from nerves before opening the door.

Monday, she was exhausted and looked like John Deere had run over her a couple of times. Large black circles hung beneath her eyes, and no amount of makeup covered them. Her hair hung limply from her scalp, looking darker than normal against her pale skin. She had lost weight already; she had been unable to eat since the newscast Saturday morning.

Walking into the office, the main receptionist, Stephanie, backed away from her, and a co-worker dropped the cellphone she was speaking into and stood to watch Amanda take her desk.

"Are you okay?"

Amanda looked up. The question had come from Stephanie, now standing on the opposite side of the room. "I'm fine. I just had a bad weekend; I didn't get much sleep."

Stephanie nodded, but kept her distance.

She knows.

Amanda ignored her co-workers, and listened to her voicemail, taking a deep, shaky breath before each message started. Scared one would be from the police. All were related to her accounts, left at the end of business on Friday.

Amanda couldn't concentrate. She couldn't help but watch her co-workers, wondering if any of them suspected, if any of them had any clue as to what she had done on Friday. What would their reaction be if they found out? Would they laugh? Would they ridicule her?

Anger began to simmer at their imagined reactions. Amanda sneered when she thought they weren't looking, plotting her revenge. They wouldn't get away with treating her like that. She had killed someone once, she could do it again. She knew where each one of her co-workers lived, where they went to work-out, where they partied. Hell, she had partied with half of them. She knew when they would be vulnerable. She could do it without getting caught. She had done it before.

They'll tell on you.

Amanda snickered, missing the looks she received from Stephanie, and the discreet call Stephanie made to the boss. Amanda continued with her plans, making notes in her steno pad.

"Amanda?"

Amanda slammed the steno shut, snapping the pencil she had been writing with in two. She looked up, her breath coming in quick a shallow rhythm. "Yes?"

It was Mr. Taylor, her boss. "Are you okay?"

Amanda nodded quickly, scanning the faces behind her boss. She knew what they were all thinking. Her plotting escalated. Maybe she could wipe them all out at the same time. Work would be the perfect place. She could take care of Mr. Taylor, too.

"Amanda?" Mr. Taylor leaned over her desk, waving one hand in front of her face.

Amanda started and slipped off her chair, her bottom hitting the floor hard, causing a run in her pantyhose. "Damn." She whispered. She didn't want to take the bus home with a run in her stocking. Someone might get the wrong idea about her.

"Amanda, I think you should go home."

Alarmed, Amanda stood up, tucking her steno under her arm protectively. "Why? Why do you want me to go home? What do you think I did?"

"Amanda, I don't think you did anything. I just think you need to go home and rest—maybe take a vacation for a few days."

He knows. He knows, and he's getting rid of you. He's going to call the police and tell them you're evil.

Amanda stared at her boss, her eyes unblinking. There was no way he'd seen her car; he didn't even know she had a garage at her condo. No, he didn't know. He didn't know anything.

"A vacation? Where?"

"Just go home and rest, Amanda. Nivens can handle your accounts for a week."

With that, Mr. Taylor turned and left. The rest of the people in the office watched her.

Amanda stared back at them. *What were they looking at?* She considered sticking her tongue out at them, but decided against it since she would have to come back to work next Monday.

They are looking at you. Watching you. Waiting for you to do it again.

The other riders on the bus wouldn't look at her.

Amanda tucked the leg with the hosiery run behind the other, clutching her gray messenger bag to her chest, daring anyone to say or think anything about it. She glared beneath her lashes at them.

She could kill them, too, if she wanted. Let them think whatever they wanted about her; she knew better.

You're an evil, evil child, and they know it.

Her apartment was quiet except for the slight hum of the refrigerator's ice machine filling. She pulled the drapes in the living room closed and turned on a single lamp.

Collapsing to the sofa, she took a deep breath. So far, so good. No one had found her out yet. She clicked on the TV and there it was, another report about the accident and the ongoing search for the hit-and-run driver.

The description was still just the dark BWM with a brunette driver. The second victim was in the ICU, their prognosis not good. The family of the victims—they had been a married couple—came on, pleading for anyone with any knowledge to come forward. The couple had two young children that would need closure once they were old enough to understand what took their parents away.

You've hurt children. Such an evil thing to do.

Amanda's breathing quickened and her head started to throb. She needed to do something with the car, get it out of her garage and somewhere no one would find it. But where?

Opening her laptop, she activated the stealth mode in her browser so no one could track the sites she went to and typed into the search bar: how to hide a car.

Not much came up, but the best solution seemed to be to drive it into a body of water.

Fuck. She lived in Arizona. Where was she going to find an isolated body of water big enough?

Maybe…maybe she could drive it out into the middle of the desert and leave it there. An isolated part of the desert. In a stretch of dry, barren land where no one ventured.

Pulling up a map of the state, she zoomed in on her city, Tempe, and then considered where she could drive in a day. She'd have to leave at night, of course, making sure no one saw her. Maybe get a can of black spray paint to cover the mess so it was not as noticeable under a streetlight.

Taking a deep breath, she closed her eyes and tried to smile. There, she had a plan.

Such an evil plan.

And since she was effectively on vacation, no one would miss her while she did it.

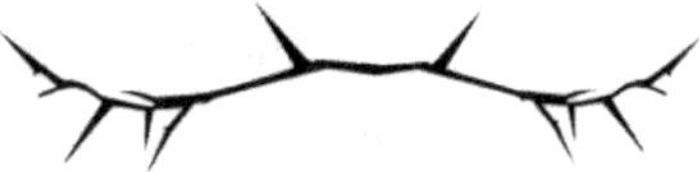

At three minutes past midnight, in the shadowed corner of her garage, Amanda shook the can of black paint she'd walked to the hardware store to buy that afternoon. She sprayed it haphazardly over the sheen of bare, twisted metal on the bumper and fender, cursing when it wasn't quite enough to finish the job.

It would have to do.

At nineteen minutes past midnight, she opened the garage door and peered around the dark shared drive before backing her BMW out. It ran a little noisy, the loose fender rattling in time with the engine.

"Fuck." Mrs. Pinterly better be running her brown noise machine. The last thing she needed was that nosy woman waking up and seeing her drive away.

She already knows you're evil. That's why she watches you all the time.

Amanda groaned and eased the car into the street. It wasn't that big a deal. She could just explain that she went away for a bit of vacation and wanted to travel in the coolest part of the day, before traffic started up.

Easy peasy.

Evil is so easy, little girl.

She drove the speed limit plus one, not daring to draw the attention of the police or even a pedestrian.

Except…

She stopped at a stoplight. There was an old wino on the far corner, weaving along the sidewalk. The man waved his arms around his head like he was fighting off flies, one hand grasping a bottle. He looked like he was talking to himself.

He reminded Amanda of her father.

The light turned green.

Amanda stepped on the gas pedal—hard.

The BMW roared forward, and she jerked the steering wheel to the right. The tires hit the curb with a sharp thud, and then the body was crumpling beneath the wheels, a dull crunching reverberating in her ears.

Maybe that would shut him up.

Giggling, Amanda veered back into the street, glancing behind her at the mess on the lonely sidewalk.

Evil feels good, doesn't it?

By the time she took an on-ramp to the interstate, she had the Sirius radio tuned to her favorite hard rock station, screaming along with the words at the top of her lungs. It drowned out the voice in her head.

She missed her exit, and that little nagging voice laughed at her for it—but she spun the BMW around in the median, tires spewing grass and mud, to take it from the other direction.

The BMW made more noise after that, a rattle singing from below instead of just the fender. Amanda didn't care; she was abandoning the car, anyway. If it broke down when she did it, all the better.

She just needed to get it far enough away to not be found easily.

She drove more carefully after that thought, though she sped up. The road wound through low shrubs and dry, dirt hills. There was no one to be seen.

And no voices to be heard.

She wondered at the silence in her head, but quickly thought no more of it. She needed to concentrate on what she was doing. Maybe, for once, the voice was helpful. Quiet.

Watching the odometer, Amanda ticked off the miles. At mile 50 she slowed, looking for the slight ruts to the right that indicated the abandoned road she'd found online.

She found it at mile 51-and-a-half, and directed the nose of the car off the tarmac and into the dirt and dry grass. She could simply drive now, letting the tires guide her along the indentations, just needing to steer around the odd shrub that grew too close to the track.

Bored with the rock channel, she switched to an FM station, curious to see if she could pick up a signal. It was faint and scratchy, every other word missing.

She took her foot off the gas, letting the car drift a bit, and listened.

The Tempe police had found the dead drunk.

They know.

The Voice was back. She wished it would shut up again.

Her stomach knotted as she stomped the brake pedal, the car sliding on loose gravel. Gasping, she stared at the radio.

Why the fuck had she done that? Hit that wino and killed him, just because?

Because you're an evil little girl who does evil things.

Sobbing, she put both hands over her mouth and closed her eyes, letting the hot, salty tears leak out. God—she was in trouble now.

But wait…no she wasn't. They didn't know it was her. There was no witness to the hit. Just the body found after the fact. And they still didn't know it was her BMW that had hit that couple. Once she had the car far enough out in the desert, she'd be free and clear.

Swallowing and sniffing hard, she gunned the engine, the back tires spinning and spraying debris behind her. She only had to follow through on her plan.

She drove another hour after that, the sun starting to peek over the horizon when the BMW ran out of gas, sputtering to a stop behind a larger bit of scraggly tree. She'd turned off the tack a while back, heading out into the wilderness where no one went.

It was quiet here, the car's engine dead, not even the AC blowing refreshing air over her face. Amanda watched the sun rise, the bright red and orange paling to pink and yellow as it crested.

It was a new day.

Smiling, she grabbed the bottle of water she'd brought and climbed out of the car. Popping the hood, she examined the engine. Would it still burn if all the gas was gone?

Only one way to find out.

Three paces back, Amanda pulled the half-empty box of matches from her pocket and lit one.

It flickered out instantly, as did the next two, but finally she got one lit long enough to toss into the engine compartment. She jogged away, expecting an immediate burst of flame and explosion.

But nothing happened.

You're evil and evil gets caught.

She watched, waited, spinning the box of matched in her fingers.

Taking a few steps forward, she pulled another match from the box and lit it, once again tossing it under the hood.

The sun was higher now, starting to warm the air. Amanda shrugged off her sweatshirt and tied it around her waist.

The car still didn't burn.

Fuck. What to do now? Why didn't that voice ever say something helpful?

She closed her eyes and took a deep breath—which is when she smelled it: rubber burning. Her matches had hit a mark somewhere.

Pacing back even farther, she narrowed her gaze, holding one hand up to block the glare of the sun, and saw the thin trail of smoke rising from the car.

Fucking finally.

Swigging half the bottle of water down in one go, Amanda started to retrace the path she'd traveled in the car. It was fifteen minutes later, the sun at her back, when she heard the car explode.

Her plan had worked.

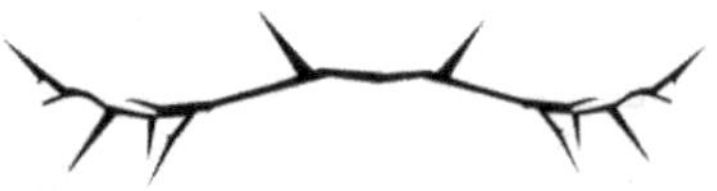

By noon, she was worried. She still hadn't found the abandoned track she'd followed to come out here. The hard packed dirt didn't show the tire tread from her car to guide her. She'd kept walking with the sun to her back, figuring she'd find it, eventually.

And her water was gone.

In hindsight, maybe she should have brought a second bottle, but her plan had included being able to trace her way back to the road and catch a ride with someone.

Sweating, she looked around; she saw nothing but yellow dirt and gnarled shrubs. She kept walking, keeping the sun behind her.

It was nearing midafternoon when she realized that by keeping the sun behind her, she'd turned herself around. The smell of hot oil and burnt rubber confirmed that she'd wound herself back towards the BMW.

She couldn't see it though, so maybe she hadn't gotten all the way back. All she had to do was turn around, keep the sun in front of her, and keep walking until she found a road.

Easy peasy.

Evil isn't easy, little girl. Evil is hard and takes more smarts than you will ever have.

She stuck her chin up and ignored the voice. She knew what she was doing. She wasn't stupid.

When the sun set, she was truly lost. Darkness engulfed her as the day's heat dissipated quickly. She pulled her sweatshirt over her head, but struggled with getting her arms in the right holes. Stumbling, she fell to her knees. Sharp rocks bit into the denim that covered her legs.

She could just sit for a bit, yeah, get her bearings before starting off again. Once she found a direction to walk, she'd be fine.

Shivering, she waited for her eyes to adjust to the dark, hugging the one arm she couldn't find the sleeve for to her chest to keep it warm. She felt hot while she trembled, her skin and soft body hair fluffing to keep her warm.

Something rustled to her left. and she swatted out at it, screaming for it to keep away.

It won't.

She spun where she sat, but the darkness remained and she could see nothing. There was no hunched form behind her, cigarette poised between two fingers, ready to press against skin. No hulking figure with fingers that squeezed her tender flesh to bruises.

But there was another rustle and then a snuffle. She scrabbled along the ground, fingers searching for something to use as a weapon. Finding a palm-sized rock, she curled her fingers around it and brought it to her chest.

It's coming for you.

"Who's there?" Her voice, sharp, echoed in the night.

No one, was the sighing reply.

"It wasn't my fault!"

What did the wino do to you?

That poor couple was just walking to their car.

Their children will hate you. They'll curse your bones for eternity.

"No one knows!"

You do. You know. You're evil.

There was laughter that boomed in her ears. *Your co-workers know it was you. That's why they sent you away. Those people on the bus wouldn't look at you. They could tell you were evil, tainted.*

Sobbing, taking in great dry gulps of air, Amanda rocked where she sat in the dirt. The sharp edge of the rock cut into her fingers, and warm blood ran down her wrist.

She slammed the rock down, winced at the pain in her hand as it cut deeper. She slammed it down again, this time hitting her foot with it. That pain was sharper, but she did it again and again.

The blood and tattered flesh on her foot and ankle felt separate from her body. It no longer hurt, and she threw the rock away.

That's not enough. The harsh whisper made her shiver even though she no longer felt the cold.

"It's not enough." She nodded in agreement, her own voice hoarse. "Not enough…"

It was still black, still night, not even the moon casting light from behind the dark clouds.

Amanda dug her nails into the shredded ankle, pressing them in, ripping at the remaining flesh. The pain was dull, far away, removed.

Not enough.

She screamed into the emptiness, slamming both hands to the ground. How could she make it enough? What was left that she could do?

Lying back, she pounded her head to the dirt, sharp shards of gravel embedding into the back of it. Pain shot through her skull and made her groan, but fleeting, flitting away with the whispers of the voice.

More…

She pounded her head harder, turning over onto her knees to repeat the movement with her forehead. Rising, the shattered ankle pushed to the side oddly. Blood ran down her face, burning into her eyes, a hot metal liquid seeping onto her tongue.

More…

For the wino.

For the couple.

For the children.

Because you are evil. So evil.

Amanda vomited, the remains of what was left of her dinner the evening before burning in her lungs and throat, dribbling from her chin to mix with the blood that soaked the ground. Gagging, heaving, her stomach determined to expunge itself from her body, she collapsed into the mess she'd made.

Something sniffed at her wounded hand, a tentative lick at the blood, a nibble at the torn flesh.

Light seared her eyelids as she opened them. A kit fox stared at her, its snout red with her blood. Part of the flesh on her hand was gone.

The animal darted back, sneering and growling at her. Its teeth sharp.

She couldn't move.

The sun crept over the horizon once more, the orange and red bathing the dirt so it looked aflame.

Hell isn't good enough for you.

Amanda stared at the small fox huddling out of reach. She shifted her arm, the one with the damaged hand, offering it as penance.

The animal darted away.

Still not enough.

Laying in the dirt, Amanda couldn't move. Even though her brain told her to, she no longer had control of her body.

The sun climbed higher in the sky, its rays beating against her. She didn't care; she couldn't care.

The kit fox came back, once again sniffing and licking at her hand. Amanda couldn't feel the nibble and when the animal tugged and dragged away a whole piece, there was no pain, just the dull sensation of pulling, like someone had carefully yanked her ponytail to get her attention.

The light faded, but the sun was still in the sky. Amanda let it come, tried to make it welcome, inviting it to stay, but it drifted, wavering. The light was too much, too hot.

Something buzzed along her ear and another something scuttled along her thigh. She should worry there are scorpions out here, after all.

Fear remained at a distance as she accepted her fate. Death was coming with the dark.

But it will never be enough.

HOTEL MONROE

K. E. JENNINGS

D^{ust.}

Where was he? There were so many excavations full of dust and dirt, it was hard to keep track of where he had been. He began to panic. The dust choked him, causing his throat to close, then open. Each minute particle invaded his body with every breath he took. He wondered if he was dying. Every time he closed his eyes in this hotel, the dust would swarm. Out of all the places that he stayed on assignments, Hotel Monroe was the grandest. An illusion. It was in the center of Cairo, ancient and beautiful at the same time. This should have been a luxurious stay for him, compared to a lower budget place they could have put him in. Instead, it hid endless nightmares and choking fits. He did not know how to escape.

The sensations of losing lung function intensified. A sheen of sweat covered his body, which the dust clung to like earth worms surfacing after a fresh rain. He took one last gasp. Resigned to the heady fate that felt inevitable, his mind raced with thoughts. Was this the end? Was he about to die? He saw the heavy curtain of darkness envelop his being.

"Reg, *Reg.* We must go. Nap time is over. Our shuttle is here."

From dust to dust.

Blue eyes flew open. The haunting words echoed in Reggie's mind as he adjusted to the open-air lobby. His colleague was staring at him, a look of disquiet on his face. He wasn't choking anymore. The air flowed in and out of his lungs easily, but he felt the stickiness of sweat covering his body. He knew dirt would be caked to his face or arms. Waking up in the lobby in such a state was embarrassing. He knew he looked like shit.

"You're soaked." Bryce said.

Reggie touched his neck. It was wet with sweat and covered in dust. He simply nodded, then sat up. Bryce gave one last uncomfortable glance to him, then headed out the front entrance steps towards the waiting van. Work this afternoon should be interesting, he thought. All he wanted was to get to the site and continue the dig. Anything to get away from sleeping in this cursed place.

From dust to dust.

Needing a reprieve from the hotel, Reg left the lobby and climbed into the van. It smelled of stale body odor and Indian curry. He recognized the notes of hing, turmeric, and cumin from countless years of eating in Indian restaurants. Which was curious, as there weren't any restaurants within walking distance of the hotel. Where could the smell of food be coming from? Possibly the driver had a takeout container. A portable fan clicked on from the front, the blades creating a rhythmic sound that dared to lull the shuttle occupants to sleep.

Reggie struggled to keep awake. He feared sleeping now. Ever since he arrived in Egypt, the incessant dreams of choking on dirt and being suffocated persisted. Nightmares came every time he shut his eyes for rest. The van sped through a section of the old town, the cobblestones bouncing everything around. Cairo stunned in the lazy light. The sun was moving downwards, its hot rays at their peak. It was why Reggie had taken a nap in the hotel lobby. He inhaled the air flowing in from a cracked window. Again, he smelled curry, almost tasting the tangy spice.

"Are you planning to be on team one again?" Bryce asked, his voice shaking with every bump in the road.

"Yeah, I do. We're close to unearthing the second burial site."

Reggie pursed his lips, deep in thought, his mind on the job. Why would his colleague ask such a question? Bryce knew how much work he'd been putting in and the long hours they all had spent on the chamber site. He'd gotten to know the fellow archeologists well, Bryce included. Archeology was a tedious profession but rewarding. The Faculty of Archeology had handpicked their team at Cairo University. Reggie had come from the U.S. and Bryce had been working in India.

"I know you will get to see it soon. Your team is doing quite good. Team two is long off from our goal," Bryce retorted.

The van finally reached the site outside of the city. Saqqara covered a huge area of the desert. It was known as the biggest open-air museum in Egypt, containing many burial sites for those in positions of honor ranging from as far back as 2400 B.C. Tourists flocked there in buses, hoping to see the burial chambers and underground galleries. There were many active dig sites as well, and out of the almost 4 miles of space, their team was in the far back, behind an exposed pyramid. There were other foreign teams working alongside them, making it a true archeologist's dream. Reggie nodded to Bryce as they went their separate ways toward the work areas. He reached up to put on his wide brimmed dig hat for sun protection and felt a stuck clod of dirt loosen from the back of his neck.

From dust to dust.

The phrase made him shiver. He wanted nothing more than to escape the words that kept echoing in his mind. Today, he hoped to get much closer to uncovering the suspected tomb in his sector. He had been working tirelessly for days. If it was indeed where they thought it was, he or someone on his team should make the discovery soon. It would be a career making moment. Many archeologists were propelled into bigger projects just by being associated with such a team find.

His hat affixed; Reg joined his team down in an open channel. They had to climb short wooden ladders, carefully carrying tools to each spot. Reggie oversaw a corner section, the size of a small car. Earth jutted outwards around the shape, as he had uncovered it to this point. He hunkered down into position, wielding a small hand brush which resembled a wide bristled paint brush with a short handle. Grain by grain, he swiped away at the earth. It was abundantly satisfying to him. Seeing the past become part of the present had to be the single most important reason he wanted to be in this career.

Time passed. The covered section of earth now resembled the shape of a coffin. Chatter could be heard from those nearby, as they found a buried cup in their respective area. The wind swirled up above, causing curry smells to float in with the breeze. Reggie frowned and looked up. Someone must have brought food into the site.

"Hey, who has curry?" He asked.

His voice carried in the air, causing those near him to stop and look. They worked in proximity to each other, but not so close that they could easily see what each member was doing. Reggie's spot was isolated, as he was in a far corner, which was positioned down a few feet into the earth. He worked faster than the others, causing his section to sink with each chunk of dirt he removed.

"Curry? I don't smell anything." A voice replied from some distance away.

He could smell it, though. It was pungent. Spicy. Notes of the food were swirling around. Then suddenly, it was gone. He frowned and shook his head.

I'm going crazy.

More time passed as he labored in his spot. He could see the line beginning to form an object below. He hoped from the outline and size that it was the burial site they had been looking for. The chief archeologists were almost certain it was here from the earlier use of ground mapping. The real question was whose tomb they were looking at.? A lost noble was rumored to be buried here but had yet to be identified at the site. Excitement began to build. With each brush stroke, he envisioned the find of a lifetime.

Just as giddiness took over, he felt a hand on his shoulder.

From dust to dust.

He whipped around and saw no one. Reaching back, he touched the fabric of his shirt. Someone had touched him. He *felt* it. Dread filled his mind, and he became scared. The nightmares were enough. His gut told him this location harbored spirits. Egypt was known for various spirits that could haunt you, especially if they were disturbed after being buried. Many local legends told of a few pharaohs that were known to haunt tourists who stepped out of line when touring the pyramids. Digging near their burial sites could easily cause such a disruption.

"Reggie! You found it!"

He heard the nearest colleague call out to him, but time had seemed to slow to a standstill.

"What?"

"The sarcophagus! It's there! The edge, you just uncovered a portion of the edge!"

Reggie glanced down at his hand. The bristles of the brush were suspended, as was the handle. He didn't feel it in his hand, only saw himself holding it. His mind spun with confusion. What was happening? He shifted his eyes and saw a golden glint that shone in the sunlight. The sarcophagus was indeed there.

"Reggie found one!!"

The other workers and colleagues were chattering now, moving closer to see the exposed artifact.

"It's just like in India."

He looked up at Ali Adel, the senior archeologist. What had he said?

"India?" Reggie asked absentmindedly.

"Sorry?" the archeologist asked, genuine confusion in his voice.

"You said 'it's just like in India'."

"No. I said it's been a long time coming."

Reggie's face became fiery.

"Are you ok? Why don't you go get some water and cool off in the van? It's here for the shuttle back to the hotel early." Ali said.

Recognizing this was not a request, Reggie nodded and carefully set his tools down in the sand. He hoped he could play this off as simply heat exhaustion. That was a common enough problem for the workers.

"Let me walk with you." Bryce said. "I want to go back early for a dinner tonight in the city."

Bryce got into step with Reggie, and they trudged through the excavation site toward the waiting van. The air was hotter up top of the dig site, and it choked their throats. Just like the dreams had induced for Reggie.

"Is there a storm coming in tonight?" Reggie asked, looking up at the sky.

"I don't think so. It's supposed to be a calm night with the stars visible. After you rest, you really should go out and look at them."

Giving Bryce a sideways glance, Reggie shook his head. He came here to experience the dig sites, not the stars. In the past, he had found wandering around in a foreign place alone at night to be dangerous. Once, he was robbed in England while out socializing after a long day in a dig. He found Bryce to be too flippant when it came to work. His demeanor was too casual, and he didn't show as much dedication as Reggie liked. The guy managed to get the best assignments though, and always got picked for another great assignment without having to apply. Reggie didn't see how unless Bryce had connections.

They reached the van as the wind whipped violently.

From dust to dust.

The voice in his head spoke urgently now, the tone laced with a vile and immoral undercurrent. Each syllable was loaded with malice. Reggie's heart thumped erratically, the force of it beating hard in his chest. He settled in a worn seat next to Bryce. The driver nodded at them both and switched on the rickety fan. Closing his eyes, Reggie breathed deeply. He just needed to calm down.

FROM DUST TO DUST!

The voice was shouting. Reggie's eyes flew open. Bryce stared at him; his face contorted into a snarl. Reggie blinked, then he looked again. This time, Bryce met him with a concerned expression.

"You really need to get some sleep. Sun exposure can drain us to a dangerous level."

Reggie couldn't think of a fitting response, so he simply nodded and let the side of his face rest on the window. For the remainder of the ride, Reggie's mind raced through the terrifying events, real and imaginary, that were going on around him. Bryce's face was pure evil for that split second, and it reminded Reggie of watching a scary movie. One where a priest would cast demons out. The voice wasn't giving him a reprieve, either. Terror gripped him as he let the thought sink in; he was being haunted. He was beyond scared and had no intention of going to sleep once they got to the hotel.

"Want me to walk you up?"

"What?" Reggie absently asked.

Bryce pushed the van door open.

"Walk you up. I am on the same floor as you. I don't want you to pass out or fall down the stairs. They said you have heat exhaustion at the site."

His limbs were tired, and his head was beginning to hurt, so Reggie conceded. He just wanted water and to sit down in the quiet. He had to think about what was going on and decide if he needed to leave.

"Here, you can have my bottle. It's unopened."

Bryce handed him a cold bottle of water. Condensation gloriously cooling off Reggie's hand as he took it. They walked through the lobby to the elevators. As the golden doors opened, Reggie caught the faint scent of the same Indian curry as before in the van, and then in the dig site. Hing and turmeric were indistinguishable, the notes of each lingering in the air.

"Curry. Where the hell is that coming from?" Reggie muttered.

"Curry is delicious. I miss that from working in India."

The doors shut and Bryce pushed the floor button. Rocketing upwards, Reggie shuffled his feet. The smell was strong now, as if he had stumbled into a kitchen where it was being prepared.

"Do you miss India? I sure do." Bryce asked.

"India? I've never been to India." he answered, his confusion mounting.

The men exited off the elevator at their floor into the long hallway. Reggie felt his forehead. It was burning up. He thought he was hallucinating.

"We need to go back there after this job." Bryce said.

"What?" He asked. "I've never been to India."

Reggie stumbled towards the number that was his room. The hallway lights flickered.

From dust to dust.

The voice was insistent. It was trying to tell him something, not just a phrase on repeat, but a warning.

"Oh yes Reggie, you have," Bryce replied.

He felt a hand on his shoulder again, just like from the dig site. Only now it was hard, clawing into his skin. Bryce took the key card from Reggie and beeped the door open, shoving him in.

"What are you doing?" Reggie cried out as heat coursed through his body.

He stumbled and fell onto the bed. Bryce didn't answer. He walked slowly towards him. Fear began to overpower the fever's effects. The scent of curry stunk now, washing over Reggie.

"Think." Bryce loudly commanded.

From dust to dust!

He strained his brain, trying without fail to figure out why Bryce had said they had both been to India. Sweat oozed out of his pores. He swiped at his forehead and felt the gritty dirt that always accompanied the nightmares he had been having when he fell asleep in this hotel. This all began when he arrived in Egypt.

I must have disturbed the dead in the tomb I discovered and now they are haunting me, just like Egyptians believe.

"Not here." Bryce retorted, reading his thoughts.

Reggie tried to stand, but Bryce held him back. They struggled, wrestling on the bed. Dust began to appear all around them. A breeze blew in the room. Realizing he couldn't get away, Reggie ceased to move.

The air stilled in the room, but the scent of Indian curry permeated.

"Hearing voices? That's me."

Bryce wrestled Reggie again, contorting his body sideways, then wrenched his neck back. Pain flooded Reggie's body.

"Having nightmares choking on sand? That's me too. I'm part of you." Bryce breathed pungent curry breath onto Reggie. "Slowly inching my way in. You thought you could unearth my bones in India and walk away unscathed?"

From dust to dust.

"And so you shall be. You'll join me in hell. I have room for another demon."

Memories flooded Reggie's mind, one more vivid than the next. It wasn't the hotel doing this to him, it was his colleague. He *knew* Bryce. They worked together in India at a sacred site, where the university he worked for had arranged a grant. Why had he blocked out such a memory? Immense pain shot through his torso as he felt a rib crack. He cried out.

"Who are you?" He begged, tears filling his eyes.

Bryce leaned down and whispered into his ear.

"Ravana, god of the demons. I am here to collect on your unsuspecting debt. When you dug me up in India, I was finally unleashed, no longer hidden in the ground. You allowed a part of my spirit to enter you through the tools you and Bryce were using. I took over Bryce's body but now I am ready to shed the human form."

The room spun as another rib cracked, and Reggie squinted as tears flooded his vision. Bryce became blurry and then fell to the floor. A dark apparition replaced him, rising from where Bryce's body was lying. This must be Ravana's true form, Reggie thought. Panic overtook him but he knew it was too late. He would pay with his life for digging up the Indian god. Sweat and dust coated Reggie's body, entombing him. Before he saw the eternal blackness of Ravana's hell, his eyes focused on the nightstand. A decorative card was folded in half on the table.

Thank you for your stay at Hotel Monroe.

HANGING ON

NATALIA K. GLAROS

I lay here, unmoving
Holding on for dear life.
My mouth gaping open
As saliva, or is it blood,
Trickles out.

I hear a lone bird singing
Its unique song I enjoy.
I take another shallow breath,
Just waiting.

I must persevere,
So someone can save me.

My eyes flutter—
I try to keep them open.
I inhale and smell something sweet,
Like a warm, fresh cookie.

Oh, I am wrong.
It is a white lilac petal,
Floating and landing
On my motionless body.

Please hold on, I tell myself.
I need to keep breathing,
Before the darkness takes hold,
And plunges me into
Either heaven or hell.

I need to hang on.

THE GOBBLE-UNS

THEA BRUNE

"An' the Gobble-uns 'll git you

Ef you

Don't

Watch

Out!"

—James Whitcomb Riley

On the night of Charlie's sixth birthday, he had to put himself to bed completely alone. He cried, and his parents knew he was scared to be alone in his room, but it was no use. He would have to get into bed and just lay there and wait for them to come in after they'd finished helping his brother, Matty, to sleep.

When Matty was first old enough for his own room and a big kid's bed, Mom would take care of him while Dad helped Charlie. But Matty cried too much and was "a handful" so little by little, Dad spent more time down the hall, and Charlie was expected to help out by setting a good example of how a big boy behaves. As Charlie learned how to do his nightly chores by himself, his parents read Matty's bedtime story. Sometimes one story wasn't enough. Sometimes they had to read two or three. Dad would read. Mom would hum lullabies in a low and soothing voice. She hummed low, but Charlie could hear them from all the way at the other end of the hall.

During Matty's story time, Charlie was supposed to be brushing his teeth, putting on his jamjams, and saying his prayers. It was a lot.

He could pull his little wooden step stool up to the sink by himself. (The one that had red mushrooms painted on it. Mom liked to laugh and say it was a "toadstool" but it didn't have any toads on it, only mushrooms, so he didn't understand the joke). He was getting better at squeezing the toothpaste out of the tube now. His hands were stronger now that he'd had a growth spurt. That's why none of his jamjams fit anymore. He'd had to stop wearing all of his footie onesies, and now he only had left the ones with no feet, and the legs were so short his bony ankles stuck out. He'd complained his toes were cold, Mom said to wear socks, and they'd get him some new jamjams soon. He'd asked when "soon" was. She'd said "soon enough" and gone back to spooning some gross looking goop into Matty's mouth while making choo-choo train noises at him.

But even though he could brush his teeth all by himself and even reach his jamjams out of the topmost drawer of his bureau, he still couldn't say his prayers by himself, because it meant he had to go by his bed. His parents thought he was saying his prayers every night… because he lied about it when they asked him. He knew not saying his prayers was bad, and he was pretty sure lying about it was even worse. But whenever he kneeled beside the bed, the way Mom had shown him, the little scraping noises and rustlings would start. Once something touched his leg from underneath. Something sharp that poked and scraped and grabbed.

Last week, his dad had gotten down and looked under the bed, but Charlie knew it was just pretend because his dad didn't see anything. There was something there, so if he had really, really looked, he would have seen it. Charlie should look and prove it, but he was too scared to do so himself. But then his dad had gone off to the kitchen and come back with a spray bottle. He said it was "monster repellent." He sprayed it under the bed, and in the closet and even behind the bedroom door, where the shadows were extra dark and made funny shapes. Later that night, when Charlie had felt the bed trembling and quivering from the restless shifting of the thing underneath, he knew his dad had also pretended about the monster repellent. When he couldn't take it anymore and had run to his parents' room, his mom had been cross with him. She'd told him she needed to get one solid night's sleep please-for-the-love-of-God, and he was too big to be running in to share their bed. She made him go back to his room and told him to stay there.

Tonight, for Charlie's birthday, while his parents gave him presents and had him blow out the candles on his cake, they kept telling him how big he was growing and how proud they were of him. His stomach turned around in knots. All he could think about was being left alone at night always from now on. All because Matty couldn't go to sleep without stories. When Mom had given some of the cake to Matty, Charlie had pushed the plate so it splatted on the floor. He'd gotten yelled at, but he wasn't sorry.

Charlie thought about all of this while he brushed his teeth. In the bathroom mirror, he could see his bed behind him through the doorway. He thought it moved a little. He tiptoed carefully as he edged around it to the other side of the room, to the dresser.

Once he had his jamjams on, he stared at the bed. His stomach felt wobbly, like that time he'd drunk sour milk. From a few feet away, he rocked on his heels once- twice- then leapt to land on the mattress without having to walk up right next to the side. The mattress thumped and the box springs protested with a loud squawk. From Matty's room, his mom yelled for him not to jump on the bed and this was why they couldn't have nice things, for Pete's sake. He heard his dad telling her in a quieter voice to go easy on him on his birthday. Then they went back to reading Matty his second bedtime story of the night.

Charlie's stuffed animals had tumbled around from the bouncing of the mattress. He picked them up and one by one and lined them along the side of the bed against the wall. They were the soldiers that would protect him in case the thing tried to come up on that side. This way, he could safely turn his back on the wall and he only had to keep an eye on the open side of the bed. He had more confidence in this system than in his dad's "monster repellent."

He said goodnight to each of his animals in turn, patting them on the head. Then he pulled the covers way up to his chin and lay there, watching the door. As the low drone of his dad's voice slowly tapered off, he heard the first faint sssk-sssk from under his mattress. A small sound, like cat paws lightly scratching. The sound moved back and forth once, twice, then stopped. He clenched his little fists around the edge of the blanket and pulled it up over his nose, so only his eyes peeked out.

Footsteps padded down the carpeted hallway, and his mom and dad poked their heads around the door. His dad chuckled to see him so bundled so far under his blanket and came and rustled his hair. His mom bent down and kissed him on his forehead. She wished him happy birthday one more time and my she just couldn't believe how big he was getting and she loved him to the moon and back.

When she turned to go, Charlie let go of the blanket to grab hold of her hand and ask if he could come sleep in their room. Mom sighed, and hugged him one more time, then told him he needed to learn to stay in his own bed, because that's what six-year-olds do. Didn't he want to set a good example for Matty? She told him she would make him pancakes for breakfast and in the morning, he would see that there was nothing he should have worried about. His dad called him "Champ." On their way out, Mom flipped the wall switch off, leaving only the illumination from his dolphin nightlight.

Silence gradually fell over the house until it was so quiet Charlie could hear the grandfather clock ticking all the way down in the kitchen. The wobbles in his stomach had hardened, like a peach pit. His fingers hurt from clenching for so long, but he didn't let go of the blanket. The noise didn't come back, and his eyes grew weary from straining to see in the shadows. Eyelids drooped and little fingers uncurled, breathing slowed…

The nightlight went out.

The mattress jerked, and a hard lump hit him in the side, as if something had punched up from underneath. His eyes flew open, but in the total darkness he couldn't see anything. He waited for the scrabbly noise to come, the scratches and whispers that always followed next, but nothing happened. He tried to breathe as quietly as possible, but it was so hard.

The covers moved. Something was tugging and shifting the sheet at the foot of the bed.

Charlie slowly curled into a ball, inching his knees up toward his chest. A tear slipped out the side of his eye and trickled down to the pillow. A hand grabbed his ankle and yanked his foot down.

Several sharp claw-points dug into his skin like knives stabbing. He tried to scream for his parents, but his throat just gulped and gulped and no sounds came out.

The hand held him in place with an unbreakable grip, but he didn't even try to thrash it off. He squeezed his eyes shut and hoped his mom and dad would come rescue him. Now rustlings started under the bedclothes. It sounded like more than one body moving around by his legs, and he got bumped and nudged from both sides. He felt something warm spreading and knew he was wetting himself. His mom was going to be angry with him in the morning.

Charlie's throat worked and finally small whimpers came out, like a puppy crying. One body was up to his chest now; it forced its way out from under the covers and he felt the pillow depress in front of his face. A warm puff of breath hit him. It smelled like the time he'd found a raccoon on the side of the road, after it had been dead a couple days.

It whispered in his ear, "Charlieee, we're going to eat you tonight, Charlieeee. We've been waiting so long…"

Charlie trembled too violently to speak coherently. "Mommy…" It was a sad, strangled cry.

"Your mommy and daddy don't care about you anymoooore." A claw scraped up his cheek and poked into his closed eyelid. "They left you to ussss… you're too big now… they don't care if you dieeee."

A moist chuckle made saliva drip onto Charlie's face. The bodies under the blanket grew agitated and started grabbing at his limbs with grasping, bony appendages. Jagged teeth began chewing on his calf.

"Pp-pp-pp-lease don't eat me," Charlie sobbed, between jagged gasps for air.

"Toooo late... Charlie… We want a juicy little boy for tonight's meal and you look so tender…" The one on his pillow was licking his face now, nibbling around his chin.

"Mm-mm-mm-atty!" he gasped out.

The rustlings stopped, all the bodies paused. Anticipation smothered the little bed like a too-warm blanket.

"What'ssss that you say, little boy meat?" The whisper was even softer now, cajoling.

"Matty…" Charlie couldn't seem to stop himself. He was so scared. He just wanted them to go away and not eat him. "Take Matty…"

The whisper was almost inside his ear now. "You don't loooove him? You don't care if he dieeeees?"

All Charlie knew was the reason his parents weren't there for him was because of Matty.

"Pp-pp-pp-lease…"

In a burst of activity, with much whooping and giggling, the bodies erupted from under the covers and scurried away. Charlies heard them careening and thumping down the hallway. The one on his pillow laughed at him for a long time before it ran after the others.

He heard Matty's door crash open. Triumphant howls and chortles couldn't drown out Matty's high-pitched shriek. Charlie's little brother screamed and screamed until the screaming cut off with a gurgle. When the sounds of crunching and wet slurps echoed into Charlie's room, his arms and legs finally started working, and he dashed from his bed to the closet. He pulled the closet door closed and hid, crouched down behind his Lego sets, his hands tight against his ears.

He felt, rather than heard, the reassuring pounding of the floorboards as footsteps raced from his parents' room down to

Matty's. Charlie sobbed in relief. His parents would stop the monsters.

But his father's bellows and his mother's shrieks were also cut off, and the entire house seemed to shudder in time with the gruesome sounds of tearing and chewing. Charlie rocked back and forth, back and forth, back and forth…

Long after, hours after, pale morning sunlight crept under the closet door. The sunlight grew stronger. The shadows it cast moved from one side of the room to the other, and the sunlight faded back out. As the darkness crept in again, a commotion came from downstairs. Banging on the door, voices calling. After a while, a crash came, and a tromping of feet up the stairs. A shout of horror, and the feet ran back downstairs.

Police sirens came from outside the windows. Eventually, the overhead light flicked on in Charlie's room. A young, fresh-faced policeman opened Charlie's closet door. He called over his shoulder that he'd found the missing boy, then he reached out a hand to Charlie, telling him he was safe now, not to worry. The bad man was gone. When Charlie didn't move, the policeman shined his flashlight around the behind the Lego sets. The man jumped back with a startled yell, stumbling and falling, then turned and ran out of the room.

Charlie thought he should come out now. His limbs stiff, he crawled out from the closet. The soft glow of the light hurt his eyes. He looked down. His hands dug into the carpet. They were tipped with long, ragged claws. Twisting his neck all around to get a full view, he saw all his limbs longer, bonier, spindlier. His knees bent out in a funny way, his skin looked grayer in the lamplight. He opened his mouth. It felt fuller than it used to, and his tongue bumped up against sharp teeth. A low raspy hiss wheezed out. He felt… hungry.

The light, though… his eyes were burning now. Directly in his line of sight, the underneath of the bed looked gloomy and inviting.

He inched forward. The darkness under the bed was absolute. The shadows went further back, on and on. So Charlie went, on and on, away from the light, hungrier with each creeping step.

THE TURK

LEE FRANKLIN

Lance Corporal Thomas Carter threw himself into the mud as the night thundered with explosions.

White flares lit the devastation around him as the bombardment made his insides spasm in ways not natural to the human condition. The reek of slow rotting flesh, and gas engorged corpses plundered his senses, with the taste of death an oil slick down the back of his throat. He pushed himself onto his elbows, his left sinking into the ruptured chest of a faceless soldier. He gagged and lay against a small rise in the slushy earth.

Despite everything, his fingers reached out to caress the letter in his pocket.

It sat there, heavy, a wedge of paper hard against his broken heart. The words, long since been washed away by the blood churned waters of Suvla Bay, were etched into his mind.

The rain bore down again, drowning out the groans and prayers of dying men. Carter shivered with such violence his teeth ached.

The bark of gunfire chewed up the ground around him, spitting mud into his face. He wasn't safe; he had to move.

He drew a deep sobbing breath and rolled himself back onto the pile of bodies. A flare flashed light onto the scene. Carter refused to look into the dull-glazed eyes of the dead. Instead, he focused on the lip of a bomb crater-turned trench, framed with barbed wire; not a promise of safety, barely a whisper.

Carter slithered to the wire with caution, his hearing shot from the artillery bombardment. Endless ringing reverberating through his skull. He whispered a small prayer to a God he both loved and loathed, and with trembling hands, he drew the concertina of barbs open as far as he could. As soon as another flare shot up, he eased his head through.

The trench resulted from an aerial bomb and had left a depression in the ground about five feet deep and five yards in diameter. The Turks had recommissioned it as a trench, fortifying it with barbed wire. A Hotchkiss machine gun lay half swallowed by the quagmire. Bodies inside the trench were twisted and torn grotesqueries of death under the white flare. They were confirmed as Turkish by the flash of a red fez.

Wriggling through the wire, Carter swore as red-hot pain screamed in his right arm and left thigh. Infection was as much a death sentence out here as a bullet. He eased his way in silence past the bodies that lie around the circumference of the depression. With his heart in his throat, Carter waited for the moment their eyes would open and they would leap up to spill his guts onto the ground. Yet they slumbered in the eternal sleep of death.

Reaching the centre of the depression, he allowed himself a moment's reprieve. His hands fumbled with the lid on his remaining canteen, and he forced himself to sip at the cold metallic tang inside. The slosh of water inside indicated only half remained, so he concentrated hard, steadying his fingers to replace the cap. He sighed and took two ragged breaths, then caressed the folded letter before allowing himself to take stock of the situation.

As his Section Commander stepped onto a landmine, his torso had been tossed into Thomas as it rode the percussive wave of the explosion. Whilst his Section Commander's body had protected him from the fragments, the impact left him stunned and battered with what he suspected was a broken nose.

Turks, alerted to their presence, hit them on the flanks, forcing them away from their lines. Dragged out from under his superior's remains, his rifle lost in the chaos, Thomas and his section rabbited across the dead land. Bullets snapped at his heels, barbed wire grabbed and slashed at his legs. Every step on that churned up earth was a roll of the dice, as his mates either fell to the Turkish Mausers or took the landmine leap into a splash of crimson mist.

A fortunate few had made it to a Turkish foxhole where the Turks' machine gun had fortunately run out of ammunition. Brutal hand-to-hand combat with blunt stabbing bayonets made for exhausting, bloody work. A short reprieve before the Allied started dropping bombs on them, driving them from their position and farther into No-man's-land.

After random pot-shots and a few more land mines, Thomas found himself alone. The sole survivor… as far as he knew. His fingers clutched at the letter in his pocket. Such heart wrenching pain that bore a desire to sink into the mire around him and embrace death like a sweet dream. Yet also in that letter, a love so fierce and tender he had to survive. He had to.

> *Dear Lance Corporal Thomas Carter,*
> *I must regretfully inform you of your wife Eleanor May Carter's passing this last March. Eleanor passed shortly after haven given birth to your son, so named David Thomas Carter.*

Doctor Dale conveyed that it was a difficult birth and Mrs. Carter was struck with childbed fever within hours. But the child is bonny and thriving.

Given that your sole surviving relative, Aunt Victoria, is quite infirm, I had no option but to petition the Governor for your immediate discharge and repatriation. In the interim, your son David is being cared for by the nuns at The Sisters of Charity in Fremantle.

If you do not survive, or return within one year of this letter's date, I will have no choice but to offer the boy for adoption.

Sincerely,
Father Nicolas Aubry

They had tried so hard and prayed so much for a child, but it was ten years until God gifted them. They had found out a few weeks after Thomas had signed to serve his King. Thomas was not surprised: he'd made a bargain with God. Give his wife the child she had always dreamed of and take his life in recompense. But God had not stuck to his bargain. It seemed instead like a twisted deal with the Devil.

The letter, along with his discharge, was floated in his face and in his hands just as Great Britain decided to use the Australian and New Zealand forces to take the Dardanelles out of the hands of the Turks. His trip home would have to wait. He was assured; they were all assured, that the taking of Gallipoli would be a walk in the park and in two weeks he would be on his way home a hero.

The cavalcade of gun fire dulled as the battle swept south. He sighed and let his head rest back against the damp earth. Exhaustion seeped into his soul, the cold chewed on his bones. Movement flickered in the corner of his eye, jerking him alert.

Thomas rubbed his eyes, the smoke, grit and settling mist distorting his vision. The shadow wavered and then solidified as it turned towards him.

Carter's gut clenched as he recognised it was a man. He reached for his bayonet, adrenalin surging through his body as he prepared to fight. A flare shot up, illuminating Carter and their surroundings, just as the man turned his head and smiled at him. A warm smile that sent a ripple of ease through Carter just before the night reclaimed the battlefield. Carter locked eyes on him. He could make out the Turks thick moustache and the fez, sitting crooked on his head.

He dared not blink. How had he not seen him? Why had the man not yet attacked him? He could see the man's eyes, dark pools in a dark night and a flash of teeth. He seemed curled over, grabbing and rubbing his legs.

Still, Carter readied himself, his hands gripping the bayonet tighter.

"Please, don't shoot. I'm a friend," the man said, raising his hands in surrender.

"You're a bloody Turk, ain't no friend of mine," Carter shouted back, relieved the man still thought he had his rifle.

"Okay, okay," the man replied. "I do not want to kill you."

"Why? You killed enough of my mates already, hey Abdul," Carter said, punctuating his point by stabbing the bayonet in the air.

"Ha, how did you know my name is Abdul?"

"I didn't know your name was Abdul. We call all you bloody Turks, Abdul," Carter answered, not understanding why something was amiss with the conversation.

"Ah, and your name must then be Johnnie. All Australians are called Johnnie."

"Yeah rightio. Wait a minute, how do you speak English?" Thomas asked as the reason for his confusion slipped into place.

"Am I speaking English?" Abdul answered, sounding confused. "I don't know. I thought you were speaking Turkish. I don't know. I don't understand."

"Yeah, whatever. You just stay on your side, and I'll stay on mine," Thomas warned.

"My legs hurt too much. Besides, too much death already," he muttered, rubbing his legs.

"You can say that again," Thomas said, his fingers reaching for the letter in his pocket.

A flare fizzled as the roar of gunfire and battle cries swung back toward them. Abdul started patting his pockets. "You want a cigarette? I have a cigarette." Thomas eyed him warily as Abdul searched his coat and pulled out a sad, mangled half of a cigarette, which he laid out with great care over his knee. He then started searching his pockets again. A mixture of pain and frustration crossed his face, and he looked at Thomas, eyes wide with hope.

"I don't have a match; do you have a match?"

Carter sighed and reached into his pant pocket. Removing them from the tin box, he unwrapped the wax paper and recovered a scratch of matches. With his bayonet in one hand, he approached Abdul from the side cautiously and flicked him the box of matches. It would be too easy for Abdul to attack from above.

"No guarantees they are dry. In fact, I think they are fireproof," he smiled at the Australian joke that had brought a moment of lightness to the battlefield and harsh conditions.

The match flared; Abdul's face seemed to flicker with the flame. Thomas saw no malice in his eyes. Exhausted and resigned, he lowered his guard.

The British told him two weeks. It had been months of dry

desert heat and now threatening snow. He had survived all that, just to finish like this. He was at least six hundred yards behind mined enemy lines, without a weapon, exhausted, and with his foe for company. If he had any tears left, he would have wept. He had failed his Eleanor, failed his David.

The food packet pressed against his leg, his stomach rumbling in response.

"I got some hardtack if you're starving," he said. His fingers gripped on the teeth-breaking-biscuit. He wouldn't have been surprised if it stopped a few bullets. It was that bloody tough.

Abdul smiled, his features softening from quizzical to relaxed. "No, you need it Johnnie. We need to get you home."

Carter laughed at the man's insane notion.

"The only way you Turks send us home is in a coffin,"

"Not tonight, Thomas," Abdul answered.

A shiver crept down Thomas's spine. How did Abdul know his name? Did he tell him? He didn't think so, but something strange was happening tonight. He removed the hardtack from his pocket and sucked on the brick-like biscuit, enjoying the saltiness.

After a few minutes, Abdul pinched out the end of the cigarette and carefully folded it back into his pocket. He pointed at the remains of the body below where Carter sat.

"You need to take his coat; the dawn will be colder still. Snow is coming," he said, sniffing the air.

Carter grimaced at the job ahead of him and put away his tucker. Abdul was right. It was getting colder by the minute and the young Turk, or what remained of him, no longer required his coat. Carter shuffled down the bank, sniffing at the smell of charred flesh. The body seemed to be holding himself in an embrace. Carter's gut churned at the sight. It was dark, but not dark enough. The man's face lay half in the mud. The side Carter could see looked like a bear attack. The skin lay shredded into flaps, fragments and patches of the skull glimmered through. His jaw locked and extended as if trying to consume the agony he'd been dealt.

Carter spat out the salty bile that surged in his throat. It was cold. He needed the jacket.

With trembling fingers, he inched the man's sleeve off his arm. Carter's heart pounded at the smell of death, the rot of seared meat burnt into his psyche. Even in the dim light, he could make out the shattered bones that poked out of the man's scorched fleshy thighs. Thomas gagged as he pulled it off the man's shoulder, the torso came with and the body rolled over, revealing a familiar face. Carter gasped; an icy chill shot up his spine. Taking a deep breath, he pushed away the dread that consumed him. Turks all looked the bloody same, anyway.

With the coat on, Carter shimmied up the bank behind Abdul. The man moved in silence and disappeared over the top before Carter could blink. Just as Carter went to ease himself through the concertina wire, Abdul's head reappeared with his fingers over his lips. He then raised three fingers, indicating three soldiers and then his palm, telling Carter to wait. Carter grabbed at the sodden earth to hold his position, wondering why the hell Abdul hadn't just left him and gone back to his mates. Trusting Abdul was Carter's only option. He was dead any other way, and he couldn't be. David needed him. Abdul's hand moved, curling two fingers towards himself, calling Carter to move.

Over the lip of the trench, Carter expected to find a squadron of Turks, Abdul at the helm, loaded Mausers pointed at his head. Yet, it was barren. Carter breathed a sigh of relief. Carter felt naked and exposed as he searched for Abdul. Twenty metres ahead and to his left, Abdul's silhouette rippled in the haze of smoke and ash as he beckoned Carter over. Carter ran, crouched over, but Abdul had moved on before he even arrived. Carter's eyes, stinging with smoke, grit and exhaustion, scanned the landscaped. He spotted Abdul even farther ahead of him, crouched low in the shadows. Carter bolted towards him.

He estimated he was about halfway there when a sudden thump smacked him between the shoulder blades, sending him face first into the muck. Gunfire cracked overhead. Carter couldn't move with the weight on his back. He heard Abdul's voice in his ear. "Stay down. Wait here. Don't look until I call you," he hissed.

Carter shivered, his mind trying to process how Abdul had got back to him so quickly, and without being seen. With a groan of pain, he raised his head, forgetting Abdul's words. In the dark haze, he could make out some movement to his right. Carter strained his eyes, but the Turk seemed to dissipate into the fog, only to reappear yards away in the blink of an eye. His hands were raised in supplication as he approached his comrades. Carter's muscles quivered with tension as he anticipated the expected betrayal; the rain of lead that would leave him another rotting carcass in the mud.

Shouts broke out swiftly, followed by a volley of shots from the Turkish Mausers. Carter flinched, trying to bury himself in the muck. When the shots cut off abruptly with a scream of terror, Carter couldn't help but look. A red light appeared to spill from Abdul himself, along with a deep guttural roar like rolling thunder. The men went screaming into the darkness.

Abdul turned his head and grinned at Carter. Flaps of skin swung like ribbons against his skull, bone glimmered white underneath. Carter froze, unable to look away even as the red light faded into night.

"Don't look" screeched through his brain, turning his guts to water. Carter buried his face in the mud.

Moments later, a hand gripped Carter's coat, jerking him out of the mud and onto his feet.

"Run," yelled Abdul, his voice seeming to come from anywhere but the figure behind Carter. With jellied legs and muck in his face, Carter ran forward blindly. He could hear heavy breathing over his shoulder and assumed it was Abdul. The image of that abomination Carter had just witnessed driving him forward in terror. Knowing, but unable to explain to himself that Abdul and that thing were undeniably one and the same, he shut his brain down and pushed himself into survival mode.

"Land mine," whispered Abdul, pushing him three paces to the right.

"Run," he commanded as Carter staggered. On they went through the dead man's land, Abdul's powerful hand propelling Carter around landmines, unseen trenches, relentless coils of rusty wire and pockets of any surviving soldiers. Exhaustion made his legs collapse underneath him time and time again. Each time, Abdul reached down and pulled him to his feet with phenomenal strength and endurance, commanding him onward.

Once more Abdul pushed him to kiss the dirt and bade him to stay, not look. Gunfire broke out. Carter raised his head to see Abdul, a shadow in the pitch of night, facing the spray of bullets untouched. That red light erupted from where Abdul stood, a flash like lightening, shooting the soldiers, stunning them. They stood there, frozen like statues, as Abdul returned. A whimper rose from Carter's throat.

"They will return to themselves in a few minutes," Abdul explained, his voice a gentle hum in Carter's ear.

"What are you? Why are you doing this?" Carter sobbed, the weight of all he had witnessed too much for his mind to take.

"No father should lose his child before even seeing them grow. The pain is too large," Abdul whispered, his voice breaking with the grief. "I know this pain. But your son will save many. This, I have been shown. But he needs you. This is all I know."

Abdul's powerful grip yanked Carter to his feet. He grabbed at the Turkish coat, tearing it from him.

"Go. You are safe now. Head in a straight line towards that mound." He commanded. Carter stumbled in the churned earth, the bitter cold assaulting his senses. Snow landed cold, wet kisses on his nose. Abdul's figure rippled as the flakes fell through his image.

"What about you?"

"My journey ends here. I can go no further. My legs hurt and Allah calls to me. Go to your son as I shall go to mine. He needs you." He said as he faded into a swirl of snow.

Carter found his feet. Was it God or the Devil himself that had found Carter in this Hellscape and saved his life? Did he care? His fingers brushed against the letter for strength as he stepped forward, toward home, to his son David.

NEVER AGAIN

ROOK RILEY

My bare foot will never again touch the sand
Nor cold salty water that
Attacks and retreats
Ebbs and flows
Like my sanity.

Glimpses of giants
Green tendrils like smoke
Alien unblinking eyes
Watching.
Waiting.

Never again will
Demons touch my bare toes
Or my barren mind
With suckers supple and moist
like Leviathans woke from
Their centuries of slumber.

Never again will they swallow me whole
Before I can kick to the surface
Starved for breath and the feel
Of land under my feet.

The nurses don't understand when
I refuse that shower
That bath
That cup of water
For They are forever seeking me.

The book the doctor gave me,
The one with the squiggly bright words,
Lit up my cell exposing the truth
And now I will never again be Their victim.

(F)LAW OF ATTRACTION

DACIA M. ARNOLD

Tiffany curled her upper lip and checked the address for the New Beginnings Women's Home. She leaned across the console to take in the looming, moss-covered Victorian house and could already smell body odor and weed smoke.

A gaunt face stared down from a third-floor window, giving her a haunting preview of the women inside. If she didn't book at least five more clients to her manifestation webinar later in the evening, she wouldn't be able to hide the fact that she'd borrowed five thousand dollars from her husband's account to catch up on her Lexus payments before her beloved LX was repossessed.

"Your thoughts create your reality," her latest audiobook played, "and don't be surprised when the thing you manifest comes to you in a way you didn't expect. This is just how the universe works."

Tiffany sat back in her seat, eyes closed, and breathed deeply. This was her fifth domestic abuse shelter in a month, but desperate women took desperate measures to turn their lives around. Even the staff wanted better lives for themselves. She needed to get into the right headspace. Practice what she preached.

Visualizing a list of two hundred forty-five names, she imagined filling the slots of her webinar. Those remaining five names manifested to reach her goal. In another mental browser, her bank transferred the money back into Ben's account.

"I trusted the universe would provide and look, it did," she said, eyes still closed with a smug smile. "I am living my dream life. I have everything I've ever wanted and more. I am truly grateful for my abundance."

"Oh, my goodness, Tiffany Manetti," a mousy-brown haired, forty-something squealed from behind baseball-sized eyeglasses as soon as Tiffany cleared the threshold. "Thank you for coming to our little town to speak with the residents. They're upstairs waiting for you. Could you sign my copy of *Girl, You're the Problem*? You make manifesting and the law of attraction so easy to understand." Mouse-brown thrusted a book in Tiffany's direction. "Yesterday, I manifested a front-row parking spot at the grocery store. Crazy, right?"

Her practiced Hollywood smile came naturally, and she tilted her head just so. "Right?! Thank you for your kind words. That really touches my heart. It is an honor that I get to do this. I appreciate you and your journey to have the life of your dreams. Here you go."

I APPRECIATE YOU AND YOUR JOURNEY TO HAVE THE LIFE OF YOUR DREAMS. LOVE, TIFFANY MANETTI.

Deviating from her standard inscription opened the possibility of a misspelling. She had to be perfect. They needed her to be perfect. A personification of everything they wanted for themselves, because they paid her to find out how to get it. Manifesting was subjective to a person's ability to maintain a high vibrational frequency, of course, and New Beginnings Women's

Home left a mountain of frequencies to climb to reach Tiffany's level of success. It was easy to think positive when you've never had to struggle, but she kept that to herself.

Mouse-brown carried Tiffany's box of pre-signed books up the stairs. Giving them away meant she was being generous. It all came back to karma or reaping what she sowed, depending on the audience's religious preference. She needed to sow some money by giving away potential revenue. Giving could also raise her vibration to match the frequency on which her money existed. Gratitude offered another vibrational boost.

"From the bottom of my heart, thank you for being here," she said to the room of thirty women who presented various levels of eagerness. In the last row of seats in the back of the room, one skeptic sat with her arms crossed over her chest, leaning back in her chair. The rest had pens and paper ready or sat upright at the edge of their seats. Almost all of them, staff included, looked like steaming piles of hot shit.

"For some of you, there wasn't much of a choice to be here. In a place like this, it's hard to envision a life of ease and comfort. I didn't come from money. I manifested my wealth, my million-dollar home, the Lexus I drive. I visualized and took inspired actions to live my best life. You can have this life, too."

Scoffs went around the room like always.

"Your thoughts create your reality," Tiffany continued, unfazed. She had comebacks for even the worst hecklers. "When you change your thoughts, you change your life. After this meeting, I dare you to look for the small things throughout your day that go right. There will still be hard times, but keep your heart open to gratitude and you'll see. You can have a moment of peace as soon as the next five minutes."

This always got their attention. Being optimistic was a matter of perception. She could get them to forget their troubles temporarily. After she walked out the door with their contact information, it was up to them to continue a positive mindset. Their inability to do so under dire circumstances led to new clients desperate for a life coach to show them the way to happiness.

"Who here is ready for that?" She scanned the raised hands and those wiping tears of hopelessness. Tiffany guided the women through her signature visualization practice.

"Now open your eyes." She continued her deep, soothing voice. "Look at me. I've been where you are."

"You're a fucking liar," crossed-arms said from the back. "My sister was your real estate agent. You bought your house as a foreclosure in 2008 for less than two hundred thousand. Inflation made it worth a million. And your husband paid for it. All of this is bullshit. You can't just think, 'I wanna be a rich bitch' and get it. Basically, you're telling all of us we're here, having the shit beat out of us regularly, because we can't think happy thoughts?"

Hollywood smile. Head tilt. This was where she made her money. "Many of us grew up feeling we had to fight to survive. We carry these beliefs into adulthood subconsciously. They manifest in our relationships." She nodded at the women, and, by design, received likewise affirmations. "But you can stop the pattern of having to fight with the power of your thoughts."

She directed her attention back to the trash from her past, the girl in the back still rolling her eyes. "To your previous point, you're right about me. That was how I came to own a million-dollar home. The stars aligned, and I got lucky. Right place. Right time. The universe doesn't care about *how* your thoughts manifest into reality. Oftentimes, your circumstances change in ways you'd never expect. My luck changed from being a dependent housewife with nothing of my own, to being the sole breadwinner, and providing my husband the opportunity to retire early without sacrificing our lifestyle. Everyone here deserves happiness, wealth, safety, comfort. Everyone here deserves to be loved and receive love. You can call it luck. Call it hard work. It all starts with your mindset and believing you can have what you desire."

Nailed it.

The traffic leaving Kansas City gave Tiffany time to decompress. Of course, her agent's sister was in a halfway house. Garbage people rarely escaped their garbage lives. The fact remained, she had what the residents of that last-ditch place could only dream of having, but they'd scrape up every penny for a chance of touching it.

Ten new emails had hit her inbox by the time the full-sized SUV was in her garage and she'd shifted to park. The garage door lowered, closing her inside the dark safety of home. Her phone glowed. She'd surpassed her goal with nine additional prepaid registrants to her webinar.

"Yes! I knew it. Thank you, God. Thank you for continuing to bless me with everything I need." She transferred five grand into her husband's bank account.

The house was satisfyingly quiet and empty. Ben, gone to his standing poker night, had left his breakfast dishes on the counter. There was likely a pair of boxer briefs on the bathroom floor, if she was a betting woman. She was. Luck was always on her side, after all. One merely had to look around at everything she owned. No, it didn't matter how she'd gained her posh lifestyle. Manifesting was about the what, not the how.

She hated recording webinars when Ben was home. He'd sometimes eavesdrop and later shit on a point she'd made or suggest what she had said was harsh or mean. Only ten percent of those on the call could even afford to hire her as a life coach. If she offended someone, they weren't her target audience.

Hair done, makeup ready, Tiffany's mouth was dry as she watched the seconds tick down to the start of the livestream. Performance anxiety crept up before her online classes, not for having less in attendance than were registered—she already had their money—but because she ignored the advice of her peers to preload her own questions for Q&A. She was afraid if she didn't answer live questions, they'd find her disingenuous. A room full of lowlife, abused women was not a virtual room of hundreds of fellow educated, upper middle-class people from all walks of life. She was already catching shit for being a rich white lady, telling underprivileged people of color that they can have it all with the power of their minds.

"Welcome. You are all exactly where you're supposed to be at this moment. Nothing is by accident. By divine plan, everything you've gone through, the sacrifices you've made, all led you here to receive this message at this specific point in your life. It is my greatest honor to share the techniques and practices I've used to build the life of my dreams. Without toiling. Without breaking my back…"

These were the lies. She spent day and night scheming, dieting, and exercising relentlessly to be the model of what a perfect life looked like. It was literally her job to appear at all times at peace, put together, and successful. Convincing them of the charade made the act a reality. A vicious, one-sided cycle.

"Before we disconnect, it's time for my favorite portion of the webinar. Now I'll take a few questions from the chat. The first one is: my husband doesn't believe in any of this and says acting like we're rich is irresponsible. What should I do if he's holding me back from manifesting? This is a question I get a lot."

Tiffany squared herself in front of the camera. No Hollywood smile. If she lied about everything else, this was a subject she could be honest about. "There are people in your life who are stuck in the perpetual lie that this is the only money they will ever have. Fear keeps them trapped in a pattern of thinking that creates a reality of poverty and lack. Sometimes, you're married to those people. They control the finances and use money to control you. I used to be a stay-at-home spouse. Now my husband stays home while I make the money. Even right now, he's playing poker with money I manifested. His tune's changed since we met," she laughed, "but there was a time he didn't believe me. Eventually, he came around. You can manifest your perfect spouse and a loving marriage, but you cannot force anyone to believe something they don't. It has to be their choice."

Another question appeared in the chat, and five comments echoed its sentiment. She nodded as she read.

"Someone in the chat asks, 'what do I do if I am stuck in a relationship because they have control of the finances? I want to leave, but I have nowhere to go and no means to take care of myself and my kids. I had to lie to pay for this webinar.'"

Tiffany pressed a hand to her heart and closed her eyes for exactly two seconds.

"To all the women who are trapped in this situation, and there seems to be a fair number of you, I have two words for you—get out. Do whatever you can to leave the situation. Your next purchase should be the book, *Gone Girl.* It's like a textbook for secretly leaving an abusive or dangerous relationship. Read that book and squirrel away money until you can safely get away."

"Look at me. Leave your spouse or else–" she stuttered, seeing the attendee numbers fall. She was four minutes over her time. A hot burning rose up her neck as the attendance plummeted. "…or else you will be stuck with someone else determining your worth for the rest of your life. I'd be lying if I said I didn't have divorce papers in my bottom drawer, just in case.

"Change is hard, but staying in an emotionally abusive place is not all life has to offer you. When you open your mind to what you can have, what you deserve to have, the universe has a strange way of meeting you right where you are in ways you would have never imagined. Sometimes, it's taking that scary step of telling him you're done."

Ten minutes over, she took a deep breath. "I know I went over time, but thank you all for coming. Remember to schedule your special discounted one-on-one consultation within the next 24 hours. I look forward to helping each and every one of you discover your dream life."

The blue light on her camera turned black. Hives erupted on her neck, along her jaw, and itched on her right cheek.

"You just went over time. It wasn't what you said," she coached herself, heading to the kitchen for wine. "Divorce isn't the worst thing you could suggest. Murder is the worst thing you could suggest, and you most definitely didn't say that."

Skinny Girl Pinot Noir washed the Clonazepam down her throat. It was only eight o'clock, but Ben would be home in an hour, and she didn't feel like talking to him. With any luck, she'd be asleep before he got home. She poured micellar water onto a cotton swab.

"$15 an ounce," she remembered Ben screaming at her one night. "Just to halfway wash your face."

His bitching would hold more weight if they couldn't afford it, but they could and more. Always more. He enjoyed golfing at the Oakwood. If he could throw down thousands for an afternoon of beers and golf balls, then she could wash her face with liquid gold.

"Half wash," she repeated, looking down to see his balled-up, navy blue boxer briefs.

She downed the rest of the wine and carried the empty glass to the kitchen. Instead of leaving the evidence with his breakfast dishes that she refused to clean, Tiffany washed the wine glass by hand and placed it back in the cabinet. Returning to the bathroom, she scooped up the underwear and slapped off the light switch. Dirty laundry placed neatly on Ben's pillow, she crawled into her side of the bed.

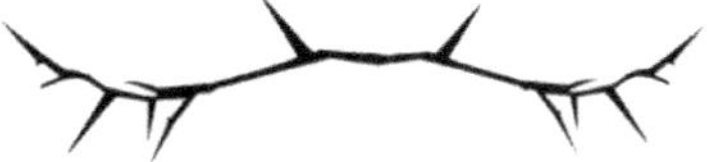

A lovely morning tune woke her at eight o'clock. Ben was already up. She silenced the alarm on her phone and counted fifty-six accepted payments for one-on-one coaching.

"Thank you, God. For this beautiful day and for providing everything I need." She threw back the blankets and slid into her robe. "And thank you for coffee."

Ben stood at the kitchen sink in a clean, identical pair of boxer briefs, loading the dishwasher. Tiffany swatted his butt and stood on tiptoes to kiss his neck. "Thank you for making coffee. It's like my love language."

"So, it went well last night?"

"About twelve grand well," she beamed.

"Great job, hon. That's amazing. You blow me away."

She needed this. The affirmation. The appreciation. The dishes done. Coffee, still hot. The daily news played live on the refrigerator's smart screen.

"Stay tuned for our shocking story. A number of murders rock the inner-city area. Could they be related?"

"It's not so shocking when it happens all the time," Tiffany scoffed.

"Hey, I checked my account last night before I came home. Did you move some money around?" He sat down next to her with his own cup of coffee.

"Oh. Yeah. I pulled money from the wrong account and didn't realize it until after my meeting yesterday. I can't believe I did that. Hope it didn't cause any trouble." Lies, but thanks to her success, they were inconsequential.

A monotone news anchor returned. "Three women lost their lives last night in seemingly unrelated domestic disputes. What the authorities have found strange about these murders is that they occurred at approximately the same time, just after the eight o'clock hour."

A picture of mousy-brown appeared on the screen with her too-large eyeglasses. Tiffany stopped listening and stared, trying to make sense of the familiar face with the words MURDER VICTIM scrawled across the bottom of the screen.

Hot coffee splashed onto her bare knee where her robe had parted over her crossed legs. Her hands shook. She put down her mug and wiped brown stains onto the smooth white silk.

"Alexa, play Easy Listening," she said, standing.

It responded. Soft music filled the kitchen.

"I don't want to lower my vibration with these horror stories," she laughed, releasing the growing anxious energy in her chest. "I'm going to start early today. There are a ton of appointments I need to schedule." She kissed Ben's cheek. Glued to his phone, he paid no attention to the disaster playing out before him.

In her office, she pulled up her list of registrants and a web browser where she searched for the names of the victims.

Heather McKillen… she read on the browser. That was mouse-brown's name. It was on her list. *Heather McKillen.* She closed her eyes and steadied her breathing.

"Sarah Givens… Sarah Giv," she choked, unable to get the name out a second time, seeing it echoed on her list.

"Mackensie Barrera…. Oh my God." Murdered by their husbands. Seemingly unrelated, but they weren't.

Tiffany's heart pounded in her throat. Her hands shook violently. Saliva flooded her mouth. She threw up into her dainty office trash bin.

"Be present," she whispered. "Be present. Be here. You are here. I am here. Keyboard." A shallow breath in and out. "Succulent." Breathe in and out. "Desk." Breathe in and out. Slower. "2021 World-Changing Coach Award." Slower breath in and out. "Calendar." In and out. "Photo of the mountains." Out. "I am here. I cannot control other people's actions. I did not murder those women. I was trying to help them. Golden picture frame. Rocky Mountains."

"Hey, honey," Tiffany called, her voice pitched inquisitively as she walked back to the kitchen. "I'm feeling drawn to the mountains. Let's hop a flight and spend the weekend in Snowmass. Like, today."

Ben scrolled once more, then looked into a far corner in thought before turning to her. "I'm actually wide open this weekend. That sounds great."

"First class?"

"What's the occasion?"

"I've been working really hard lately and want to recharge before I dive into other people's problems for the next six months," she asserted.

"That's responsible. Sure. But no working while we're gone."

"I was just thinking I'll leave my work phone at home and not bring my computer. Just you and me." Tiffany felt better already.

Within a few hours, they were on their way, away from the horror. With every passing mile, Tiffany gave gratitude for her comfort to combat the cortisol that flooded her with worry when she remembered the women who'd died. She whispered words of thanks for the money she'd received to hide away in the woods hundreds of miles away, the luxury of gourmet food delivered for dinner, and the fine wine stocked in the cabin to enjoy at their leisure.

After the first bottle was gone, they lay together, spent from afternoon sex. The house phone rang.

"We didn't order anything else, did we?" Ben asked, getting up, not bothering with clothes. He returned. Before Tiffany could ask who'd been on the phone, it rang again. After the third time, Ben came back with the whole thing in his hands. He opened the bedroom closet and set it on a stack of quilts.

"If they need us, they'll come and get us," he declared and hopped back into bed.

Tiffany disagreed. She didn't want anyone to come get them. That was the point of their trip. She kissed him, a long one that involved open mouths. Ben was safety.

Her cell phone rang. "Seriously?! Of all the places to have service." She didn't recognize the number, but answered. No sooner than she had the phone near her ear, beeping began for an incoming call. Givens, Michael. She clicked over.

Nothing.

Ben's phone rang.

"Don't answer it." She pressed hard on the power button and swiped her phone off before snatching Ben's and doing the same. Getting up, Tiffany opened the closet and placed the two mobile devices next to the landline, slamming the door.

"What's going on, Tiffany?"

Too flustered, she struggled to come up with a solid, rational lie. "Maybe this place is haunted. That was freaky. Besides, I thought we were unplugging for the weekend. I need a break from being so available to people. I just want to be available to you." She gave him a soft, pouty smile. "Want another glass of wine?"

"Okay. I'll find a movie," he said, getting up and donning a robe.

"Pick a comedy. Something light," she said, following him in the living room, then on to the kitchen to fetch a fresh bottle. Hawkstone Merlot was the path of least resistance. She poured two glasses and returned.

"Oh… we have cable," she said, seeing a news report transition back from commercials.

"They're running a story about you," Ben said, his eyes wide with glee. "You made national television, honey."

"No." White heat burned her forehead. There was only one reason she'd make national news.

"What?"

"No, Ben. Turn it off." It was too late. There she was. The recording of her webinar.

"Leave your spouse or else you will be stuck with someone else determining your worth for the rest of your life. I'd be lying if I said I didn't have divorce papers in my bottom drawer, just in case."

Ben looked from the TV at her.

"The universe has a strange way of meeting you right where you are in ways you would have never imagined. Sometimes, it's taking that scary step of telling him you're done."

Ben pressed his mouth into a line. His face grew red, but neither of them moved or spoke.

"The three women tragically murdered in Kansas City last night met famed life coach, Tiffany Manetti, during her tour of women's shelters in the weeks prior to their death. Sources say Manetti has a track record for targeting underprivileged and endangered women for her life coaching business. These were the last words they heard before their husbands ended their lives."

Ben shook his head, listening to the newscaster. "I drew up those papers to divorce you, Tiff. You told those women a lie. They took your advice, and it got them killed."

"No. I can't control people's actions." She couldn't look at him. So frozen, she couldn't wipe the tears pouring from her eyes. He glared at her. Her safety. Her security. It was crumbling from under her.

"How many times do I have to tell you? You are not a therapist or a counselor. You can't just tell people to get a divorce. *You* won't even get divorced. I've left you five separate times, Tiff. Every time you beg me not to go."

He disappeared down the hall.

Tiffany couldn't move.

When he returned, he was dressed and powering on his phone. Without a word, he walked out the front door, slamming it behind him.

"Manetti is currently unavailable for comment," the newscaster droned on.

"Sarah Givens. Remember that name."

The thought was her own, had come from her own mouth, but the sensation of speaking was foreign. She hadn't meant to say anything.

"Heather McKillen. Remember that name. MacKensie Barrera. Remember that name." Her own voice growled with anger despite her own defeated ache.

"I didn't mean…" she sobbed. Her mind was fracturing. "I didn't mean to get them killed."

"You're a fraud. You pretend to have it all. It's a performance, an act," Tiffany answered her own pleading with disdain. The hate for herself warring for control over self-pity.

"I'm lucky to have what I have." A weak attempt at resolve.

"You trick people into giving you things you don't deserve," she spat. "You don't even know how to run a business. You're so far in debt, you have to steal from Ben to cover your ass."

Tiffany vomited into the kitchen trash. Stale acidic wine ejected from her mouth, some through her nose, burning her eyes.

"Everyone sees who you are now." Her voice was deep and sore from throwing up.

"No," she cried.

"Your clients are going to see you for what you are, a liar. A Fake. A murderer."

"I didn't kill those women."

"You pushed them over the edge. We survived by submission. It was you who moved them to rage. You who guided their hands for blood. You killed us, Tiffany Manetti. You killed us. And now he's going to kill you."

She clasped her hands over her mouth. "What? No."

"Ben is going to kill you."

"He wouldn't."

"What you think becomes your reality, Tiffany." Her voice turned sweet, a soft innocent tone like she was speaking to a child instead of audibly arguing with herself. "Your outer circumstances are a direct reflection of the ugliness inside you."

"This is just a thing that happened to me. It does not define me."

"Ben is going to kill you, Tiffany."

"Stop it. That's a lie."

Ben is going to kill you. He's going to kill you. The three voices of the dead women echoed in her head.

"No. No. No." Hands pressed to her ears, she ran to the bathroom.

He's going to kill you. He's going to kill you, the voices continued.

She opened her overnight bag and dumped the contents of her makeup bag into a pile on the rug. Her Clonazepam wasn't there. Ben must have taken them to keep her from overdosing herself. He wouldn't kill her. He was trying to keep her safe.

You forgot the meds at home. You put it back on the shelf instead of putting it in the bag. Ben is going to kill you. You emasculate him. You lie to him. He sold his company to support your coaching business and you lie and tell people it was you who amassed wealth. You amassed shame and lies. You collect fear of failing and exploit women. Heather McKillen. Sarah Givens. MacKensie Barrera. He's going to kill you. He's going to kill you.

"No. No. No." Tiffany turned on the sink faucet as far as it would go. But the voices continued their chant. She stepped into the shower, still in her nightgown, and turned the water on.

He's going to kill you. He's going to kill you.

Tiffany huddled on the shower floor while spirits of the women tormented her for what felt like hours. She wanted Ben to come back. Needed to know he was okay and wasn't furious with her. She needed him to hug her. Forgive her again.

He's going to kill you. He's going to kill you.

"He's going to kill me," Tiffany said finally.

The voices stopped.

The front door closed.

She turned off the faucet and left the shower. Pools of water followed her every step. She opened the bathroom door and there he was in the hallway. Hands in fists.

"I am so sorry, Ben. I'm so sorry."

She walked towards her husband, arms out to hold him.

Ben grabbed her wrists before she could press her soaking frame against him. He pushed her arms down, and she lost her balance. Her bare feet slid on the wet tile of the hallway floor, sending her legs up into the air as her body fell back.

CRACK.

The house went black. Her head was quiet. She blinked, willing her vision to return. In the darkness, she saw her reflection. Her head rested in a pool of dark blood; her neck bent at an impossible angle. She blinked again. A glass surface. Two glass surfaces, identically round, less than an inch apart. Too-large eyeglasses surrounded by mouse-brown hair caked with blood. Two other faces came into view.

"It was an accident," Tiffany whimpered.

"Your thoughts create your reality," they said in unison. "And don't be surprised when the thing you manifest comes to you in a way you didn't expect. This is just how the universe works."

"Where am I?" Tiffany blinked harder and more women came into view. Their mouths moved but all she could hear was a low hum that made her sick to her stomach.

"You are a part of the collective consciousness," the three said.

She stood. Women surrounded her. Thousands, as far as she could see in all manner of dress, bikinis, wedding dresses, regular clothes, and so many were naked. They were all dead, most violently, moving their mouths. The hum grew louder but stayed the same low vibration. Tiffany stopped resisting the vibration. The mantra. Then she finally heard what they were saying and she couldn't help but join in.

"He's going to kill me."

ENDINGS AND BEGINNINGS

JANINE K. SPENDLOVE

Then

I'd lunged out of the way of the shuffling corpse. Hitting the dirt, I let out a hiss of pain when my back slammed into the gnarled tree roots beneath me. My hand had flown out to my side, grasping for my shotgun as I looked up at the moaning undead creature before me. Its skin was pallid and gray, a perfect canvas for the vivid red and orange autumn leaves stuck in its hair and the blood and gore encrusted clothing.

It had reached for me the same moment I heard the mechanical clacking of a shotgun pump. The moaning stopped.

"It's ok, Neil," my favorite voice in the entire world had called. "You can come out now. The scary zombie is dead. Permanently this time."

I rose to my feet and wiped dirt and leaves off my backside. "Dammit, MJ, I thought I told you not to leave the compound."

Maria Julieta merely smiled, her rosy lips quirking at the corners as she efficiently reloaded her shotgun. "And I thought I told *you* not to leave the compound. You know the deal. You stay, I stay.

You go, I go." She toed the corpse before her and tucked a stray lock of dark brown hair shot with gray behind her ear. "Look at his clothes. Brand new. The pendejo tried to get some fresh supplies and got bit in the process." She looked up at me. "Probably he was alone when it happened, too."

I pulled off my ball cap, recently appropriated from one of the creatures as I'd lost my last one in a scuffle, and ran my fingers through my graying hair. I would think that after nearly twenty-two years of marriage I'd be used to a tongue lashing from MJ, but as usual, that was not the case.

Giving a non-committal mumble that sounded as close to "I'm sorry" that I could manage, I'd scooped up my weapon and immediately set about inspecting it, making sure it wasn't damaged.

"We don't have time for that, Neil. Sun's nearly set." Maria Julieta placed a tanned hand on my forearm. Puckered and faded scars and burns from nearly three decades of running a bakery crisscrossed her pale hand and disappeared under the green flannel of the long sleeve shirt she wore.

I'd stilled my movements as a low moan came from our left, followed by two more directly behind us. The sun was nearly down, and the undead got active at night. Slinging the nylon strap jury-rigged to my shotgun over my shoulder, I followed her, and we set off at a quick trot through the sparse woods back to the compound.

It didn't take long before the inquisition I knew I deserved came.

"Why'd you go off alone?" MJ huffed between breaths.

I took my time in answering. I knew this was coming, but had hoped it wouldn't. "You remember what tomorrow is?"

"Of course." She pulled me to a stop. "Don't tell me you went to find an anniversary present for me!"

I grunted and held up a gold, heart-shaped locket I'd found in an abandoned house.

She leaned toward me, her eyes blazing with fury, and it was all I could do to not kiss her.

"Neil Winferd Allen, you *do not* go outside of the compound *without* me, most especially *not* to get me a gift. *Do you understand?*"

I nodded my head, not breaking eye contact. She shook her head, chuckled, and leaned in, pressing a kiss on the tip of my nose.

"Estúpido," she murmured, and I grinned.

"I'm always an idiot for you," I pulled her into my arms, determined to thoroughly kiss her when a closer moan from the next berm over brought us back to reality.

We started running again.

"Neil," she gasped between strides, "the best gift you could give me is a twenty-third year of marriage. You promised me. Don't forget our deal."

I nodded my head, stomach churning.

She glared at me, stopping my head mid-nod. "*All* of our deal. No hesitation, no goodbyes, no 'I love yous.' Just shoot."

"I promise, MJ." I didn't want to think about our deal. I didn't want to think about anything except how much I loved this woman.

Now

My worn fingers lace through the ice-cold chain link before me. The fence looms several feet over my head and as I look up, wondering how easy it would be to scale, a frigid winter wind blows my ball cap off my head. I force my stiff fingers to uncurl from around the links and lean over tiredly to scoop the hat up.

It's easy to find despite the late hour. The stars shine brightly, illuminating the compound behind me. The compound itself is a series of interconnected underground bunkers that all lead to one place—an old, decommissioned military armory. Once upon a time, this used to be a weapons range. Now we expend our ammunition on moving targets.

When the virus first broke out five years ago, there was a bit of worry because it seemed to spread so quickly. But there had been plenty of epidemics prior to this and the human race had always gotten those under control, eventually.

Not this time.

I'd seen the writing on the wall and when Mike called, telling me about Tera and the group she was putting together in North Carolina, and that they could use a good auto mechanic and a baker, well, I answered. I helped MJ close up *Dulce*. About killed her to say goodbye to her bakery—it'd been her life's work.

That was over three years ago. Been nearly six months since we've seen another enclave of humans.

The old, burned fields before me are empty all the way out to the tree line. I run my fingers through my graying hair, pulling the fringe that falls before my eyes back and neatly under the ball cap as I tug the hat back on my head.

Another stiff wind blows right through my threadbare winter coat, and just as I wonder if spring is ever going to come, I freeze in place.

A low, haunting moan emerges from the tree line, along with the familiar dragging shuffle that accompanies one of the creatures when they arrive.

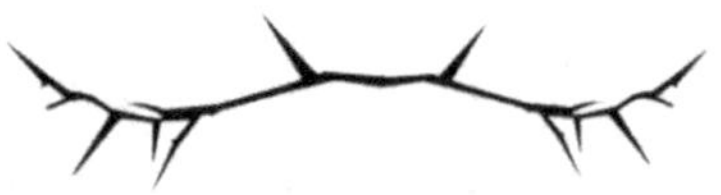

Then

We'd broken through the last of the trees just as the light was waning and ran across the uneven, burned ground toward the compound chain-link fence. We kept at least fifty feet of the ground clear around the entire fence with controlled burns so the creatures couldn't hide there during the day and bite us. We'd lost too many survivors that way.

"Hurry up!" Tera, a tall, thickly built, black woman, called to us. She kept her keen eyes on the tree line and I realized, as I heard the faint sound of an engine running to my right, she wasn't looking for shufflers, but the main foraging party. As the camp commander, Tera was strict about when the main gate was closed and barred. She'd leave a person out to fend for themself all night rather than risk letting the compound get overrun.

It was cold, but responsible. And that's what we needed if we wanted to survive.

Just as we reached the gate and slipped past Tera's withering gaze, a battered military five-ton truck broke through the tree line. There used to be a well-maintained road there, but years of rain and the occasional snow and freeze had left it pitted and difficult to navigate. The truck stuck in a deep rut that the drivers usually avoided, but in his haste, Mike—a retired Marine CH-46 pilot— appeared to have forgotten about. Kicking the door of the truck open, Mike jumped down to inspect just how badly he was stuck.

I could tell there would be no moving the truck tonight and that Mike and the rest of the party just needed to get into the compound—the moans were getting louder and closer. Mike turned back to the cab of the truck, and just as the words, "Come on," were leaving his mouth, a gray, decomposing arm from underneath the five-ton had grasped his leg and jerked him away from the truck.

It was over before I could fully process what had happened. For being slow-moving, once the creatures had you in their grasp, there was no getting away. Sato, Mike's wife, leapt from the truck bed, and blew the head off the undead feasting on brains of her now deceased husband.

Collapsing to the ground, Sato's long black hair spilled around her like a waterfall of ink. Her shriek of grief rent the air and chilled me to my core. MJ took my hand in hers and I clung to it like a lifeline. Sato had to be carried off by her brother.

We got the rest of the party in the gate, and MJ shot Mike in the head to make sure he wouldn't rise again. We'd burn his corpse in the morning.

The last of the light was gone.

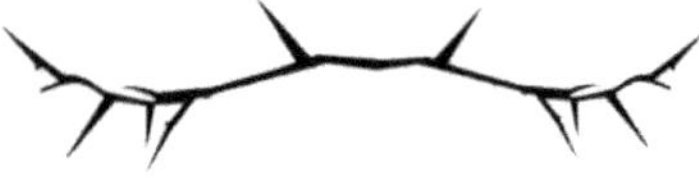

Now

My heart leaps as my hands involuntarily grab at the fence again, pulling my body close to the metal's biting cold.

The creature emerges and my heart sinks.

It wasn't her.

It's never her.

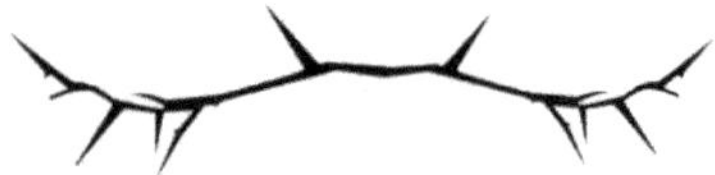

Then

I think it had been just over two months after Mike was taken—time becomes meaningless when you live day to day— when Tera sent me and Maria out to get some more ammo and anything else useful we could find. There was a depot in

Fayetteville and since that compound had been overrun about nine months back, they didn't need ammo anymore.

I patted the dash of the old Ford 100 series truck as its engine coughed and sputtered. Primer gray and just a cab with an open truck bed. It was a beat-up old thing, but she ran just fine, usually, and she was simple enough that I could fix her when need be without a full mechanic's shop.

The truck's engine resumed its normal clacking hum, and I dropped my hand to Maria's hair and stroked the silky strands. She'd stretched out as much as she could on the torn old bench, her head pillowed on my thigh, and her legs curled up at the door. Our trusty shotguns hung in the rearview window.

It was odd to think that this was normal, but as Maria said, this was as good a "date" as any these days.

We hit a bump, and jolted from her nap, Maria sat up. The gold from the locket I'd given her peeped out from under her collar as she stretched as best she could in the tiny cab. It was still a sore subject between us—the locket—but she wore it all the same. I couldn't help smirking.

"What's so funny?" She stifled a yawn with her hand.

"Your face."

Her eyes widened. "Oh, really?"

"You've got track marks all over your cheek from my blue jeans."

Her hand reached up and felt her left cheek, and she smiled. "So I do." Her smile was so brilliant it had melted my heart the first day I'd met her, almost twenty-five years prior.

She'd been broken down on the side of the road, the rear of her yellow VW beetle steaming, as she leaned over the engine.

I'd pulled in behind her, and when she looked back at me, her long brown ponytail brushed across her bare shoulders, a pink tank top bright against her tanned skin.

"I didn't call a tow truck." She'd frowned at my rig.

"I know, ma'am. I was passing by." I'd pulled off my old ball cap and scrubbed my dirty blonde hair out of my eyes before replacing the cap. I was past due for a haircut. "Thought I could lend you a hand."

She bit her lower lip and eyed my truck again. "I can't pay you. At least not right now."

I smiled and shook my head. "I don't think you'll need a tow, anyway. These little engines are so simple, usually you just need a bit of chicken wire and a hammer to fix 'em."

She crossed her arms and popped her hip to the side while raising an eyebrow as if calling me on my bull.

"Well, maybe I'll need more than just a hammer. Got any duct tape?"

That cracked her, and a brilliant smile stretched across her face. She didn't have a lick of makeup on and I thought was the prettiest girl I'd ever met.

I stuck out my grimy hand, and she didn't hesitate to grip it in hers and give it a hearty shake.

"I'm Neil."

"I'm Maria Julieta. But you can call me MJ."

Now

"They never come out all the way anymore." Sato walks up next to me, disturbing my solitude. "It's like they've learned."

I can't bear to look over at my old friend. I know what her round face, framed perfectly by her pitch-black straight hair, will look like. I'd see myself reflected in her eyes, and that is simply too painful. So I fix my gaze on the creature at the edge of the treeline, and eye the one joining it hopeful, though I know it won't be her.

"Do you think…" I hesitate, afraid to voice the question. But if anyone would understand, it's Sato. "Do you think that maybe there is still a bit of them left in there after… after they turn?"

"You know there isn't." Her hand settles on top of mine, and she gently pries my fingers off the fence and turns me to face her. "I miss Mike every single day, and you know how much MJ meant to me. If I thought there was any chance…" Sato brushes an errant tear from the corner of her eye and looks back up at me. "What's really wrong? It's not just that you miss your wife. I miss my husband, but it's not like this. You seem like you've been carrying a great burden." She grips my shoulders. "You know you can tell me anything, right?"

I swallow hard. I want to tell her. I need to tell someone. It's eating me up inside. And if anyone would understand, it's Sato. She hadn't been able to do it either.

Then

For our first date, nearly twenty-five years ago, I thought going to the movies would be a great idea, and MJ seemed to agree. Little did I know it would be a terrible film that left us both questioning my sanity in bringing us to it. Needless to say, we'd left early, and I'd asked if I could at least drive her home.

"Do you mind swinging by the bakery first?" She'd reached back and pulled her long wavy hair up into a ponytail. "I need to get the bread in the proofer for Sato."

"Sure!" Too bad I wasn't looking where I was going instead of at her bare arms while she did her hair, since I'd walked right into the concrete pillar. Thankfully, Dulce was just around the corner, and MJ was able to get me a dishtowel full of ice for my bloody nose.

I sat on a barstool next to a massive metal baker's table as Maria Julieta bustled around the room, moving trays of bread dough from the freezer to a glass encased contraption that looked like some sort of sauna for the dough.

"What the heck does that thing do?" Except I sounded more like, "Wha da heg duh da ting do?"

"It's the proofer, and it's a way to control the humidity and how quickly the bread rises." Maria Julieta looked at the clock on the wall. It was a lot later than I'd realized. "Sato has the early shift, so when she gets in, these should just be ready to pop into the oven and be out in time for me to make the first delivery run later tomorrow morning." She looked at the clock again. "Rather, this morning."

"You have to work tomorrow?" I felt bad for keeping her out late.

"Yup. But then I'm the boss. I always have to work." She flashed me a brilliant smile as she put the last of the dough in the proofer and then came to stand in front of me. "I had a good time tonight, Neil."

I'd raised an eyebrow, clearly disbelieving.

"Despite the movie," she'd clarified. "I'm picking next time."

Next time? My heart soared!

She pulled off my ball cap and swept aside my dirty blonde hair as it fell into my eyes. "You need a haircut. Now let me get a look at that nose."

The skin on the back of my hands tingled as her fingers brushed against them when she pulled the dishtowel from my face.

"Looks like the bleeding has stopped."

Taking a chance, I crossed my eyes, trying to get a better look at my nose. "I don't know, MJ. I think maybe it needs to be kissed better."

It was a line, a terrible, cheesy, horrible line that should have never worked.

Except that it did.

There, in the back room of Dulce, with the smell of yeast and fresh dough in the air, Maria Julieta gave me another brilliant smile before leaning in and pressing her chapped lips lightly on the side of my nose.

I wrapped my arms around her and pulled her in close. My seat on the stool had lowered me enough that our heads were at the same height, and I could see her dark brown eyes sparkle as I moved to kiss her. She'd enthusiastically kissed me back, and my world was forever changed.

It was the best damn day of my life. Hell, it was the start of my real life.

Now

"I couldn't do it, Sato." I turn away from my old friend and face the slowly growing crowd of undead on the other side of the field. There are at least half a dozen of them now, and their howling angst seems to perfectly express just how my heart feels.

I grab onto the chain link and lean my head against it, letting out a slow breath. It frosts before my eyes. "I just… even dead, she's still my wife. She'll always be my wife."

"I understand, Neil. You know I do." Her words are calm, perfunctory even, but that is how Sato always is. The feel of her shaking hand on my arm is enough to clue me in to just how upset she truly is.

"I couldn't shoot Mike. MJ had to do it."

"I know I shouldn't blame myself—"

"No, you shouldn't." Her grip tightens.

"Except that we'd promised each other—" My voice cracks as the newest creature walks into the starlight.

Could it be?

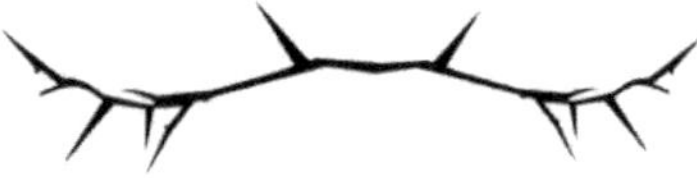

Then

It was near our fifth anniversary that I'd learned what really mattered to me.

"Neil?"

My favorite voice in the world! I'd rolled out from under the truck I was working on and went to scoop MJ up in a hug, but she stopped me with a plate of white chocolate macadamia nut cookies, my favorite.

"Cookies, MJ? You trying to fatten me up?" I'd smiled as I tore into the first one, gobbling it down. They were still warm! Years of eating these and I still couldn't get enough of them. Or my wife. I looked up at her to thank her and froze.

On the surface everything looked ok. She was in her standard shorts and a tank top, a baking apron still wrapped around her waist, and her now blonde hair was up in a pony tail per the usual.

Her face had appeared calm, but there was a tightness around her eyes, and her usual smile for me was nowhere to be seen. She stood stiffly, hands at her side, fingering the hem of her apron. She was about to break down in tears, and I knew how much she hated crying in public.

Quickly looking around, and seeing my boss' office was empty, I set the cookies down on the hood of the truck I was working on, and quickly escorted Maria Julieta in there.

Closing the door tightly behind me, I barely had time to wrap my arms around my wife before she burst into tears.

"What's wrong, MJ?" I ran my hands up and down her back while she tucked her head underneath my chin.

But she didn't answer at first, just shook her head and continued to soak my navy grease-stained jumpsuit with her tears. I didn't mind one bit. I loved holding my wife, but I hated that she was hurting. I just wanted to fix it. I just wanted her to be happy.

"Come on, MJ, it can't be that bad. Whatever it is, we can fix it together."

This was apparently the wrong thing to say. Her sobs came harder.

Finally, after a couple minutes, she calmed herself down, pulled out of my arms and got a tissue from the top of the metal bookshelf in the small office's corner.

"I can't have kids, Neil. Not ever."

I felt a wave of relief roll through me. I'd momentarily worried she had a terminal illness or something she'd been hiding from me. Sure, I wanted kids, as much as the next guy, and of course there would be disappointment to work through later, but I wanted my best friend and wife even more, and the relief I'd felt that I wasn't losing her was consuming.

"I want a divorce."

"What?" My legs gave out, and it was fortunate there was a chair behind me, or else I'd have ended up on the floor. "Where the hell is this coming from?"

She finally turned to face me, tears streaking down her cheeks, though her words were once again calm, as if she'd been rehearsing them. "I know how much you want kids. I can't give them to you. And I won't keep you from that. You're going to be the best dad ever, but not with me. So I release you."

"No." I surged to my feet.

"What?" This seemed to surprise her.

In one step, I was before her, gripping her biceps in my calloused, greasy hands. "No. I married you because I loved you and I want to spend forever with you, not because I wanted a baby factory. I'm not leaving you and you're not leaving me—at least not for this. You can leave me for the toilet seat being left up, for forgetting to take the trash out, for making dinner too spicy for you, but not for this—not because we can't have kids. It's not you that can't have kids. It's us. Because we're a team."

She broke down into sobs again, her grief over her inability to bear children clear on her face, but there was also a small smile there. My smile. She wrapped her arms around me and I held her tight, pressing light kisses on the crown of her head.

"Don't you dare leave me, MJ. Don't you ever leave me. Where you go, I go. That's our deal."

"Deal." She nodded against my chest, sniffling.

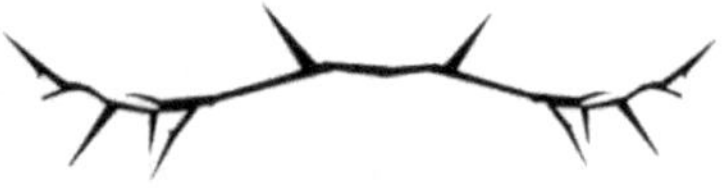

Now

She emerges from the woods much like the others had, shuffling and dragging her feet along the ground as if they are made of lead. Even after months of deteriorating, I'd recognize her anywhere. Her once healthy, tanned skin is gray and sagging on her bones. Her lank gray and brown hair is still pulled up in the last ponytail she'd ever put it in—her broken and battered fingers certainly don't have the dexterity to do it now. A bright flash of gold gleams at her collarbone. The heart-shaped locket I gave her for our anniversary.

A ghostly moan tears from her shredded lips as she looks right at me. And for a moment, it seems almost as if she recognizes me.

A gasp sounds from Sato and I hear her raise her shotgun. Before I even realize I'm doing it, my hand wraps around the barrel and I jerk upward.

"No, wait!"

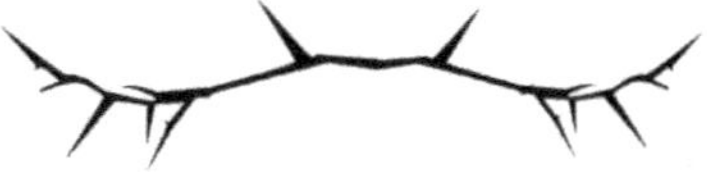

Then

We'd considered adoption, but initially couldn't afford it. And then we bought Dulce, so instead of being just the manager, MJ was also the owner. Of course, the bakery promptly ate up all the money we had saved, as there was always something that needed replacing or fixing and nothing was cheap. So we ended up being cool aunt and uncle to all our siblings' and friends' kids, and to be honest, we were fine with that.

At least we learned to be. Truth be told, I was happy just having Maria Julieta in my life, and I told her that all the time, but I think maybe she always harbored a bit of sadness over it, and it broke my heart. All I ever wanted was for her to be happy.

For our seventeenth anniversary I'd wanted to do something special, so I took her back up to Wilmington, North Carolina, to the very bed-and-breakfast where we'd spent our honeymoon, the Front Street Inn. We stayed in the Georgia O'Keeffe suite, which was a bit out of our budget, but I wanted this to be a special weekend, and she was MJ's favorite painter.

I was in the kitchenette popping the tab on a Natural Light when I heard the television come on in the small living room. The news was reporting an update on a recent virus outbreak in Arizona, but MJ changed channels before I could hear any more.

Pouring the beer into champagne glasses, I heard my wife laughing in the other room and the familiar atrocious dialogue from a movie I thought we'd never see again.

"Neil, hurry—this is hilarious," MJ called from the other room. "It's just as bad—no, it's worse—than when we watched it on our first date."

I rounded the corner and handed her a glass. We clinked them together, and I grinned. "A classy drink for my classy gal."

The years had been kind to my wonderful wife. All her laughter and joy showed in the beginnings of lines around her eyes and mouth. Her arms and hands were dotted with various scars and burns from nearly two decades of working at a bakery, and she prized them all. Her hair, brown again, with the occasional stunning natural gray highlights, hung loosely around her shoulders, something rare indeed.

The Lord knew I loved this woman more than life itself.

I settled my arm around her shoulders and turned toward the awful film on the television. "We really gonna watch this?"

"Only if you don't have something better planned."

"Well, I was kinda hopin' to get you drunk and then see if you'd take advantage of me."

"Hmm, tempting. But we never saw the end of this movie the first time around." She grinned into her glass and gave me a coy side glance. "Maybe if you're lucky, I'll let you get to second base—I'm not wearing a bra."

We never did make it to the end of the movie.

Now

"Don't shoot, it's MJ!"

"No, it's not, Neil. It's a mindless shuffler. Maria Julieta is dead." Sato tried to jerk the gun's barrel from my hand, but I held tight. "Let go. I can end this for you."

I ripped the shotgun from her hands and threw it far behind us into the night. It crashed against the compound's solid brick walls with a clatter that was sure to wake everyone nearby. I didn't care.

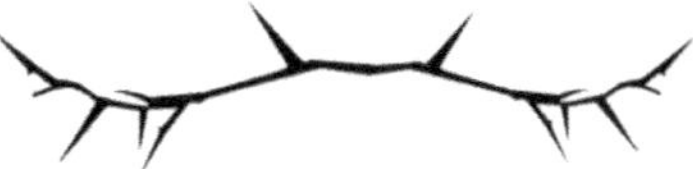

Then

It was my worst memory. The one that haunted me at all times. Still, it started out nice enough.

"You need a haircut." MJ had ruffled her long, thin fingers through my hair. "I'll give you one when we get back."

"Only if you promise not to give me another high-and-tight." I slammed the tailgate on the truck shut. "Took me two months to grow out that ridiculous cut. I'm not in the military. Never was."

She wrapped her arms around me from behind and pressed a kiss on my neck. "I know. But I thought you looked cute." She let me go and I re-thought my aversion to a crew cut.

"I'm going to get one more load, then we can go." Maria Julieta turned back to the armory, and I looked up at the sun, more anxious than normal after the shufflers had got Mike.

"Better hurry. Sun's setting."

"You know I will." MJ slipped through the hole we'd cut in the fence and then through the askew front door.

I walked a quick circuit around the truck to make sure it was in top shape for the trip back. Plenty of tread on the wheels, gas tank full, and for good measure, I turned the ignition. It started like a champ.

Then I stiffened as an icy wind blew through my thin coat.

I heard a moan.

"MJ…" I scooped up my shotgun and whirled toward the sound. "MJ! Time to—"

Her scream rent the air and I was running toward the armory.

I shot the creature before it could take another bite of my wife.

The world seemed to tilt as I slid against the wall down to the filthy concrete floor beneath me.

My lungs felt like they caught fire, and I took an involuntary breath. It tasted stale and musty. It tasted like the end of the world.

The end of my world.

She collapsed on the ground before me. Her pale pink skin graying and shrinking against her bone and sinew before my eyes. Life was rapidly fading from her as she stretched one claw-like hand out toward me.

"Pl-please…" The rest of her words came out as an unintelligible garble.

I pushed myself to my feet and leveled my shotgun at MJ as she looked up at me, darkening brown eyes begging me to put her out of her misery.

My vision blurred, and I felt wetness on my cheeks. My hands trembled as I pumped my shotgun.

The last of the light faded from my wife's eyes and she died.

I lowered my shotgun and walked back to the door. I paused when I heard a moan come from behind me.

My wife's moan.

Now

The gate is locked, as it always is at night, so I start climbing the fence.

Sato grabs my leg. "No! It's *not* MJ! All it wants to do is eat you!"

My boot slams into her shoulder—not hard enough to injure—and I resume climbing.

I hop over the top of the fence, and getting back to my feet, I snake my fingers through the chain link to grasp my friend's. "She came back, Sato. She found me."

Sato's eyes, gleaming with tears, meet mine, and she shakes her head. "No, Neil. Don't do it."

I could see others emerging from the compound in varying states of undress, all hefting weapons. I was out of time.

"Goodbye, Sato," I say with a smile, finally feeling content.

I run toward MJ, somehow not tripping on the icy, uneven field. Her arms are extended as she takes a shuffling step toward me, and I swear there is a smile across her sagging face.

I pull her into my arms, hugging her tight to me.

"Where you go, I go," I tell her.

The last thing I hear as my wife bites into my neck is the mechanical click-clack of a shotgun being pumped.

I smile.

DARK MISTS

QUERUS ABUTTU

Coyotes sing for the second blood moon,
and the red James rises.
From beneath the Earth
near Hatton's cross
a strange presence eulogizes.

Through cracks of rock,
the Dark Mists come,
swirling grim fingers down the river run.
slinking along her wild banks
stalking brains to overcome.

Did the Dark Mists ever find you?
Transport your mind to
sharp teeth terrors
inside caverns
of your chest?
Smell the rot?
Taste the death?
Did you feel the flies?

Ice crystals glazed,
across your eyes?

Some draw breath to tell the tale,
found on the shores,
masks of dread.
Some disappear—where, no one knows.
Others wash up,
dark blue and dead.

Beware the Dark Mists,
slithering the James
when coyotes sing, and
the blood moon ascends.
One touch, you'll be demonically changed.

Beware the Dark Mists,
leaving behind a mangled mind tattoo,
Or transporting you, wandering, to some hidden place—
Or discarding your body on the watery shores—
Dark and blue.

EDIE OF WITCHES POND

SIRRAH MEDEIROS

Ringing in Becky's right ear persisted after turning off the hearing aid. She tugged at her earlobe, hoping it would help, but the irritation continued. Frustrated, she went back to work. Cool wind carried brittle orange leaves around Becky Brenton's boots as she tied a knot on the bulging leaf bag braced against her legs. The overgrown yard was littered with the remnants of two years' worth of tree debris. She looked back at the house. Her house. It needed work, but she was thankful for the purchase and getting such a fabulous deal in an otherwise hot market. She pulled on the bag, dragging it toward the corner of the house.

"Holy fudge!" Becky jumped as Mark, her young son, tugged at her jacket hem. "You scared me. Don't sneak up like that."

"Mom, I've been calling you. Did you turn off your hearing aids again?"

She could see his little neck straining as he spoke, but he sounded far away. Switching the device on, the yard came alive with the soft rustling of leaves falling through the branches, birds chirping, and a nearby squirrel scampering under the acorn tree. "I'm sorry. What did you say?"

"Can I fish at the pond?" Mark pointed to the water at the edge of their yard. "I saw some bass big enough to eat."

"Stay on this side where I can see you. I unboxed your fishing gear and put it on a shelf in the garage." Becky followed behind him as he ran toward the back door.

"Thanks, Mom."

"Grab the small cooler. If you catch something, I'll cook it for dinner."

A few hours later, Becky sat at the round dinette table, just large enough for her and Mark. Smiling, she wiped her hands across the tablecloth to clear the new wrinkles from the fabric and then placed a single candle in the middle of the table. Memory of a candlelight dinner with her husband flitted through her mind. She missed him terribly, but she and Mark were going to be okay now that she was living near her brother. She heard Mark swing the back door open, banging and slamming the cooler into the wall as he trudged into the house. "Careful, I mopped the floors a while ago. Wipe your feet."

"Sorry, Mom. I'll clean up the mud. Look, I caught three fish. They're big ones, too!"

Becky helped lift the cooler to the kitchen sink. "How did you get this to the house? It's so heavy. No wonder you were banging about as you came in the door."

"Edie helped me carry it most of the way."

"Is Edie the lady who lives next door?" Becky pulled one of three largemouth bass from the cooler and turned on the faucet to rinse the muck off their dinner.

"No, Edie's much older and smells funny. But she was super nice, Mom. Edie said it's been a long time since a child lived in our house. She was happy to meet me."

"That's nice, sweetie. I hope you remembered your manners and didn't comment on her odor."

"Of course, Mom. I'm not an idiot." Mark rolled his eyes, then pulled open drawers, looking for a knife to help his mother prepare the fish.

"I'll clean the fish for dinner. Before you tackle the mud on the floor, take off those dirty clothes. By the look of these fish and your clothes, you must have wrestled them into the cooler." Becky tossed her chin toward the muddy floor with a chuckle.

"Oh, yeah. I forgot. I'll clean it up just like I promised."

Several hours later, loud shrieking pulled Becky from slumber with a start. She'd fallen asleep at the kitchen table. The house was dark. Moonlight peeked through the tattered mini blinds of the solitary kitchen window. Instinctively, Becky reached up to turn down the hearing aids but found none in her ears. Another shriek bellowed as if the person stood beside her, and she'd had her hearing aids on full blast. Becky covered her ears as she turned this way and that to find the source of the noise until sudden silence surrounded her again. She caught sight of her hearing aids on the counter and placed them back in her ears as she called out for Mark.

Without a reply, she rushed upstairs to his bedroom and found Mark fast asleep. *How could he sleep through those maddening screeches?* Becky ignored the pounding in her head and moved closer to her son. She pulled the blanket up tight under his chin and gave Mark a kiss on the forehead. He didn't stir. Becky sat at the edge of the bed, gazing at her son's chest as it rose and fell with each breath. He looked so much like his father. Soon he'd be a teenager arguing about curfew and exerting his independence. How she wished his father could see him grow up. For now, she longed for him to stay a young twelve-year-old by her side.

Becky left her son and eased the bedroom door closed. She stood on the narrow landing at the top of the staircase. The shrieks had stopped, and she wondered if the commotion was all in her head or remnants of a dream. She was exhausted. The yard work and unboxing had worn her out so much, perhaps she confused a dream with reality. Satisfied with her conclusion, Becky stepped on the first tread of the staircase, causing the stair to groan in reply. A shadow darted across her view at the bottom of the steps. She paused and sighed, massaging her temple. *Oh, great. I'm seeing things now, too. I must be tired.*

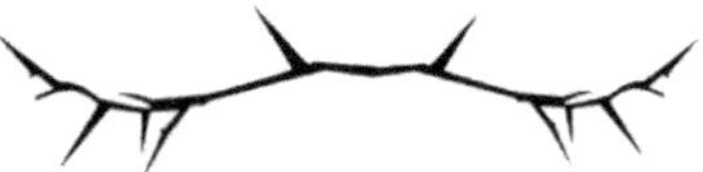

The hint of winter drawing near spread across the crisp wind the following morning. More leaves swirled about the yard as Becky cleaned their breakfast dishes and Mark pulled on his boots. The doorbell's raucous chime rang out, giving them both a start.

As Becky grabbed a kitchen towel, Mark raced to answer the door.

"Oh, hi there. I'm Nora Dickson, your neighbor on the left." Nora tipped her chin toward her home and looked at Mark with a smile. She noticed Becky coming toward them, wiping her hands. "I'm sorry I'm late with introducing myself, but we were on vacation when you moved in. We got home last night. I hope you like Italian. I made you a lasagna."

Becky accepted the dish Nora offered and stepped to the side. "Thank you. That's truly kind of you. I'm Becky Brenton and this is my son, Mark. Please come in. Care for a cup of coffee?"

"Thanks. I'd like that."

"I'll put this in the refrigerator. Mark caught fish out of the pond for our dinner yesterday. I have yet to make a good run to the grocery store." Becky put the dish away.

"Oh, I'm glad you're enjoying the pond. The previous owner—an old man, a bit frail—was odd about the pond on your property."

"Really? Is there something wrong with the water?"

"I don't think so. We moved in six months before he passed away. He was in poor health and had a live-in nurse. Sometimes, while getting out for some fresh air, he would ramble incoherently about the pond until he got so agitated the nurse had to bring him inside."

"The fish were big and tasted great. Right, Mom?" Mark piped in as he came around the corner with his jacket on.

"That's good to hear." Nora looked at her phone. "Sorry, my husband is ready earlier than I thought. I need to take a raincheck on coffee."

"Sure. Anytime." Becky nodded and followed Nora to the door. She watched as Nora met up with her husband by their car. Her new neighbors looked at her. Becky waved and received a wave and nod before Nora ducked into the dark shadows of the interior.

Becky and Mark spent until early afternoon raking more leaves and bush trimmings into bags and then dragged them to the curb for the next day's trash pickup. There were a few daylight hours left in the autumn sky when they made it inside the warm house. Becky made hot chocolate as Mark glanced longingly toward the pond.

"Mom, can we get a boat soon? I found an old one in the weeds, but it's all beat up."

"Maybe when your uncle returns from his training exercise and comes by to see our new place. You and he can pick out something together."

"Aw, Mom. It's another week before Uncle Joe can visit. Can't you and I go? There's something in the middle of the pond, like a platform just under the surface. I wanna check it out."

"That'll have to wait." Becky jabbed a finger by her right earlobe and shook her head. The ringing had started again.

"Come on. Please?"

"Enough about the boat, Mark. I need to run to the grocery store. You can either come with me or stay here, but if you stay, don't leave the house and keep the doors locked. So, which will it be?"

Mark flopped himself onto the couch and crossed his arms with his chin tucked into his chest. "I'll stay."

Becky grabbed her purse and paused, glancing at her son, who suddenly looked like a toddler with his lips drawn into a pout. The ringing in her ear grew more intense as she viciously shook her head in response. "I won't be long."

It was dark by the time Becky returned home. "Mark, come help me with the groceries." Becky called out as she slammed through the doorway. "The traffic is a nightmare in this town. Trying to turn off Richmond Highway to get home took over twenty minutes."

She placed the bags on the table.

"Mark?" Becky stood still, waiting for a reply or sound of movement. The ringing, starting again in her head as she came through the door, blasted across her temples as she walked up the stairs, then turned toward his room. As the door creaked open, she eyed his body sprawled on his bed. A sudden pain shot through her head, buckling her knees. Catching herself, she leaned against the doorway as a dark shadow caught her eye beside Mark. "Who-who's there?"

The stillness unnerved Becky as the ringing in her head intensified. She squinted, trying to conjure the shadow into a discernable image. Moonlight filtered in through the blinds. Becky ran a hand over the wall, feeling for the light switch. Just as an old woman's image formed from the shadow, a shriek reverberated through Becky.

Her finger found and flipped the switch on. The room lit up, leaving Becky in silence—the shadow gone. She sucked in quick gulps of air—her pulse pounding in her ears. Yet Mark remained sleeping. Her ears no longer ringing, replaced with the dulling thud of her heartbeat, Becky shook off the fear threatening to engulf her and pulled a blanket over her son. As she moved to leave, she stopped to close the window and latch. In the distance, the mist wafting over the pond highlighted a roiling darkness in its center—a woman's billowing figure rose, hovering over the shimmering fog. A sudden merciless screech filled Becky's mind. A sound not from the outside, but from within.

She jumped back, stumbled over Mark's shoes, and slammed her head against the bedpost on her way to the hardwood floor.

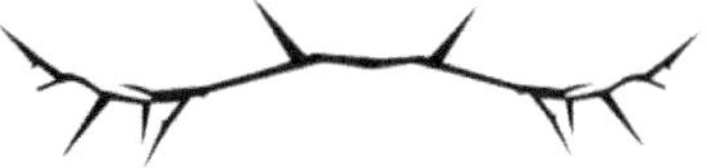

Becky woke to Mark talking to someone on the phone. She rubbed her head as she overheard him—his voice shaking.

"She's mumbling and not making sense, Uncle Joe. There's some blood on her face and neck, but not too much."

A long pause.

"I don't know. It can't be too bad. I didn't hear anything. I fell asleep when she went to the grocery store." Mark turned toward his mother and noticed her trying to lift herself. "She is moving. Yeah. I can ask Edie or Mrs. Dickson for help until you get here."

Becky noticed Mark coming toward her. "Wha appe?" she asked.

Mark cocked his head and furrowed his brow. "Mom, I can't understand you. Are your hearing aids on?"

She nodded. The fingers of her left hand curled in at a strange angle, but she couldn't straighten her hand to prop herself up. There were bloodstained smudges on the old carpet where she'd tried to spread her hand open. Her eyes remained on the dark smears for several seconds.

"Should I call an ambulance or a doctor?"

Becky gazed up and struggled to keep focus on her son's face, but she shook her head. "No. I… m okay." She was struggling to speak. The thought was there, but the words came out staggered and incomplete, skipping like a record player.

"Uncle Joe's coming by to check on you, but it won't be until tomorrow." Mark noticed his mother nod before he squatted and braced his shoulder under her left side. "Push off me and let me help. Uncle said to get you on the bed and put ice on your head. I'm going to find Edie or the lady next door before it gets too late."

They struggled to get Becky onto the bed. Once Mark placed a pillow under her head, Becky tapped him with her shaking, curled up hand. "Wa-rr."

"You need some water?" Mark brushed the hair out of her eyes. "Mom, you're shaking. I'll find you a blanket."

A few minutes later, Mark came back with a folded quilt Becky didn't recognize and a glass of water with a straw. He held the glass as she tried to grasp the straw, but couldn't. With a sigh, Mark held it so his mom could get a drink.

She took a long pull on the straw, then another. Exhausted, Becky leaned back and closed her eyes.

Becky stirred, unsure of how long she'd been asleep. She felt more alert and soon remembered how her hand was curled and unresponsive earlier. Now, her hand opened and closed as if nothing were wrong. Shrugging, she pulled the musty quilt off, raised up, and sat on the edge of Mark's bed. As her feet touched the floor, she felt something slide under her foot. She turned on the bedside lamp. An envelope, yellowed and wrinkled, lay on the floor.

Becky picked it up and turned it over. Where could it have come from? She put a finger under the flap and slid it across the edge. The papers were as yellowed as the envelope, but the handwriting was a beautiful script written with care. She clicked the bedside lamp to its brightest setting and read. Her eyes moved left to right, the paper shaking in her grasp as she read on, her eyes darting faster and faster.

"No. No, this can't be true." Her gut told her otherwise, and she suddenly tossed the letter on the bed and stood, screaming for her son. "Mark? Mark, where are you?"

Frantic, Becky searched the entire house, turning on every light while yelling for Mark. After scouring their modest home, she ran back to his room, unsure what to do. The clock read 1:43 A.M. Where could he be? Her eyes caught sight of light reflecting off the pond. She froze. The billowing figure hovered over the pool of water, and enveloped in the crook of her murky arm was Mark.

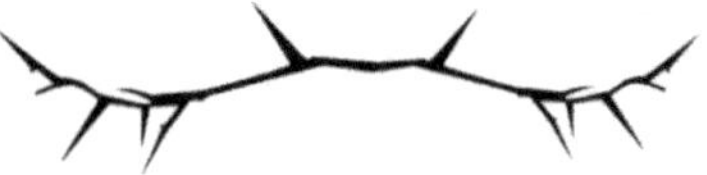

Joe Brenton leaned at the base of the acorn tree with the afternoon sun in the autumn sky scattering light through the trees while several uniform police taped off the backyard. The yard smelled of musk and decay, fitting for the grisly scene he had found. He'd called as soon as he saw his sister's body near the water's edge. He was desperate to find his nephew, but the sheriff insisted he stay outside until a unit was on site to inspect the house and surrounding area. As police cars continued to arrive, no one had spoken to him except for the first officer, who asked him to wait by the tree for the sheriff. Irritated at having to wait for hours, Joe pushed away from the tree as he glimpsed an older man in uniform plodding toward him from the back door.

"Did you find my nephew? I can't just wait here and do nothing."

"Sir, I understand you're anxious, but please let us manage this and we'll find your nephew. The deputy you spoke with brought me up to speed on your statement. I'm Sheriff Pannell." He held papers balled in his hand as he walked past Joe toward Becky's body. When the sheriff was within a few inches of Becky, he bent over and studied the scene. "Well, I'll be damned if that isn't the oddest thing."

"What?" Joe followed the sheriff and stood nearby, but couldn't bring himself to look at his sister.

"Her ears. They're ruptured just like Mrs. Mason, who used to live here. Her body is in the same position, too." The sheriff groaned as he stood straight. "Now, I'm not one for old-wives' tales, but this sure is mighty strange for both women to die in the same fashion by the water. People in this county call this here pond 'Witches Pond' for all the disappearances, I suppose. Especially the—"

"Especially what? Children? You were going to say children." Joe grabbed the sheriff's shoulder and pulled him around.

Sheriff Pannell looked at Joe's hand and politely said, "Now, sir. I know you're upset, but you best get your hand off me. Yes, I was going to say 'children,' but that don't mean your nephew's been taken by a witch. This ain't no fairy tale, after all. We'll find him."

Joe pulled his hand away and ran his fingers through his hair. "Sorry, Sheriff. I don't know what to think of this. Becky and Mark moved here to be near me so I could help Becky raise my nephew. Her husband passed away a year ago. I've got to take care of her boy."

Sheriff Pannell nodded. "I understand, son. We'll sort this out. Just odd is all—your sister looking precisely as Ms. Mason did when she passed. Ms. Mason used to complain of all sorts of odd things—ghosts, shrieking, items moved or missing from the house. They lost a little girl, too. Poor folks. Mr. Mason lived here by himself for decades after, keeping the local kids away from the pond. He swore the old stories were true." The sheriff looked down at the crumpled papers in his hands and offered it to Joe. "Oh, I forgot. One deputy found this letter in a bedroom. It's old and signed by Jake Mason. I don't reckon it's of any use to us."

"Becky was hurt. That's why I came by to check on her. She wouldn't have been reading an old letter. Mark was supposed to get help from a neighbor, Mrs. Dickson or Edie? I don't know either of them since I hadn't come to visit yet." Joe glanced at the letter the sheriff held out for him. He grabbed it and put it in his jacket pocket.

"Mr. and Mrs. Dickson live next door, but Edie, you say? That's a mistake. He must've heard the old stories. Children get things mixed up. We see it all the time."

Joe looked up. "I'm sorry. I don't understand."

The sheriff cleared his throat and squared his shoulders, straightening his posture. "Edith is the witch from those old tales—Edie for short."

"Mark said there was an old lady named Edie. I'm certain of it. She helped him carry his catch from the pond up to the house a few days ago." Joe motioned from the pond to the back door as if that helped solidify that the woman was real.

The sheriff paused to consider what he had heard, then shrugged. "I'm sorry for your loss, sir. I have little else to go on until we get the autopsy back." Sheriff Pannell nodded to the medical team to proceed with removing Becky's remains. "An alert has gone out about your nephew with photos we found in the house. We'll be in touch. You said you're local, right?"

"On the military base, yes. But I'd like to come by and make sure the house is looked after."

"Once my men finish with it, you're free to come and go. We found a house key under the rock where Mr. Mason used to keep it."

"Thank you, sheriff." Joe took the house key and shook the man's hand. "I'm going to stick around until your men are done."

Sheriff Pannell waved as he turned away, walking back in the direction he'd come. "Suit yourself."

Joe sat on the back steps staring at the key in his hand until the sky's colors finished changing and sunlight faded out of sight. He couldn't help feeling guilty for not showing up sooner. His mind played Mark's call over and over, searching for something he missed or forgot to ask—anything that might have warned Joe it was an emergency.

An unopened bag leaned on the bottom step. Food offered by Mrs. Dickson once she'd learned of her neighbors' sudden tragedy and that Becky's brother was at the house with the police. Although she was friendly enough, Joe grew jaded when Mrs. Dickson confirmed she hadn't seen Mark or knew of his sister's fall. She left soon after her arrival, allowing Joe to relinquish himself back to his thoughts. There were too many questions and no answers.

He stood, stretched, and rolled his neck, weary from the day. Frogs and crickets began their evening concert in the tall grass beyond the property line. The hoot of a nearby owl rattled Joe with its sudden, throaty cry. Then, below the crickets' chirps and the other critters, a soft ringing filled his ears. Almost indiscernible, but he felt it in his core as the sound grew louder. He looked about for a source and froze as his eyes found a murky darkness forming over the pond. A towering figure of gloom rose, itself formed out of the smoky mist, and leaned toward the house, malevolent and menacing. Joe stepped aside the steps, nearly snagging his feet, and braced himself against the house.

Faces took shape around the mysterious billowing figure, children's faces—a dozen or more and they grew more discernable by the second. One apparition stepped out from the shroud of night, causing Joe's knees to buckle. His nephew, Mark, stared longingly at him, then glanced at where his mother's body had lain.

Joe's cry rang out through the trees. His grief tore at his throat as he wailed into the night. His fists balled tightly. When he dared look back at the pond, Mark offered a gentle wave, then fell apart like smoke, and drifted back into the shadow's fold.

His right hand throbbed. Joe unfurled his fingers as blood dripped from his palm, the house key sat in a growing pool of crimson as it glistened in the moonlight. Fury mixed with his despair. Joe curled his fingers around the key once again as he made a solemn vow to himself. *Not another child will fall victim to Edie under my watch.*

DEVIL'S HIGHWAY

V. L. JONES

Rico Torres had driven down this highway for years without incident. This nightmare isn't real, he thought, as his heart hammered in his chest. Tonight, for whatever reason, an urban legend comes to life in a black sedan. A sedan, complete with beaming pumpkin eyes, chased him down a deserted highway. *Yeah, I've seen everything now.*

After two long weeks of meetings and contract signings, Rico was ready to head back home to Tucson. He planned a stop at Wilcox, which was the halfway point. It broke up the monotony of a long trip and allowed him to stretch his legs. If he needed to, the stop also allowed him to grab food and gas up the car.

When he turned back on the highway, fingers of reds, oranges, and yellows lit up the eastern horizon. The colors interlaced in blues and pinks painted a desert masterpiece. When the mantle of evening fell; the night took on an air of mystery. The highway empty, except for the occasional lone driver like Rico.

Arizona sunsets were the most beautiful in the world. He had seen many of them throughout his military career. Even the ones in Afghanistan could not match the fiery ones of the Southwest desert. The last rays of the sun-kissed the horizon with streaks of crimsons, oranges, and yellows. Although born and raised in Arizona, Rico never got tired of watching the intense sunsets. He loved how the warm colors of the day melted into the cooler blues and lavenders of night. The evenings took on the scent of sand mixed with dew. A unique fragrance that only the desert can create.

And yeah, a little eerie, too.

He had crossed into Arizona when something rammed him from behind. His late model eggshell blue Toyota Tacoma weaved to the left. Rico fought the wheel for a few tense minutes before regaining control. *What the Hell?* Rico checked the rearview mirror in time to see a black car hit his bumper again. *Where the hell did that car come from?* Moments earlier, he'd checked behind him, and there was no car. *There is no way it could have come on me that quick. So, where did it come from?*

Rico pressed harder on the accelerator, trying to coax more speed from the old truck. At the same time, he lowered the window and waved the car to pass. He hoped it would go around him, but it bumped him again. Rico swiveled around in his seat, straining to see who was driving. A long, sleek sedan with tinted windows hit him again. *Damn. Not able to see the driver.*

He let loose a string of cuss words because his imagination had to be running away with him. The headlights did not look like real eyes glowing in the darkness, but sentient pumpkin orange glittering eyes were staring right at him. It was a play of light or shadows, but they were not real eyes. They couldn't be.

He turned his attention back to the road, sliding over to the right lane. It changed lanes with him, speeding until right on Rico's bumper. The sedan rammed his truck so hard it shoved the Tacoma off the road and onto the shoulder. So much for wishing the sedan would drive around him. Instead, Rico wrestled the truck for control as the back end of the pickup fishtailed.

He maneuvered the truck back on the road after a few tense and scary moments. He tried to put the stupid legend out of his mind. But all the childhood stories kept flooding back. Rico pushed harder on the accelerator, forcing more speed out of the ole girl. The Tacoma responded with coughs and rasps as the truck gained momentum. Not built for speed caused her to shimmy even as Rico tried to coax her to go faster.

The legend couldn't be true. It couldn't. In the old days, this road used to be highway 666 or the Devil's Highway. Arizona Highway Department renamed it Route 191 in some places and Route 491 in others in an attempt to calm nervous drivers growing up on the stories. The ole 666 had a history of high accident rates. A mystery, as the highway was straight for hundreds of miles. Yet, people claimed to see strange lights. Truckers reported weird green storms, and of course, the Devil's car.

The desert always had an aura of mystery at night. This stretch of highway was remote and desolate, so it didn't surprise Rico to hear the stories. He passed them off as driver hallucinations and dismissed the rumors. Plus, he had been making this run for five years with nothing out of the ordinary ever happening.

Now, here he was, racing down the road, chased by the Devil's car. *Why now? Things were getting better for Isela and I.* The truck and sedan continued their macabre chase down the dark Arizona highway with the silvery rays of a full harvest moon lighting the way. Rico tried to conjure a map of the area in his mind and see what was nearby. *If my memory's right, the Sunrise rest stop should be coming up. Then what do I do if I managed to beat the sedan there?*

Call the police? And tell them what? The Devil's car is harassing me? Rico thought about his options as he raced down the interstate. The sedan from legend was hot on his bumper.

Yeah, he could call the police. But, of course, the million-dollar question is, would they believe him? Hell, he didn't believe it, and he was the one the Devil's sedan was chasing.

He weaved between the lanes, praying the sedan would pass him and go on its merry way. But it didn't. It stayed on his ass, bumping him now and then like it was taunting him. The Toyota was not capable of more speed, so trying to squeeze additional momentum would not work.

The damn car was not going around him, and he needed to escape whatever was chasing him. It kept tapping him and backing off; he saw when he glanced in the mirror. The driver was teasing him. Not good. *Stay calm, Rico. Stay calm.* He had no idea what the hell the sedan wanted or why it was chasing him. Ten years as a ranger never prepared him for this. He'd fought flesh and blood enemies, not urban legends. Urban legends that appeared to have come to life and liked stalking him. He glanced down at his fuel gauge—half a tank.

A half tank should be enough. It would be two hours to Wilcox if Rico survived that long to get there. The bad thing about legends was you didn't know what was true or false. In the stories his grandfather used to tell him when he was little, Rico couldn't remember if people died in them or not.

Ahead, the sign for the Sunrise rest stop informed Rico he was still five miles away. If he stayed ahead of the sedan long enough to reach Sunrise, he might have a chance of staying alive.

But, instead, the sedan tapped his bumper again, and Rico struggled to keep the Toyota on the road. After what seemed to be eons later, he reached the rest stop. He slowed down as he pulled into the parking lot and halted in shock.

Impossible as it seemed. In front of Rico, the sedan was there, blocking his movement forward. That stunned him. *How the hell did it get in front of me?* The sedan was right on him.

He checked moments before he turned off. Now it was in front of him, preventing Rico from pulling into the rest stop.

Those creepy pumpkin eyes sent chills down his spine. Weird clicking noises from behind him drew his attention back to the rearview mirror. Four black Rottweilers were glaring back at him with luminous crimson eyes through the window. They were standing shoulder to shoulder in the truck bed. *Now, where did they come from?*

They stood motionless, staring at him, unnerving him. He had never seen dogs stand so still, their attention focused on Rico. Okay, he didn't remember anything about dogs with glowing red eyes in his grandpa's stories.

The sedan jerked forward at Rico numerous times, like a leashed animal waiting for its master to let it loose. Rico sat there listening to it rev its engine, playing with him. The dogs in the back weren't getting in through the rear window. When in Afghanistan, Rico survived explosions and the enemy firing at him. But he still carried the night fears. So, when he bought the truck, he replaced the windows with reinforced plexiglass. Plexiglass was near impossible to break.

Nope, Rico was not worried about the dogs. On the other hand, he had no idea what the sedan wanted or what it would do. So, the sedan was the immediate problem. As if it knew what Rico was thinking, the sedan charged forward. Rico put the truck in reverse, and as fast as the Toyota moved backward; the sedan advanced. The sedan stopped, and so did Rico. Now they were both involved in a waiting game. He could feel the sweat dripping down his back, soaking his best dress shirt. The same shirt he had worn to the conference meetings at the hardware store.

He had a tough time adjusting to civilian life after returning from Afghanistan. Isela, knowing how much Rico loved plants, suggested starting a nursery. They created a business specializing in growing high desert plants. The growing season for high desert plants is much shorter than low desert plants. High desert plants experienced harsher weather conditions than low desert plants. The plants they grew had to be hardy to survive the extreme weather conditions of the high desert.

Trial and error plus numerous financial setbacks almost closed them down. But Torres Nurseries stayed alive, selling plants to landscapers, home builders, and other small businesses. Then a few weeks ago, Rico received a call from a buyer. The buyer was looking for high desert plants to purchase for a local hardware store. He invited Torres Nurseries to attend the vendor conference sponsored in Albuquerque.

Rico wasn't the only vendor invited to the conference. So, he was glad he brought samples from his nursery. After the meetings, he signed a contract with them. The buyer loved his plants and the variety his nursery grew. Torres Nursery was now their lead supplier for high desert plants. Their nursery would be supplying plants to the Albuquerque District. Even better, they also purchased the rest of his nursery's Christmas Cactus, Rosemary Trees, and Poinsettias.

Rico and Isleta's hard work paid off. But instead of being at home celebrating with Isela at a restaurant tonight? Rico was here playing chicken with an urban myth. Minutes dragged by, one after the other, while sweat continued to pool on his forehead. Still, Rico sat without moving, his gut warning him he needed to keep his wits about him. His instincts honed by numerous campaigns in Afghanistan, which had often saved his life.

He knew that, like Afghanistan, he would have to fight for his life, and he needed to keep his cool. He could not afford to let his guard down, not even a little. And those spooky Jack-o'-lantern headlights staring at him weren't giving him warm, fuzzy feelings either. Worried about the gas level, Rico glanced at the fuel gauge and calculated the distance to Wilcox.

The last thing he needed right now was to run out of gas. He was down to three-eighths of a tank and still about two hours from Willcox. *It would be close.* He looked back up at the vehicle in front of him. Then he checked on the Rotties in the back. Rico had an idea, and before he could talk himself out of it. He put the truck in reverse and drove backward before doing a quick 180. The sudden turn threw the dogs out of the cab with startled yelps and thuds. He slammed the truck into drive, lurching the truck forward. Rico pushed the pickup as fast as he could force it to move.

He merged onto I-10 too fast and almost lost control of his vehicle. Rico continued speeding down the highway, steadying the truck as he drove. The sedan was not far behind. But he was hoping to build a sizeable lead ahead of it and the creepy mutts. To his right, Rico could see red glowing eyes watching him as he sped down the highway.

Eyes that kept pace with him when no human-dog could run that fast. The sound of an approaching engine and a quick look in the mirror showed the sedan gaining. No average car could move that fast, either. As much as he hated to admit it, it seemed like an actual ghost haunted him. The Devil was chasing him down the moonlit highway at breakneck speeds. He wasn't even sure he believed in anything ethereal or ghostly.

Right now, Rico was concerned with staying alive. An exit sign for a Navajo casino/resort loomed ahead. Without a second thought, he tapped the brakes and whipped down the exit, heading for the casino. Casinos were open twenty-four hours, providing a place for Rico to hide until morning came. Statues of grizzlies lined the entryway on both sides. But when he entered the parking lot and drove up to valet parking. Their heads swiveled towards him with unblinking, glowing red orbs.

Impossible, yet his eyes weren't lying to him. Once inanimate statues are now staring at him. Rico couldn't believe it. He didn't dare stop at the resort now. The stories his father told him didn't say if these creatures would follow him inside or not. Would they harm unsuspecting gamblers if he stayed at the casino, or were they only after him? He could not take the chance, so he kept going and hoped he had enough gas to make it to Wilcox.

Rico was not religious, but not because he didn't believe in God. It was because he didn't have any use for him. Why would a loving God let his entire unit die and not him? Why did he get to live, and they didn't? Isela had told him once during a rough patch of depression that God had a plan for him. There was a reason he was the only survivor, even if Rico couldn't see it for himself. Rico had to have faith. On his big 5-0, as a present, Isela had given him a silver cross and nagged him to wear it. He did too. Not because he believed what she told him, but because he loved his Isela. He knew God did not give a damn about him.

But the cross gave him an idea. The Devil could not go on hallowed ground, nor did he like holy water. Further up the road, a wooden bridge spanned a small stream. What if he threw the cross in the stream? Wouldn't that transform the ordinary water into holy water? In theory, that would stop the sedan. Right?

He might have a chance, but what about those mangy curs? Being evil, they should not be able to cross the stream either. The only problem with that logic is there had been no mention of devil dogs. His grandfathers regaled him with stories about the Devil's Highway many times.

No devil dogs, so where did they fit in with the legend? And would holy water even work on them? Guess he would find out soon enough.

As he raced down the road, Rico glanced behind him to gauge the sedan's distance from him. It was catching up to him way too fast and would be on him in seconds. There was no way he could push more speed out of the truck. He had the accelerator to the floor. Noises coming from the engine were worrying him. It sounded close to blowing. Off to the right, he noticed the glowing eyes kept pace with the truck. *Not good.* Glancing at his gas gauge again, he noticed he was now down to less than one-eighth of a tank.

Time was not on his side, and he was running out of it. The stream was just up the road.

Rico took another quick look in the mirror. Then ripped the cross off from around his neck. Transferring it to his left hand, and prayed as he raced to the bridge. He didn't care if God believed in him or not; Rico just wanted to live through the night. Another quick look back showed the sedan less than a few hundred yards behind. It would be on him in seconds.

The hell dogs loped out of the desert, acting confident that he had nowhere to go. They formed a small wall in front of him, trying to box him in, and that was not happening. He drove straight at the dogs, staring defiantly at him from the middle of the road. Rico swerved onto the shoulder around them at the last minute, continuing his breakneck race down the highway. Rico heard the angry snarls and growls as he sped past the devil dogs and couldn't help the smile forming on his lips. Pleased at outsmarting them lifted his spirits. He knew it was still a long way to go before he would be safe. Rico could see the bridge ahead of him. Another quick look in the mirror showed the sedan was seconds from catching up.

The driver's window rolled down; Rico tossed the cross out the window. It sailed over the bridge rail down into the stream below as he sped across the bridge to the other side. He checked on the sedan. It had stopped. Rico let out a major sigh of relief, which was short-lived.

In the desert night, he saw glowing red eyes glaring at him. Of course, silver wouldn't affect them.

That was fine by him because now Rico was getting angry, and he had a surprise for those hell dogs. He opened the glove box, grabbed the handgun inside, placing it on the seat next to him. Another thing Rico loved about Arizona; it was an open-carry gun state. He took the next exit off I-10 and followed the road further into the desert. Away from any homes or businesses until he felt he was far enough away, then stopped.

He rolled the window down, grabbed the gun, and crawled onto the hood of the truck.

This weapon had hollow-point bullets designed to cause maximum damage to the target. Rico hoped that it included a pack of devil dogs. With the gun and extra ammo in hand, he waited. He scanned the sparse foliage surrounding him that dotted the desert. A full moon tinged the area with a slight silvery hue. It provided enough light for him to see the mutts when they decided to come at him.

He heard the growling first from his right. A slight shift of his body and Rico was pointing the gun in that direction and waited.

He heard rustling noises from behind him, but he was not buying it. His guts were telling him that the noises were a distraction. The mutts were trying to pull his attention off the movement in front of him. The rustling noises continued, then he heard growling noises in front of him. He felt the sweat dripping off his body in gallons onto the hood as he laid motionless. The gun pointed at the empty desert. He knew they were there—all four of them.

One of the dogs had detached from the group, making its way cautiously towards the truck. It stopped, sniffing the air like it was trying to smell him out. As much as Rico was sweating, he would be surprised if the damn thing didn't smell him. The dog lowered its head before moving forward again. Fifty feet. Forty-five. Thirty-five feet. Within thirty feet from his hiding spot, Rico aimed for the center of its chest and fired.

The shot knocked it back another three feet, where it laid twitching. To Rico's relief, the dog didn't get back up; it laid there squirming and yelping. It disappeared moments later in a flash of brilliant ruby-red light. A loud clap of thunder followed immediately. *One hell dog down and three more to go.*

The other three were not happy about losing one of their own. The dogs came charging out of the darkness. Rico sighted the middle one, which was closest, and fired. The bullet knocked it back where it laid still, and then it too disappeared in that same ruby-red light and thunder. The remaining two stopped their charge, going low to the ground. Flat on their bellies, making it difficult for Rico to see them. Their shapes merged with the desert surface. He searched for them, camouflaged in the darkness, straining his eyes.

Their coat color, combined with the night, hid the little shits from him. He could hear dragging noises as they snuck their way across the sand. Where Rico waited on top of his truck, but dammit! He couldn't see them, and he did not want to give his position away by moving. But Rico couldn't stay up on the roof of his truck all night, either. He began inching backward across the hood. Then slid through the driver's window and back into his seat.

Rico rolled the window up before turning the keys in the ignition. And in reverse, he headed out of the brush wand back onto the highway. The beasts from hell snarled in frustration, which made him smile. Until he remembered, he had a long way to go, and that removed the smile. Rico couldn't afford to get cocky about his continued survival. Still, he couldn't help feeling better about his odds. But he knew dropping his guard was when mistakes happened.

Afghanistan taught him that.

His unit was rotating out of Afghanistan that day. Gassed and ready on the tarmac was the helicopter taking them home. They filed into the chopper, thrilled and excited to still be alive and going home. That was when all hell broke loose. An incoming mortar took out the chopper, killing everyone but Rico. The concussion from the explosion blew out his eardrums, taking most of Rico's hearing with it. He couldn't stop wondering why he was still alive over the years.

The shrinks told him it was survivors' guilt. Now, this. Not superstitious, Rico couldn't help thinking that was why the Devil was chasing him. His brothers died that day, and Rico didn't.

He escaped the death destiny had planned for him. That day, he was to have died with his brothers. Now the Devil was here to collect his soul. *NO!* Rico might not understand why the Devil and his pets were chasing him. He may not deserve to be alive when his men weren't. But going to hell wasn't in his future either, because Rico wasn't an evil person.

They were racing the sun to Willcox. The red glowing eyes kept pace with him on his right side. Rico also noticed that the sky was getting lighter in the east. Noting the time on the dash 6:15 am. Even devil dogs can't outrace daylight. Wilcox's lights were up the road and approaching fast. His pounding heart began slowing. The truck stop appeared to the left, off the interstate. And that was the exit he took.

Rico pulled up to the gas pump and got out, looking towards the desert. The remaining Rotties stood near a line of sagebrush, glaring at him with glowing eyes—their bodies fast becoming transparent. As Rico watched, the Rotties faded as the sun rose until they disappeared.

He had made it. He had survived.

Rico thought long and hard about what to tell Isela as he drove the rest of the way to Tucson. He knew she would be worried about him getting home later than usual. In the end, Rico decided not to tell her anything about his crazy night from hell. Isela was still asleep when he got home. He took a long hot shower, and afterward, he made a cup of coffee. Then took his cup and thoughts outside to the patio.

Isela found him hours later, still sitting outside, and joined him. Where they sat in comfortable silence, drinking their coffee. That was one of many reasons Rico loved Isela. Her ability to know when Rico wanted to talk and when he didn't. After twenty years of marriage, she knew him inside and out. The problem was, would Rico ever be ready to talk about what happened?

Last night made him question what he believed. If the Devil was real, then that meant God was real too. That meant Isela might be right as well, he thought. God might have a plan for him after all. He wasn't ready to go there yet. So Rico would stick to his original plan of taking Isela out to dinner. Then tonight, over dessert, he'd share the good news. Torres Nursery was now an official vendor to an Albuquerque-based hardware franchise.

Later that evening, while driving to the restaurant for dinner. Isla broke the silence after Rico had checked his rearview mirror for the umpteenth time. "What's going on, Rico?"

He searched the desert surrounding them, looking for glowing red eyes. Rico didn't know how to answer her. In their entire marriage, he'd never lied to her. Not once. No matter how bad or scary things were. He'd always told Isela the truth. Did he dare tell her the truth now?

"Rico?"

He ducked his head, took a deep breath. He looked over at Isela, sitting quietly in the passenger seat.

"I'm sorry, my love, but I'm not even sure where to begin."

"Start from the beginning, love; that's always the best place to start."

He laughed. "Yes, you're right," but then he sobered. "Isela, I'm not sure what happened last night, let alone how to explain it to you."

"Open your mouth and start talking. We will get through this as we've gotten through everything else."

"Have I told you today how much I love you?"

Isela laughed, and it was pure joy to hear her laughter. "No, my love, you haven't, so I will wait for you to do so."

Rico laughed in response. "I love you, Isela." Then he told her what happened last night, from beginning to end. Afterward, he asked her. "What do you think? Do you think I imagined everything, or maybe I'm crazy?"

"Rico, don't be silly. You are the most grounded man I have ever met. But you have seen and done things in Afghanistan. Things that have made you question your spiritual beliefs. So, your grandpa's stories came to life. To force you to face your fears and decide what you believe."

"So, what now?" He asked, confused.

"What do you believe?" Isela pressed.

"I don't know," Rico replied.

"Well, you don't have to decide tonight. Let us enjoy dinner, and everything else will work itself out."

That's what they did, too. It was a wonderful evening; the food was great, and so was the conversation. Rico enjoyed the expression on her face. When over Tiramisu, he told Isela the excellent news. Then they toasted the new contract with the store. They talked about adding an addition to the nursery to keep up with future orders. Life at that moment was good and filled with hope.

Afterward, Rico and Isela walked hand in hand to the front door when he stopped. Frozen in his tracks because lying in the middle of the "welcome mat," the moon's light making it glow, was Rico's silver cross.

GHOSTS OF WRITTEN WORDS

PAMELA K. KINNEY

Ghosts conjured by
Written words,
Haunting pages of
Imagination.
Rising from the
Author's terrible nightmares,
Or forgotten dreams,
Ghostly tales for
Winter nights.
Stories full of
Chills,
For readers' own
Thrills.
As readers know,
Skillful writing
Entices fear,
Birthing:
"It's alive, alive!"
In the reader's own
Terrified mind.

LORELAI

LANE BLEVINS

"You have to leave," she told the swollen mound of her belly.

An elbow pushed against the confines of the womb and traced a horizon on Marta's abdomen. It reminded her of the chubby boy at the bus station four months back who'd dragged his thumbnail from one side of his throat to the other, a circle of his friends jeering at his old-fashioned threat. Even though she knew the gesture wasn't directed at her, Marta felt it'd been a bad omen. A reminder of the world her daughter would soon stumble through, as Marta had. As Marta still was.

Marta was forty weeks along now. The August 19th due date had already come and gone. The humble nursery where she now spent most of her evenings, as if finding sanctuary in its possibility, was cobbled together from donated clothes and consignment furniture, one of her two bedrooms in the apartment dedicated to the granulated face from the ultrasounds. *Lorelai*, she'd whispered the first time that face showed up on the screen while the warm goo slid down her hip. Marta hadn't even glanced at names yet, but this one rose from her bones, fully formed and ready to be stamped onto the birth certificate and stitched into customized blankets.

Marta had rearranged her entire life around this rabbit-quick heartbeat fluttering inside her stomach, but after all the weeks of cramped spine and acid reflux and uncontrollable hunger, she was ready for her body to be hers and hers alone, again.

She knelt beside the crib with her hands clasped together like she was at church. Stars like pinpricks through a black canvas gleamed at her from the window. Sheer lilac curtains danced in front of the dark sky whenever the oscillating fan turned their way. The pink stuffed elephant on the hand-me-down rocking chair stared at her, its black eyes shining with the amber glow of a nightlight. "I know it seems like a big scary world out here, little one, but it's not all that bad, not really."

Already she was selling false promises to her daughter, but what else could she do? Tell her about her daddy's temper, or the judgmental stare of the manager of the grocery store she worked at, or the landlord from her previous studio apartment in Charlotte who'd threatened eviction if she didn't give him a quick handjob on her threadbare couch?

Tears slipped down her cheeks. Her palms pressed so tightly together she could feel her knuckles whitening. "It'll be so much better with you out here with me. We can be a team. Been so long since I felt like I had anyone else in my corner but me, you know? I don't mean to saddle you with all my shit, honey, I don't. I'm just… I'm excited to meet you is all."

Her back throbbed with a hot, needling pain. The itch on her belly from the jagged fissures of stretch marks was so powerful she feared it might drive her mad. She felt as if she had a pebble lodged at the back of her throat, something that constantly rattled around and nudged against her gag reflex. Everything smelled like matchsticks to her; it'd been like that since week—what—thirty-two?

She had an app on her phone and every week it chimed with a new notification. *Baby is the size of a blueberry. Of a kumquat. Of an apple. A cabbage. Watermelon. Exceptionally large watermelon.* It'd been her lone marker for tracking the passage of time. She had no family here. No baby showers, no gender reveals, no pregnancy photoshoots or birthing plans or maternity leave. She had this room, and the room inside her belly—this tiny space in a two-bedroom apartment on the third floor with four neighbors who didn't know her name. It was all she had to give.

She swept her palm along her protruding stomach. "It's long past your time, *mija*. My body can't hold you anymore. You must leave."

No, she heard Lorelai whisper back.

Week forty-one. Baby is the size of a pumpkin. The kind of pumpkin that gets left in the gutter with the flies gathered along the corners of its carved-out eyes. Baby's fingernails are now long enough to scratch at your organs. Baby can hear everything, even your most private thoughts. Baby can smile in utero but chooses not to.

Marta rode the bus to and from work. Her black slacks were marked with mustard along the hems from where she'd mopped up a spill on the condiments' aisle—the motion of sliding the mop from side to side on the floor had caused her muscles to knot like a vice gripping her spine. The pain persisted and grew as her abdomen stretched each week. Her belly was so big that she had to wear an elastic band to hold it up. Sometimes she feared that, without the band, her womb would tear away from her body like a giant blood-swollen tick, leaving her exposed intestines to unravel onto the grimy off-white floors of the grocery store. The rumbling of the bus soothed Lorelai, coaxing her from the desire to somersault and cartwheel in protest of Marta's breakfast.

She heard Lorelai often now. Her whisper was alien, her vocal-chords and lungs unpracticed, and her perception of sound distorted by the meat separating her from the outside world. At the bus stop, a homeless man sang about Jesus in a beautiful, doleful croon, and Marta idly wondered how differently the man's voice would have sounded if she heard him from the bottom of a river.

"Look about ready to pop," an old woman said, a jade green fascinator hat bobby-pinned to her hair. She wore fuchsia lipstick drawn on with a shaky hand, but her smile was genuine as she gestured towards Marta's belly.

Marta forced herself to smile back, something paltry and polite to ward off any more conversation. Her stomach gurgled with the sudden urge to spew scrambled eggs and decaf all over the bus floor. Instead, her smile widened to display all her teeth, even the molars, until her eyes watered with the effort. She knew if she didn't keep smiling, she'd lose every bit of her breakfast and Lorelai would suffer for it.

Or was it Lorelai doing this to her? Pulling at her strings until Marta was a marionette?

At her last appointment with the obstetrician, the midwife had prattled about one of her patients going into labor three weeks early because a bit of bad shrimp made her vomit so hard, her water broke. Marta yearned for that. Yearned for the gush of fluid clearing up even the slightest bit of space in her body so she wouldn't feel so overstuffed. Wouldn't feel like her skin was on the verge of splitting.

Marta had asked to be induced at once, but the midwife shrugged and said, "She'll get here when she's ready. No need to rush her!" Something had been off about the woman's slightly downturned smile with her frizzy hair curtaining her eyes, which had not once throughout the duration of the appointment met Marta's. Something about it said, *I'd rather save my schedule for the mothers who aren't already failing. For the mothers with health insurance, who haven't scheduled appointments with WIC.* The midwife had triaged Marta from their very first appointment and had categorized her "expectant": best to send the chaplain over and leave the medical resources to the patients who had a chance.

"Oh, I'm ready," Marta finally said back to the old woman who had since looked away and busied herself with the contents of her purse.

Week forty-two. Baby is the size of a gangly foal born steaming onto the hay. Does it sometimes feel like you had the wind knocked out of you? Like your heart can't quite expand enough and all the blood is getting backlogged in your lungs? Don't worry, that's just the baby standing inside of you, thrashing against its fleshy coffin.

Marta dreamed she was in the middle of a still, gray ocean. The briny water lapped at her throat and her feet searched for sand but merely found a bottomless sea.

In the dream, she pressed her hands against her belly and, for the first time in months, felt no movement. No flutters or trembles or somersaults from her little girl. For a moment, Marta felt a terrible dread plummeting through her body—dread, but also maybe relief, if she was being honest, because what if Antonio found her again and she had to leave Lumberton in a hurry, what if rent went up or she couldn't afford Lorelai's daycare, what if she couldn't go back to work right away or lost her job or lost the apartment the nursery the hand-me-down crib?

None of the books you read can help you, Lorelai whispered. *I will never sleep in the crib you worked two extra shifts to purchase. You will never bathe or swaddle me. You will never slip a spoon of pureed apple between my lips and laugh at the excess that dribbles onto my chin. I will never drink from your breast. My beginning is your end.*

Cramping pressure exploded in Marta's pelvis as Lorelai dropped lower and lower in the birth canal. Plummeted like an elevator car without cables. No contractions, no dilation, just instant labor. Marta screamed and the bitter water filled her mouth. She clutched her belly, but it was no use. She took it back, she took the relief back, took back any moment when she'd privately wished she'd never seen that little blue plus sign, ever wished she'd scraped the money away to afford the morning-after pill on the days when Antonio hid her birth control. Now all she wanted, desperately wanted, was for Lorelai to stay.

The pain set her nerve-endings ablaze, and the iron tang of blood blossomed in her mouth as she bit her tongue so hard her incisors met. Something slid from her body, twisted and bigger than Lorelai should be, even at forty-two weeks. Something slick and taut slid from between Marta's thighs, then reached up to coil around her torso, her arms, her throat, flexing like a bundle of exposed muscle.

Lorelai. Not a girl in the fetal position with the pinched face preparing to issue her first piercing wail. Not a girl suckling her tiny thumb and peering into her mother's eyes with a look of calm wonderment.

Marta had birthed a tangle of eels. They squeezed so tightly around her throat she could hear her heartbeat drumming in her ears. A pair of them manacled her wrists and ankles, their heavy bodies wrapping themselves in knots to tug her down. The eels jutted their mangled faces away from the surface, lunging their phlegm-slick, gray bodies with the might of ancient things. The water rose to her chin. Her mouth. Her nose. They dragged her down to the depths of the sea. The filmy-eyed morays could breathe underwater, but she could not. That didn't matter to the carnivores. They were monsters, but they still needed their mother.

Week forty-three. Baby is the size of a V8 engine. Your body temperature has spiked to 104° F. Baby now wears your flesh like a Hazmat suit, walking around in your boneless, loose-skinned legs and shaking your employer's hand. Baby already has a political party and is running for the role of HOA treasurer.

The single craving that had persisted throughout Marta's pregnancy was the craving for rare beef—beef only, because it was the one variation satisfying enough to warrant the risk of listeria and e. coli. If she could afford steak tartare, she would have eaten it for every meal. When that taste of iron gushed into her mouth as she chewed the gristly tendon of her almost-cool sirloin, some part of her wondered if it was her craving, or Lorelai's.

"Is that why you won't come out?" Marta asked the fetus kicking her insides. As she bit into her late-night snack, rust-colored juice dribbled from her chin to the enormous protuberance jutting from her waist where Lorelai slept, if Lorelai slept. Her belly looked like a massive, fleshy balloon marbled with bluish veins. "Still trying to tenderize me?"

She balanced the plate on her knees and rocked in the creaky rocking chair in the nursery, laughing a laugh that didn't sound like her. So much of her had been changing lately. The dark splotches on her cheeks from the hormones. The streak of gray hair sprouting from her temple. Her fingernails were growing faster, but that only meant she had to chew them more often. Sometimes she wondered if Lorelai was a fetus at all, and not a malignant teratoma growing teeth and hair and nails of its own.

The dream had persisted each night—the gray sea, the absent heartbeat, the agony, and the eels dragging her under. She dreaded sleep now, and tried to busy herself with nesting tasks like organizing the stuffed animals, rewashing and folding baby clothes, dusting the blinds. Her manager had stopped including her on the schedule. The general manager told her that, with her "condition," she could no longer be relied on. *Best to wait until after the baby, then we can get you caught up on hours.* Marta suspected her boss didn't want to risk her water breaking in the frozen food aisle.

"Your daddy called me last night," Marta said to Lorelai. "He called but didn't say anything. Speechless, breathing, listening to me breathe. You know, at first, I thought you might be the thing that would convince him to change. Do right by us. But now I think he'd gut us both if he thought he was smart enough to get away with it."

It gets so lonely, Marta thought, and she knew Lorelai could hear her think it. In grade school, Marta had been prone to flights of fancy. No magazine about wedding planning or travel or better homes and gardens went unstudied. She didn't want anything lavish. Only a life where every second was cherished. Not one where the clock ground her bones down one tick at a time, as it had done to her parents. They'd labored in someone else's vineyards and fields just to get by—then they'd dropped dear in their fifties, likely because of those vineyards and fields and the unyielding sun. She wanted a home to call her own. A husband who would find beauty in her flighty smile and snaggled canines. Children who would find comfort in her loving embrace.

She looked around the nursery at its well-intentioned shabbiness. Thankful for the utter quiet of the apartment interrupted only by the neighbors having yet another argument about whose turn it was to let the dog out for a piss. Even the shabbiness would be okay if she had someone to hold her. Was this apartment the extent of her possibilities? Was she born simply to restock grocery store shelves and serve as a vessel for the thing in her belly that changed the sound of her laughter and no longer let her sleep? "Thought things would be different. Thought I'd be different," she said, as an apology.

Week forty-four. She is arriving now. She is ready.

Sweat coated Marta's skin when she woke on the scratchy carpet of the nursery floor. The room smelled of well-water. Rattlesnake dens. A shedding. She watched the fan rotate above her in wobbly circles.

A baby blanket was bunched up around her waist. It was soaked. She didn't have to look down to see the amniotic fluid flecked with blood—that was the smell—that primordial smell of the bogs where the first organisms sprouted limbs to climb from the muck. Marta tried to reach for her cellphone on the rocking chair, but pain tore through her like a scythe. The contraction was so intense, so urgent that she knew it wouldn't matter whether she called for an ambulance now or not. She would be doing this alone.

Marta glanced down at her belly. The baby's feet kicked violently. Pulling the soaked blanket away from her body, Marta struggled to prop herself up on her elbows, setting a pillow under her hips and placing her feet as far apart as she could. She wasn't ready—would she ever have been ready? Ready to get it over with, but she never would have been ready to say goodbye, so instead of even thinking that word, she thought, *I love you* over and over like she was reciting a rosary. She hoped Lorelai could hear it.

Sometime between five and seven million years ago, the first woman crawled towards her cave under the light of the moon. She lay on her back and grunted through childbirth without ultrasounds or sterile hospital sheets or bassinets or pink stuffed elephants with flat black eyes, without even the notion of a name. That first woman had nothing but instinct.

The sweat-soaked corner of a blanket gritted between her teeth, Marta steeled herself to prepare for the next contraction, no longer bothered by the lingering smell of pet dander that she hadn't been able to shampoo out of the rocking chair, or the missed calls from Antonio's number, or the hard life she'd had, or the hard life she'd pass on to Lorelai. She wasn't haunted by the thought anymore: *This is why I was born?* She'd sublimated it with a sturdy whisper that might have been hers and might have been her daughter's: *This is why I was born.*

The skin of her stomach, stretched so thin it had practically become translucent over the past several days, rippled with movement. Her daughter had no interest in passing through the narrow birth canal, shifting her little bones around to accommodate her mother's body. Instead, something pressed from the other side of Marta's belly—a small hand pushed against the whisper-thin muscle separating Lorelai from the outside world. Tears clung to Marta's eyelashes, prisming the room with the amber glow of the nightlight until it looked like a hundred stars hung from the ceiling.

So much love she felt for someone she'd never know. So much she wished she could say to her, this thing that was emerging, fully formed, from the womb. She set her hand against Lorelai's as her belly convulsed, spreading pulsating pain from her core as Lorelai split her abdomen down the middle like a cocoon.

Marta's ribs bent back, cracking and splintering as two hands sprouting from the deflated sack of her body. They looked like red tulips to her. The pain felt like she'd swallowed a Molotov Cocktail, her belly full of fire and broken glass. Blood from her pulverized organs filled her abdominal cavity, saturated her lungs in an instant, and splashed against the back of her throat as she coughed. The carpet fibers were soaked, transformed from beige to red. Fingers the size of vulture talons reached out of her torso to grip hers and she gasped her daughter's name repeatedly, garbling until the syllables swam together.

Marta's breathless chant of her daughter's name grew quiet as Lorelai's scream echoed through the apartment.

JOY AND OUR PATCHWORK LADY

ROOK RILEY

Joy stood in the shadow of the open kitchen door, stunned. Broken dishes littered the floor. The air was heavy with the scent of spoiled milk and aerated violence. Devony texted, "*PLS*" and Joy had dropped everything, flying over here in the middle of the night. No makeup. No prosthetics. Just her in the giant oversized hoodie she'd sworn to burn if she ever got the cash for top surgery.

She stepped over the glass and righted a kitchen chair. How Devony'd let it go this far, Joy could not fathom. How many times had she begged her cousin to take Oskar and leave that pig of a man? Too many. She paused to tighten the sink's knob and stop the dripping water. Too many. But Dev was afraid to be alone. Afraid to be a single mom. And afraid of what Vaughn Cobb would do to her or Oskar if she left.

Joy was afraid of what he would do to them if they stayed.

Blood was spattered across the hallway. Pictures were torn, and the glass shattered in their frames where they fell. This was bad, the worst she'd ever seen. Black scuff marks and dented holes in Oskar's door signaled Vaughn's determination to knock it down.

She hoped Dev had made the man suffer. That it was his blood on the walls.

She sniffed back tears and took a deep breath, mentally preparing herself, before knocking.

"Oskar?" her voice soft as her mind pleaded for him to be okay. "It's me, Auntie Joy. Your momma sent me."

The lock clicked almost immediately, and the door swung open. Oskar stared up at her with an old man's eyes, not those of a teary kindergartener. She knelt down to hug him, but he shied away. Red fingermarks striped his upper arms.

He dropped a blood-stained washcloth on the floor.

His voice was hollow and monotone as he asked, "Where's Daddy?"

"Oh baby," she picked him up, and as he struggled against her, she struggled with the words. "He's at the hospital with your mom." It was the truth, as far as she knew.

"Is he coming back?" Oskar asked.

Joy nodded. "Yeah. And we don't want to be here when he does, right?"

She put him down so he could open the little crawl space door in his closet and grabbed out his special go-bag. It was black and red vinyl, featuring a screaming eagle with metallic talons. A tough guy backpack for an undersized five-year-old.

Devony didn't want Oskar to be picked up by CPS and put in foster care, so she was always careful to take the fight outside— down the block, if possible. Oskar knew to hide in the crawl space and wait for Joy. But this had to be the last time. Dev had to understand that.

He refused to be carried to the car. Instead, he walked with his shoulders back, head up, and held onto Joy's hand like a lifeline. As she bundled him into the car seat she'd bought so many months ago for this express purpose, he reached out and put something small and hard into her hand.

"We have to go see Momma," he said. "She can't get better without it."

Before she asked him what it was, she knew. The streetlight picked up its silver twinkle.

"It's her tooth, Auntie."

By the time she'd driven home, Oskar was asleep and Joy was raging, racking her brain to come up with a way to get Dev to come to her senses. She tucked the sleeping boy into her bed in case he awoke in the middle of the night and was scared.

Her own sleep was start and stop, marred by nightmares of finding Oskar and Dev dead. No rest. No refresh.

Barefooted, she went downstairs in the morning to find Bubbe, her adopted grandmother and landlady, and her best friend Andrick at the kitchen table.

"Joy, you remember? Remember what I told you when we thought you were a boy?" Bubbe asked.

It could be any number of things since Bubbe Lubov was a fount of wisdom from the old country and a retired pediatrician. She knew medicine and stories from all over the world. Joy hadn't found any topic the geriatric spitfire didn't know at least something about. And after Joy's parents had kicked her out, Bubbe rented the upstairs apartment to her. These early morning philosophy sessions were normal. But Joy wasn't in the mood today.

"If this is about how my mother shouldn't have worn hats while pregnant, I don't want to hear it." Joy poured herself a cup of coffee and stirred in a spoonful of vanilla sugar. "Hats cannot affect gendering before or after 12 weeks. It's ridiculous, Bubbe."

The old woman waved her gnarled, arthritic fingers, dismissing Joy's comment. "Such a smartass *devushka*. Don't mock the folklore. And no, I meant the time you and Andrick threatened the White girls. Remember?"

Andrick, sitting opposite Bubbe, blew the steam off his coffee and shrugged. "That was 20 years ago. How am I supposed to remember that?

"They were heinous bitches. That's what I remember," Joy added. "Why're we wasting time on them?" She took her cup and sat down with them at the worn Formica table.

Bubbe's voice quavered with frustration. "You two were laying on that floor right over there in front watching some propaganda show and speaking violence against those girls."

Andrick laughed. "Oh, you mean that cartoon eagle that saved bears, lions, and unicorns. It was the only kid show on—like ever."

It really was possible because when Andrick's parents died in a car accident, Bubbe had raised him. Joy had spent many afternoons here watching General Freedom save animals from various predicaments.

Bubbe's hand shook as she sipped her tea. "One of you threatened to punch Becky White in her face. Do you remember now?"

Joy's thoughts caught on the strand of memories of middle school and those preacher's kids had latched on to her for being different. They'd tormented the shit out of her.

"Look, I don't have time for—" Joy started.

"They were assholes. Terrorists with braces even, Bubbe. But you know I wouldn't hit one of them," Andy finished off his cup of coffee. "I'd have cut my hand on their braces and caught Asshole Mouth. Plus, you would have probably ripped out my teeth for the fairies or donated my sac to the Patchwork Lady. "

Oh no. He'd done it now. Our Lady was supposed to be off-limits, but he had stuck his foot right in the big middle of it.

"Oh, laugh at Her will you, ungrateful children. Laugh then. But if it were up to me, Devony would be rid of that man by now. If I could walk the path, I would."

"Gather the bones, clever the path," Andrick began as he grabbed his postman's jacket and headed for the door. "Post the letters."

Joy shook her head. He was off to deliver the mail and she would be here trying to get Bubbe to chill out while babysitting Oskar and checking on Dev's condition.

"Thanks, Andy. You're less than awesome," she called to his back.

With a wave, he was out the door.

After settling Bubbe with her recorded shows, Joy made a quick call to the hospital. Dev was still unconscious. Vaughn had been arrested. If she thought the court's elders would give her custody of Oskar, she'd fight for him. But that would not happen. And she knew that as soon as Dev woke up, she'd bond that piece of shit out of jail again.

"He'll kill her, you know," Bubbe said as a matter of fact, without taking her eyes off the ancient console television. "And he'll either kill Oskar too, or train him up to be his father's son."

Joy shook her head and leaned against the rocking chair where the old woman sat. "I know Bubbe. I know. But what can I do?"

"Do you remember what I told you about *Loskutnaya Ledi*, Our Lady?" she asked.

She did. Of course she did. And what she didn't, Bubbe filled in.

Joy wrote it all down.

She called out sick to work and stood outside Dev's house. In the daylight, it looked normal. Just a regular house on a regular street, broken pavement and all. The outside was freshly painted and the landscaping perfect. Vaughn's truck wasn't in the driveway. She took a steadying breath and went in through the kitchen door. Without last night's panic, it was less scary. Wounded walls, sagging sad furniture. This place hadn't been happy in a long, long time.

She dug Vaughn's fancy dress boots out from under their bed and took the box cutter out of her purse. The blade chewed through the shaft's double stitching to remove it from the foot. She took that and the half-hidden bottle of Jack's Old Number 13 from the nightstand with her to the kitchen. On the counter were a bunch of unpaid bills and a couple of unsigned IOUs. On the fridge were pictures of Oskar. Joy flipped through the envelopes, looking for anything handwritten.

Nothing.

Was she really this desperate? Believing in some ridiculous folktale? Joy couldn't laugh because this might be the only way to save Devony's life. She was worth fighting for, even if Dev couldn't see it for herself. She could just wing it. Nothing ventured, nothing gained. There probably wasn't a Patchwork Lady, anyway.

Back at home, Bubbe brought what she had hidden behind her back out with a flourish.

"From Hector next door's prized rooster," Bubbe explained as she laid the blue-black feathers on the kitchen table. "When a dog gets in his yard, sometimes that bird drops his whole tail to get away."

"And your sweet Leela the pit bull had nothing to do with it, I'm sure," Joy said as she tightened the lid on an old pickle jar, watching the strip of skin she'd shaved off her leg swirl around the glass before putting it down next to the feathers, boot leather, a bottle of Jack Daniels whiskey, and Dev's silver tooth. All she had left to get was his name written by someone that loved him.

Oskar looked up from playing Xbox and smiled at her. She had the sudden urge to have him write his father's name for her. That was sick, though. And if he ever found out what happened, he'd blame himself for Vaughn's death. She had the paper and crayons in her hand, but couldn't make herself ask.

Just when she thought everything was lost, Andy came through.

"Here," he said and laid a blue envelope on the table. "You need his name in love, right?"

There it was, Vaughn Nathan Cobb, written in a shaky hand. Inside was a birthday card signed Love, Momma. Perfect.

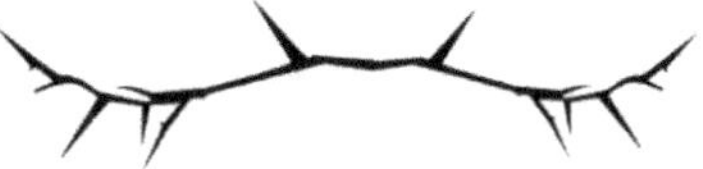

Joy took special care getting ready. Everything had to be perfect: her hair, makeup, even what she wore.

Oskar's backpack held all her offerings. Bubbe had drawn Joy a map. It didn't make sense that any of this existed, let alone existed in broken-down, left-behind suburbia. Beyond the abandoned apartment construction, she was to follow the creek through the underbrush until trees wove together and blocked the sky. There she was to find the light. Bubbe didn't know what it meant, or how far to go because she'd never walked it herself.

Old Tyvek wrap hung from ancient, abandoned construction and fluttered in the chill wind. As she hiked up the thin path, the glow of her flashlight bobbed along, highlighting bushes and overgrown shrubs one moment—rusty nails and broken beer bottles the next. Three smooth stones, about the size of her fist, marked the crossroad of the path. Here was where she was to wait.

Joy smoothed back her hair and pulled the ponytail holder out to let her hair cover her neck. She unpacked the pillow and crazy quilt Bubbe made, arranging it to wrap around so she didn't have to sit on the hard ground. She pulled her phone out from her front pocket and settled down to wait. She browsed the web and checked out her normal sites and looked up. Outside the glow of the screen, the night was still. The earlier breeze had stopped. She couldn't hear the cars barreling up Highway 80 or 30, even though she knew she was less than a mile from that interchange.

She slipped the phone back into her pocket, turning it off to save battery in case she needed Bubbe to rescue her. How that would work, she had no idea. Bubbe's bad hip and general fragility weren't exactly the hero squad. And Andy could never find her. According to the story, no man could.

She glanced up the path and noticed a small flickering light, like a fire in the distance. She left the pillow but kept the quilt wrapped around her shoulders like a cape of protection as she wandered on. Instead of the broken path she'd seen before, this one was neatly swept. Flat stones in sets of three marked the way to go. And that way had not been there earlier. Joy was sure of that.

Sweet vanilla drifted down from the cracked, almost empty Yankee Candle that lit the neat path. As she walked out past its glow, a cat yowled in the distance. It set her teeth on edge.

There was nothing for her to fear here. Our Lady will exist and accept the offerings, or she won't be real at all. The grade continued to climb and Joy stumbled. Across her path lay a long bone. Joy hadn't had an anatomy class, but it looked a lot like a tibia to her. She picked it up, tucked it under her arm, and kept going. A few steps later, another bone blocked the way. The air seemed thinner now, and she felt a little dizzy. The third bone, the tip of a finger perhaps, was stuck out from under a pile of dry leaves. She put it in her pocket, unsteady on her feet for a moment.

Bubbe's instructions had been another part of the poem.

> Gather the bones
> Clever the path
> Seek me
> In the witching hour
> He cannot atone
> For these sins
> Summon me
> He has earned our wrath
> Pay me.
> Pain for pain.
> I rise again.

She steadied herself against a tree and took a slow, deep breath to re-center. Up another steep hill, a candle glowed. This time it was lavender floating on the cold wind. As she moved towards it, the night grew colder. Her feet crunched through frozen leaves. Her breath came out in a little nimbus. Outside the edges of the trail, something was stalking her. She couldn't catch the movement facing it. Only from the corner of her eyes would she catch a glimpse of something darker than the night. As she left the safety of the candle's glow, she could hear the creature getting closer. Joy fought the urge to run. The wind picked up about her ankles, scattering sharp-edged leaves blowing around her. The leaves blew up under her skirts, slicing through the leggings she wore beneath. It hurt, but not enough to stop her.

She pulled her coat's collar up, gathered the woolen scarf to wrap around her face, and kept the quilt around her shoulders. As she moved on, she could feel blood weeping down her legs.

In the dark, the stalking beast howled.

Joy struggled forward against the wind, the leaves cutting and sticking in freezing clumps to her face, her hair, and hands. Her night vision returned and, through a break in the trees, moonlight illuminated a huge gray wolf lying in wait for her. She kept her eyes on the stalking animal. Garbage bags, soda cans, plastic jugs, and other discarded trash from the area formed the beast. It crept towards the path, a low eerie growl vibrating the very ground under her feet.

She was afraid to take her eyes off it to look for a stick, a rock—any sort of weapon, but she did. There was nothing. It crept closer, staying low to the ground.

She took the fear that had piled on since this ordeal started and flipped it, turning it into anger. She mimicked what she remembered her mother doing to strays.

Stomping her foot, she threw her arms open wide and yelled, "Scat! Go on, get out of here!"

The garbage wolf stopped, cocking its head at her. It whined.

She looked down at the bones in her hand and shook her head. "No, wolf. That's not for you."

Instead of attacking, the beast came to sit at her feet. The demonic glare in his eyes was gone. Nothing there but the gray eyes of an animal. She secured the bones in the backpack and leaned down to have a closer look. That's when she noticed it wasn't animated trash. There was an animal trapped inside all that other crap.

"You weren't going to hurt me, were you?" Joy whispered. "You needed some help."

She found the cold to be much easier to bear as she knelt down to untangle knotted fur from all the garbage. When she finished, it wasn't a wolf at all, but a big, friendly dog who rewarded her with a lick on her hand. Looking at it in the face, it was hard for her to understand what she had been afraid of in the first place. Obviously, there's no such thing as a garbage wolf.

The night traveled on and so did they, the dog at her side.

Ahead, the path split. Guttering candles in broken jars lit both ways.

Neither path looked particularly better than the other. Jagged broken concrete flickered in and out of sight. She chose the rising trail and started upwards, the dog following at a distance. Weeds and grasses choked their way between the chunks of broken sidewalk and more trash. Abruptly, the trail vanished. She found herself under the low branches of overgrown shrubs. Ahead was a rotten wooden fence. She reached out to touch it and found the moss on it wet and spongy. The wood gave a little under her hands.

She turned to go back the way she'd come, but there was no path behind her. Nothing to follow. Even the dog was lost to the night. The vague idea of going down was all she had and so down she went. But she was also curious about this fence and the ornamental overgrown landscaping.

There was a gate, but it'd been locked or was stuck. She forced her shoulder against it and the wood gave way with a screech. She stumbled forward into a wild backyard. Honeysuckle and brambles stretched from the patio to the fence. A wrought iron post light warmed up to a golden orange. Carefully, Joy picked her way over to the stretch of flat concrete. A rusted-out barbeque grill, crumbling dog toys, and the remains of a picnic table littered the patio.

Disappointing.

She was tired. The late hour and the earlier adrenalin dump were taking their toll.

A firepit on the other side of the patio caught her attention. Amid the ring of bricks, a shiny bit of metal caught her eye. She tucked her hair behind her ear and knelt down to inspect the pit. Silver slag and half-melted coins lay all along the bottom. On the opposite side of the pit were empty whiskey bottles—many with candles shoved into their neck.

A faded portrait of the Patchwork Lady was painted on the ruined back fence. This was the shrine. She was surprised it was in a place like this, but it didn't matter.

She thought back to the poem, the little sing-song Bubbe'd taught her.

> In love, it was written
> In vengeance's flame
> It shall wither and blacken
> > The name
> Upon hisself, it was worn
> > The leather
> From you, it was torn
> > The skin
> Liquor ignites the burn
> While silver pays
> For what you yearn
> > Vengeance

She pulled the bones from the backpack and assembled them on the patio. Of course, things were missing. There was no ribcage, no pelvis, or skull. Joy could only lay down the arms and legs in the approximate spots she thought they should go. She took the skin out of the pickle jar and laid it across the bones, and poured the whiskey over all of it. Jack was only 80 proof, and that would not set anything on fire, so she brought lighter fluid to be sure. She squeezed the can, traced the bones, and lit a match.

The light from the lamppost brightened, illuminating the yard as she spoke. The fire leapt up. In the flames, Joy could make out the shape of a woman.

She hid her fear and did as Bubbe instructed.

"Our Patchwork Lady," she began. "Hear the cries of the abused and forsaken voice of our sister who needs your help."

She tossed in the boot leather and the fire's greed made short work of it. The gray smoke held no trace of a burning smell. Instead, it was sweet vanilla, or maybe lavender.

"I have skin for your bones, whiskey for your thirst, leather for your shoes, feathers for your hat, and the silver for your payment."

Joy carefully sat Dev's molar on a brick by the fire.

"I even bring you a tooth for your bite."

As she watched, the flames wriggled into the bones, setting them to glowing with embers floating out from the joints. Hands formed and stretched the skin like stockings, rolling it up and over the bones. Even without a skull, Joy could see the head forming and a blank, featureless face.

"Daughter and sister," a hole, a mouth opened into the bright orange fire, "why do you wake me?"

"Vengeance." The strength and venom in her voice echoed, resounding in her head.

The lady's fiery glow dimmed as she assumed a more solid form.

Joy held still as the goddess reached for her with the ancient fires of vengeance. She fought the urge to close her eyes or shield her face from the heat. The scent of burning hair distracted Joy. It had taken so long for it to grow out. The goddess peered into Joy's eyes. Mirrored in the flames, Joy saw images of Vaughn slamming Devony against the kitchen sink. She saw Oskar fly into the wall from a backhanded slap.

At first, she thought it was the wind whispering against her ear. But then it was as if the words were forming in her mind and then ripping free of her throat, screaming into the night.

"Daughter, you have chosen … wisely."

White-hot pain filled her body as the goddess slipped inside. The super-heated air scorched her lungs as she felt consciousness slipping away.

A myriad of voices speaking one atop the other urged her body forward. Joy floated inside her mind while her body lurched forward on unsteady legs. The awkwardness didn't last. Within moments, she sped through the woods and back up the path as if her legs could fly.

It wasn't as though the goddess wore her body like an old coat. It was more like Joy was there, riding along in a glorious battle-ready Valkyrie. Revenge heated her corner of the mind, and she was ready.

The broken pavement under their feet.

A fresh coat of paint over the cracked foundation.

Perfect hedges.

Vaughn's truck in the driveway.

Joy never touched the front door. It smoldered and turned to embers and ash as they approached. Carpet melted and burned as they flowed across the floor.

"What the fuck?" Vaughn staggered into the room, more than half drunk by the look of him.

Joy wanted to answer him, to shout out that it was her. But no words would form.

He sneered and lunged.

The air shimmered between them.

The curtains billowed on the air current and started to smoke.

The voices. The patchwork quilt of voices egging her on roared.

"Vengeance!"

Flames shot from their mouth, engulfing Vaughn. His face blistered and blackened, and the skin melted, sloughing off onto the floor.

Joy woke alone and cold, laying on the sidewalk facing a mailbox and home that were not her own. Across the street, Dev's house was engulfed in fire. It was everywhere; the roof, the doors, and the windows. It glowed a deep red and amber to livid purple.

She pulled herself up on wobbly legs to take one last look. The paint peeled and blistered on Vaughn's truck. Glass in the windows exploded. Neighbors came out running towards the fire.

Joy walked past it all toward home.

AFTERWORD

SHAD MESHAD

Society at large with the medical community has recognized the arts as therapeutic, not only for the artist, but often for the recipient or viewer. Creating something beautiful out of pain, using a medium to heal or amplify a message, is a tremendous driving force toward understanding and well-being.

Creative arts are extremely effective in establishing a safe zone for feelings to emerge and to express oneself. If you look at the number of biographies, novels, story collections, manuscripts, and poetry collections that veterans or veterans' family members have published, you get a sense of how important a creative outlet can be for healing.

This anthology, crafted by women veterans and supporting women veterans, demonstrates the power of the written word and visual arts. Collectively, they use their voice and skill set to amplify messages relating to life's horrors and hopes, while giving back to other veterans. Bringing the message full circle to support others—it's what we do at the National Veterans Foundation (NVF)—veterans supporting veterans.

But how did we start?

As President and Founder of the NVF, I've advocated for vets for over 50 years. We operate a national toll-free crisis and information hotline for all vets and their families. We also run a Street Outreach program in our area, plus a national Prison Outreach program for incarcerated vets.

The non-profit NVF began in 1985 as the Vietnam Veterans Aid Foundation. We changed the name in 1991 to focus on *all* veterans. The first goal was to establish a toll-free national hotline so vets could find the services and information they needed. Now called the Lifeline for Vets, it was the first of its kind.

My first encounter with women vets was in Vietnam, where I served as a psychology officer in a MASH unit. Working alongside U.S. Army nurses at night with all the trauma of war coming in through triage was horrifying. I got to experience it for several nights, so I can really understand—that was *all* the nurses dealt with *every* night.

After the war, many of the nurses I had befriended contacted me. All were experiencing severe emotional problems. Even though we didn't have a definition of Post Traumatic Stress Disorder (PTSD) in the seventies, the thinking of that time was that their trauma was unwarranted because they weren't war fighters. I knew I had experienced trauma, not in the field, but in the field *hospitals*. I understood women vets needed to realize they were as much a veteran of war as anybody. And they needed to be recognized as war veterans and given access to the same medical treatment and counseling their male counterparts received. Luckily, five or six women with whom I served were in the LA/Orange County area. I started running rap groups with them, just as I had with their male counterparts.

A rap group, in this context, is a gathering of veterans to talk openly about their experiences in the military. When I first began working with Vietnam vets, I used this vet-to-vet model for counseling groups of veterans on the streets of LA. Developed early in my career when I worked with incarcerated vets deemed to be the most dangerous at Leavenworth, this method became the central core of the Vet Centers, community clinics away from Veterans Affairs (VA) hospitals, where veterans can drop in for counseling. Under the Carter Administration, I co-authored the Vet Center program for the VA and opened the first centers. There are now over three hundred Vet Centers operating across the U.S.

Meeting with these nurses and listening to their journeys after the war gave them a safe place to open up about their experiences and how they were dealing with the aftermath of war. Many of them were drinking excessively. As nurses, they knew about, and could sometimes get, different kinds of drugs to calm their trauma. As far as I knew, I was the first therapist *ever* to work with female Vietnam veteran groups. I recognized it didn't matter whether you were a woman or a man in war, nor did it matter exactly what you did in the war. If you participated in war, you could easily be traumatized.

After 9/11, the government allowed qualified women to be inducted and brought into the military as combatants. Today, about 13% of the military armed forces are women. The 20-year wars in Iraq and Afghanistan involved women in combat zones, and many of them in actual combat.

But there were other consequences besides being traumatized by killing or the very real prospect of being killed. Women were experiencing trauma during the war but also during regular military duty because of sexual assault. Women started reporting military sexual trauma in such numbers that this got its own acronym: MST.

In 1994, legislation passed in the United States that mandated that the Department of Veterans Administration (VA) screen all veterans for MST. But it wasn't until ten years later, in 2004, the Veterans Health Administration began screening men and women vets for MST at national VA facilities. This meant the issue went unreported and untreated for a decade after being formally recognized as a major issue within the military.

According to the Department of Defense, "Despite efforts to prevent and address MST, high prevalence and low reporting persist; the Department of Defense received only 3374 reports in 2012 of an estimated 26,000 active-duty members experiencing unwanted sexual contact." Those 26,000 incidents included rape but were not limited to rape; harassment was included in those estimates. Even so, 26,000 was outrageous. The military has addressed MST during the last 10 years, but it's still almost impossible to put a complete halt to it because of the mixing of young men and women in units together. That's not a popular thing to say, I realize. But proximity is a factor, especially in high-stress conditions.

I found out through our national hotline, the NVF's Lifeline for Vets, that women veterans were having trauma not only from war but also, a majority of them had experienced sexual trauma. Trauma is trauma, as I have long said.

We started getting calls from women because of my work with women Vietnam vets. Several times we had a couple come into our offices and as I worked with them, they brought in other colleagues who had served. Understand, these weren't only nurses, but women combatants from all branches of the service.

The stories of the assaults and how the VA didn't address it or understand it were strikingly similar. The basic fact that the VA is 90% male and the fact that they had been assaulted by males made it extremely difficult for women vets to get the treatment they needed and had earned. Many were harassed just walking into a VA facility. You must remember how male-centered the VA was.

Between 2000 and 2010, there were no licensed therapists to work with PTSD, sexual trauma, and harassment. The NVF's Lifeline for Vets had been around since 1982. Our presence traveled by word of mouth, mostly. Women share information and resources, and our toll-free number was passed around. We were "the only game in town."

Over the last fifteen years, I hired women to address those calls because callers were more comfortable talking to a woman, either a woman vet or a professional woman trained in trauma. We have a female mental health professional who addresses calls from women veterans that require more in-depth knowledge of the particular issues facing women vets, but especially women who have been sexually assaulted or harassed.

I have personally spoken to the VA's national committee about having trained women trauma experts available at all VA hospitals and Vet Centers. My voice is still loud, but it's a slow process. Somehow, they don't see it as necessary as they did when I first came to the VA in the eighties. The thinking now is "we've got psychologists and social workers who know how to work with anything." That is not true. I am a trauma expert. I belong to the American Trauma Association. There are things specialists know that generic mental health workers do not know.

We continue to address the need for trained trauma professionals, and we'll continue into the future. We're not where we'd like to be, but we'll get there. We blog about women vets and their experiences, and we include their stories in our newsletter. Our website, www.nvf.org, offers both support and resources for women veterans and can be found under the Resources tab on our home page.

Last, the counselors on our Lifeline for Vets can help women veterans find services local to them. Best, our counselors provide a listening ear.

Shad Meshad
October 2023

BIOGRAPHIES

QUERUS ABUTTU, "Dr. Q." Is a retired military Navy veteran with 28 years of service. Dr. Q. writes strange dark tales, speculative fiction, and weird sci-fi. She is a midnight poet, savior of road turtles, and a solitary green-gray witch living on the wooded banks of Iron Shores. When she's not writing, Dr. Q. explores the wilds of Virginia and interviews interesting individuals for her next novel "As Above, So Below." Before her deployment to Afghanistan in 2010, Dr. Q. graduated from Seton Hill's MFA program in Writing Popular Fiction, and recently became a lifetime member of the Horror Writer's Association (HWA). She loves foraging for wild foods, designing edible landscaping in her yard, and trying to find 101 ways to thwart deer from eating her plants. You may find her at a local wine tasting or in a local pub drinking craft beers talking to random people and writing furiously in a tattered notebook that she keeps under her pillow at night. You can discover more about her at www.QuerusAbuttu.com. Check out her previous works on Amazon: https://www.amazon.com/stores/Querus-Abuttu/author/B009NDJ2RM

DACIA M. ARNOLD is a ten-year U.S. Army veteran. As a combat medic, she served in the Baghdad Emergency Room during a 15-month deployment with the 86TH Combat Support Hospital. During her second deployment as the Noncommissioned Officer in Charge (NCOIC) of the busiest outpatient clinic in Southern Iraq, her best friend lost her life to domestic violence. While *(F)Law of Attraction* might suggest otherwise, it is important to understand the blame for such abuse is solely on the hands of those inflicting it.

Arnold is a cross genre author who writes to remedy the years of disassociating the horrors of war and loss by reassociating hard lessons and themes in her writing. Accounts of her time in the Army have been published in the New York Times (November, 2019) and Full Magazine Vol III (January, 2021). She is a two-time ChapterBuzz Award Winner for her debut novel, *Apparent Power*, and its sequel, *Shifting Power*. Arnold currently lives in the woods of Western Pennsylvania with her husband, two children, and a fat beagle named "The Unsinkable" Molly Brown. https://daciamarnold.com/

LANE BLEVINS has served in the United States Army for 14 years as a Combat Medic. Born and raised in Ocala, Florida, she has since been stationed in Hawaii, Texas, North Carolina, and Georgia. She has taken part in training exercises in Poland, Bulgaria, Germany, and Romania, and has served in two combat tours, one to FOB Warhorse, Iraq, and one in Kandahar Airfield, Afghanistan. She is a Sergeant First Class stationed in San Antonio, working as an instructor and senior enlisted leader. She has published three short stories in various literary journals. When not writing, she's spending untold hours at playgrounds, watching movies, and letting her daughters apply glitter to her eyelids. Lane is currently working on a horror novel entitled *Foremother*, seeking publication in 2024.

RACHEL A. BRUNE. As a military journalist, Rachel A. Brune wrote and photographed the U.S. Army and its soldiers for five years. When she moved on, she didn't quit writing stories with soldiers in them, just added werewolves, sorcerers, a couple evil mad scientists, and a Fae or two. Rachel is the founder and Editor-in-Chief at Crone Girls Press, an indie horror micropress specializing in anthologies, as well as the Senior Editor of Falstaff Dread, the horror imprint of Falstaff Books. She lives with her spouse, two daughters, one reticent cat, and two flatulent rescue dogs. Her werewolf secret agent novel, *Cold Run*, was published in 2022 by Falstaff Books.

THEA BRUNE served as an Electronic Warfare technician in the U.S. Navy. After separating, she followed the path of many, many sailors before her and straightaway moved back overseas to settle down in one of her favorite ports of call. Now she resides in Abu Dhabi, United Arab Emirates, with her excellent cat, Scruggs the Third. She spends her summer days hiding from the desert heat and reading and writing horror in hopes of generating enough chills to save on the AirCon bill.

LT SAM CASEY is a Surface Warfare Officer (Nuclear) in the U.S. Navy, currently teaching in the English Department at the United States Naval Academy as a Military Instructor. Prior, she was attached to USS ROOSEVELT (DDG 80) from 2017 to 2018 and USS George Washington (CVN 73) from 2019 to 2022. She enjoys writing poetry and prose in her free time and is excited to share her first attempt in the horror genre! She has been published under the pen-name Porter Jenkins with The Minison Project: Sonnet Collection vol 4, and Wrong Turn Lit. Her Poetry

Collection, *Erotic Trauma*, will be published with the Naked Cat in October 2023.

SARA CROCOLL SMITH (she/her) served in the United States Air Force from 2008 to 2012 as a Logistics Readiness Officer. Smith is the author of the ghostly gothic horror series *Hopeful Horror*. She's also the award-winning editor of the *Love Letters to Poe* anthologies. A few notable publications include stories in Cloaked Press's 2022 *Spring into SciFi*, Ghost Orchid Press's *Chlorophobia: An Eco-Horror Anthology*, Bag of Bones Press's *206-Word Stories Horror Anthology*, as well as an audio production of her story "The Swallowing of Graves" on Thirteen Podcast. Visit HopefulHorror.com for more about her work.

LEE FRANKLIN is an Australian Army veteran, having served ten years in logistics support, including two tours in East Timor. Lee delights in writing fast action, blood-soaked short stories and her debut was a military horror novel called "Berserker—Green Hell," all with a distinct Australian flavor. She is owned by three dogs and is raising three sons with her Argentinian husband.

NATALIA K. GLAROS is a U.S. Army veteran, having served three years as a Private First Class in Arizona and Virginia. Natalia was adopted at a young age and came to the United States to start a new life with her new family. As she grew up, she learned to be courageous and strong, which led her to join the Army. Natalia holds a bachelor's degree in criminal justice and investigative forensics from the University of Maryland Global Campus. She enjoyed listening and reading scary and ominous stories as a young girl, which led her to write her own crime fiction books. Natalia is the author of *Douglas Faye*, the first in a crime series, published in 2015. As a child, she wrote poetry, but then wanted to focus on bringing stories to life. Natalia is wrapping up her Douglas Faye series and looking forward to writing her next spine-chilling series.

BRENDA HUETTNER was in the U.S. Army Reserves when Desert Shield began and served in the headquarters unit for the 94th ARCOM for the duration of the Desert Shield/Desert Storm operations. Since then, she has been an independent technical communication consultant as a writer, editor, trainer, and manager for both software and hardware companies. She's a principal of Microwaves101.com, an online encyclopedia of microwave engineering knowledge.

Brenda is a Fellow of the Society for Technical Communication, and a Senior Member of IEEE, active in the Professional Communication Society, the Engineering Management council, and the Tucson section. She's also a member of the Usability Professionals Association. Brenda has published several books and articles, and presented half-day, full-day, and multi-day courses on writing, project management, usability, and career management. She also participates in NASA's volunteer Solar System Ambassador program.

K. E. JENNINGS served in the U.S. Army as a Chaplain Assistant NCO from 2004 to 2012. While on active duty, she completed assignments in the continental U.S., Germany, and a 15-month deployment to Iraq during the surge where she was assigned to a combat engineer battalion. She has written over six full-length novels and various short stories. Her genres include thriller, mystery and action. In her off time, K.E. enjoys spending time at various beaches, skateboarding with her son, and hiking up mountains with her family. You can find her online on Instagram @kejennings7787 and Twitter @ke_jenning3137.

V. L. JONES is a paranormal enthusiast and horror writer. She grew up in a haunted house in Washington State, which fueled her passion for the supernatural and monsters. Verona now lives in Tucson, Arizona, which she uses as her home base to explore haunted sites with a history.

Verona enlisted in the U.S. Navy out of high school in 1975 as a Cryptological Technical Technician (CTT), a nice way of saying a communications technician. Her first duty station was in the highlands of Scotland, and talk about hitting pay dirt. Scotland and England are about urban legends and ghostly hauntings. Fascinated by the history of these places, she often writes about her spooky findings.

Her explorations fuel her imagination, and she writes horror stories with elements of urban legends, cryptids, and folklore blended in. Verona loves anything about cryptids, such as Bigfoot, the Ozark Howler, The Black Dog, and the Mothman, to name a few. Verona also loves the paranormal and the supernatural worlds. As her schedule permits, she plots the next trip to a paranormal hotspot.

PAMELA K. KINNEY joined the U.S. Army in 1976, when the military was no longer drafting, but had become an all-volunteer force. She gave up long ago trying not to listen to the voices in her head and has written award-winning, bestselling horror, fantasy, science fiction, poetry, along with nonfiction ghost books ever since. Her horror short story, "Bottled Spirits," was a runner-up for the 2013 WSFA Small Press Award and is considered one of the seven best genre short fiction for that year. Her horror, fantasy, and science fiction stories, poetry and nonfiction articles were published in various anthologies and magazines, she has an urban fantasy novel, a science fiction novella, five nonfiction ghost books and a nonfiction book about shapeshifting cryptids in the United States. Her poem, "Dementia," that was in the HWA Poetry Showcase Vol VII, got her a mention in Best Horror of the Years. Vol 13.

Pamela and her husband live with one crazy black cat (who thinks she should take precedence over her mistress's writing most days). Along with writing, Pamela has acted on stage and film and investigates the paranormal for episodes of Paranormal World Seekers for AVA Productions. She is a member of both the Virginia Writers Club and Horror Writers Association. She is an Army veteran. You can learn more about her at http://www.PamelaKKinney.com.

K. P. KULSKI is a Korean-American author born in Honolulu, Hawaii. She's embarked on many career adventures: the U.S. Navy and Air Force, video game design, and history professor. Her fiction is often inspired by stories of the past; most evident in her gothic horror novel, *Fairest Flesh*, from Strangehouse Books and novella, *House of Pungsu*, from Bizarro Pulp Press. She now resides in Northeast Ohio with her husband and children in a house in the woods. Find her online at garnetonwinter.com and on Twitter @garnetonwinter.

ELIZE MCKELVEY is a Marine Corps veteran and freelance artist. She graduated college with a BFA in illustration in 2012 and left for boot camp the day after graduation. Elize served as a combat artist in areas such as Iraq and Baghdad, helping to connect civilians to the front lines and the in-between moments of the military. Her exceptional acumen has led to opportunities to work with companies such as VETtv, Wacom, Michaels Art Craft Store, The Smithsonian Channel with Paramount, Pilot pen, and many more. Today, she continues to participate in the combat art program as a civilian artist. Though no longer in uniform, she still carries the same passion to tell stories. Read more about Elize McKelvey's story and see her amazing work at InkStickArt.com.

SIRRAH MEDEIROS served in the U.S. Marine Corps from 1985 to 1990, trained as a Marine Water Dog. The experiences in water purification inspired her toward environmental studies, and she later graduated from the University of Maryland with honors. After many military moves and career changes, Sirrah retired from defense work as a program manager and technical communicator. She now pursues her passions as a writer and editor of dark fiction, and is the owner and Editor-in-Chief of Tundra Swan Press. Sirrah is the author of the Cristiane Bradford dark urban fantasy series— the most recent in the series, *Secrets of Mother*, was a 2022 Pinnacle Book Achievement Award winner. You can see a list of her published horror short fiction and other works at https://www.sirrahmedeiros.com.

TARA MOELLER lives in Norfolk, Virginia with her husband of 31 years, David, and their brindle Bullmastiff, Delilah. She served in the United States Navy from 1991 through 1997 as an electronics technician, honorable discharging after the birth of her and David's only child. Serving aboard the Norfolk Naval Base, she and her husband made the area their home for almost thirty years.

After leaving active duty, Tara attended Old Dominion University, ultimately obtaining a Bachelor of Liberal Arts in English. Upon graduation from ODU in 2000, she started work as an editor for Naval Facilities Engineering Command in the Criteria Office. In late 2007, she started work as a technical editor at

Operational Test and Evaluation Force and now works at its sister command, Marine Corps Operational Test and Evaluation Activity, out of Quantico, Virginia.

Tara has published several short stories in various anthologies, novellas, and a full-length novel—not all of them horror, but they do have horror elements. When not writing or working, you will find her reading or wire-wrapping jewelry.

KRISTINA OSBORN is a talented graphic artist and U.S. Air Force veteran residing in Washington State. With over 15 years of experience in the multimedia industry, she brings a wealth of expertise and a keen eye for design to every project. Alongside her professional accomplishments, Kristina embraces her role as a devoted mother to a toddler, finding inspiration in the beauty and challenges of parenthood.

Armed with a BA in Communications and an AA in Digital Media, Kristina possesses a solid educational foundation that complements her practical skills. She thrives on collaboration and actively seeks opportunities to work alongside fellow creatives, valuing the dynamic energy that emerges from a team effort. Learn more about Kristina and Truborn Design at www.truborndesign.com.

ROOK RILEY is a U.S. Army veteran who served six years as a linguist in Military Intelligence. They are a book coach, a game enthusiast, and an author trained in Krav Maga. They split their time between teaching middle school in the Dallas area and helping on the family farm where the bulk of their writing is done. They are a member of Missing in America, the Horror Writers Association, and the PTA. Their hobbies include binge-watching Netflix and collecting tattoos. You can find their short stories in several anthologies available through Amazon. https://www.authorrookriley.com/

ELLA B. RITE was born and raised in Detroit, Michigan. She retired from the U.S. Navy, raised two sons, and earned a bachelor's degree before embarking on her writing career. She writes horror, science fiction, mystery & fantasy. Her favorite books contain what she calls "Scooby-Doo Scares": horror wrapped in a whodunit with a bit of comedy. She can't resist stories about haunted houses & cursed objects. Currently, she is working on a book series about a rogue witch who constantly irritates her coven.

JANINE K. SPENDLOVE is a retired United States Marine Corps KC-130 Pilot. In the writing world, she is an award-winning author primarily known for her *War of the Seasons* fantasy series. She has several short stories published in various speculative fiction anthologies, to include the *Star Wars* tie-in story "Inbrief." Janine is also a member of the Science Fiction and Fantasy Writers Association (SFWA), Women in Aerospace (WIA), and BroadUniverse (BU). A graduate of Johns Hopkins University: School of International Studies (SAIS) and Brigham Young University (BYU), Janine loves pugs, sewing her own clothes, making the occasional costume, and playing Beatles tunes on her guitar. She resides with her family in Northern Virginia and is currently at work on her next novel. Find out more @janinekspendlove on social media or janinekspendlove.com.

T. R. WHITNEY, Sorrento, Louisiana, has been writing for a few years. A retired U.S. Army Master Sergeant, she began writing as part of her PTSD therapy. Her pieces include some with a military flavor and others with various generic themes.

She has published two books of poetry, *A Soldiers Journey Home* and *A Journey of Healing*. Tanya is a 2018 National Veterans Creative Arts Festival Gold Medalist and 2022 Silver Medalist in Creative Writing categories. She has written award-winning poems and short stories which are published in various anthologies in the U.S. and England, including *Reach of Song*, *Treasures Found in a Cedar Chest*, *Sandcutters*, *Ink to Paper* Volumes, and *Tears O'er A Tin Cup*. She is at work on both a collection of short stories and her first novel. Find her online at www.trwhitney.com and follow her on Facebook at TR Whitney-Poet & Author.

DONNA ZEPHRINE was born in Harlem, New York and grew up in Bay Shore, Long island. She went to Brentwood High School, graduated from Columbia University School of Social Work in May 2017, and currently works for the New York State Office of Mental Health at Pilgrim Psychiatric Center Outpatient Intensive Case Management as a Bridger.

She is a combat veteran who completed two tours in Iraq. She was on active duty in the U.S. Army stationed at Hunter Army Airfield, Savannah, Georgia, 3rd Infantry Division as a mechanic from October 29, 2002 to January 31. 2006.

Since returning home, Donna enjoys sharing her experiences and storytelling through writing. Donna's stories have been published in the New York Times, Writers Guild Initiative, Military Experience, The Arts, Suicide, The Seasons, Lockdown, New World, Qutub Minar Review, Summer, War and Battle, Bards Initiative, Radvocate, Oberon, Long Island Poetry Association and, The Mighty. Donna has participated in various veteran writing workshops throughout NYC. Recently, Donna was featured in USA Warrior stories, and took part in Warrior Chorus and Decruit, which encourages self-expression. Donna is always seeking new experiences to learn, such as Toast Masters, which focuses on public speaking. She is involved in World Team Sports, Veterans of Foreign Wars, Wounded Warrior Project, Team Red White and blue, Team Rubicon, Project9line, Provetus, and Convene Communities. In her spare time, Donna plays sled hockey for the Long Island Rough Riders. Donna serves as an advisory board member for Heroes to Heroes.

ACKNOWLEDGEMENTS

To the dozens of women veterans who submitted stories and poems for our inaugural anthology, THANK YOU.

To the almost two dozen women whose creativity and passions fill these pages, your teamwork, vision, and professionalism throughout the development of this book were outstanding. I couldn't have asked for anything more, you all were a joy to work with on this project. I hope your pens and artistic prowess continue to haunt for years to come.

To Red Lagoe (Death Knell Press) for introducing me to the amazing talents and cover design magic of Kristina Osborn, Truborn Design. Thank you for bringing us together!

To Vince Liaguno for answering my messages and giving me a guiding nudge whenever I asked the smallest question. It wasn't often, but when I asked, you answered. Thank you.

To Jenn Moffitt (U.S. Marine Corps veteran), a huge thanks for getting me in contact with Elize MeKelvey, InkStickArt, and her amazing ability to capture the heart of each story in her artwork.

ESTEEMED APPARITIONS

Thank you to all our Kickstarter Backers! Without your support, getting this project off the ground would have been a much more arduous endeavor. We're grateful for you and your funding of this campaign. To each of you noted below and those who opted not to have their names listed, we thank you.

Kimberly Mulan Ginty • Amanda Eschmeyer

Richard Novak • Brad Center • Amber Steet • Lisa Kruse

Jace Chre • Professor James Musgrave, E-4, USNR

Charity Tahmaseb • John Jason Lau • Kevin A. Davis

AingealWroth • Vanessa Quinones • Melanie MccraeCrate

Davy Van Obbergen • Red Lagoe • Richard O'Shea

Steve Pattee • Eron Wyngarde • Jean Marie Ward

Roboghostworld • Kristina Meschi • Zack Fissel

Ryan T. Jenkins • Brett Burkhardt • D. J. Stevenson

Lea Walker • Katie Slocum • Edward Abbott

Michael Rook • William R. D. Wood • Bob McGough

Caroline Coriell • Maggie Allen • Olivia Coleman

Jesse Braxton (Elder Gamer) • Jacob H. Joseph

Sara T. Bond • Elizabeth Donald • Colleen Feeney

Bill McCloud • Logan Denault • Carol Gyzander

Zen Hance • Debbie Chen • C. Fatley • Jennifer Andberg

Melissa DePriest • Kyleanne Hunter • Brad Kabosky

THE HAUNTED ZONE

Kimberely Briggs • Vince A. Liaguno • Christopher Roman
Kristi Wilder • GhostCat • Sara Crocoll Smith
Christina Maria Fernandez • Natalia K. Glaros
Richard Leis • Dustin Hegwood • Esapekka Erikkson
Jennifer L. Pierce • Elena Medeiros • J. E. Erickson
Lazarushorror • D.J. and Alexis Henshaw • Regina Weber
Stephen Medeiros • Cheyenne Lynn • Dino Hicks
Paul and Laura Trinies • Jessica Retherford

TUNDRA SWAN PRESS

Tundra Swan Press started in 2021 as a platform to publish Sirrah Medeiros's longer works of fiction. However, in 2022, an inkling sprouted, a single root, with the idea to lift other voices. In 2023, the roots grew and flourished with more ideas, and the goal was set to publish anthologies that amplify voices and support causes while publishing quality dark fiction. For more information about Tundra Swan Press and what we have planned, please visit:

https://www.tundraswanpress.com

www.ingramcontent.com/pod-product-compliance
Lightning Source LLC
Chambersburg PA
CBHW071242300726

48975CB00002B/519